Mr.
&
Mrs.
Witch

Mr.
&
Mrs.
Witch

A Novel

GWENDA BOND

St. Martin's Griffin
New York

First published in the United States by St. Martin's Griffin, an imprint of St. Martin's Publishing Group

www.stmartins.com

Library of Congress Cataloging-in-Publication Data

Names: Bond, Gwenda, author.
Title: Mr. & Mrs. Witch / Gwenda Bond.
Other titles: Mister & Mrs. Witch
Description: First Edition. | New York: St. Martin's Griffin, 2023.
Identifiers: LCCN 2022039387 | ISBN 9781250845955 (trade paperback) |
    ISBN 9781250845948 (ebook)
Subjects: LCGFT: Novels.
Classification: LCC PS3602.O65648 M7 2023 | DDC 813/.6—dc23/
    eng/20220829
LC record available at https://lccn.loc.gov/2022039387

Our books may be purchased in bulk for promotional, educational, or business use. Please contact your local bookseller or the Macmillan Corporate and Premium Sales Department at 1-800-221-7945, extension 5442, or by email at MacmillanSpecialMarkets@macmillan.com.

First Edition: 2023

10 9 8 7 6 5 4 3 2 1

*To all of us who've ever tried to twitch
our noses and make things happen*

*And for Kami and Sam, because I can't
dedicate the books we're writing together to you*

I am a witch. A real house-haunting, broom-riding, cauldron-stirring witch.

— *Bewitched*

Witch. From the Anglo-Saxon word *wicce*, German *wissen*, "to know," and *wikken*, "to divine." The witches were at first called "wise women," until the day when the Church took it unto herself to follow the law of Moses, which put every "witch" or enchantress to death.

—H. P. Blavatsky, *The Theosophical Glossary* (1892)

Now

1

✦✦✦

Savvy

This is the most *something* day—weirdest, definitely the *weirdest*—of Savvy's life, and it's barely past noon.

"Do you think your flower crown should have more hemlock?" Savvy's best friend Brie squints at her in the rearview mirror of the car she's driving along the dirt-and-gravel road.

Savvy's in the back seat with a garment bag holding The Dress, capital letters, and another with the pink dress Brie plans to wear in her role as maid of honor. There's also a duffel her other best friend Elle, short for Louise, handed her as they piled in to leave for the venue.

"No, it will overpower the rue," Elle says. Elle is in her chic suit already and has planned this entire day within an inch of its life.

Underlying their fussing is the actual question her best friends are not brave enough to ask her: Is Savvy hexing Wilde *really* about to get married? To a regular human man?

Savvy never indulged in fantasies about her wedding while growing up. There were some other little witches who swooned over the fairy tale of the pitiful frog who could be transformed back into a much-reformed prince by the right witch and then put a ring on it. Or the story of the witch who saved the father and his three stepdaughters by banishing bad fairies from their chimney and then married the oldest daughter and they all lived happily ever after. The girls might have gone to sleep afterward dreaming of the charmer who'd steal their heart.

Savvy took away a different moral from those stories.

She believed in witches saving the day. It was her entire job, and, until recently, her entire life. She figured she'd be fine on her own. Forever. Her mother always assured her that was the best, safest way to be. She never thought she'd need to marry a prince or princess, or, well, anyone, to keep saving the world in small and large ways every day. She has C.R.O.N.E.—Covert Responses to Occult Nightmares by Enchantresses—for that.

But here she is, being driven to the Atlanta C.R.O.N.E. chapter's extensive property outside the city. They're headed to the rustic barn venue on the outer edge, used for social occasions where outsiders are invited. The entire property, with its rambling houses, barns, other buildings, fields, and forests, is known to the witches as the Farmhouse. Its iron-clad, blood-bound protective spells will prevent any guests from getting lost or seeing any secrets they shouldn't. On this, her wedding day. Because apparently *it* can happen to anyone. By which she means love.

Griffin changed her plans . . . and, after some major freaking out, she's surprisingly okay with that. Savvy can be impulsive, which occasionally gets her in trouble. But usually also back out again. You have to think on your feet when you could accidentally release a magic plague into the sewers of London or need to keep an angry dragon from burning a town in the Balkans. At first, the idea of marrying Griffin a year after meeting him felt on the same level as those things. A catastrophe in the making.

Then she looked at him, across the dinner table at their favorite Mexican place, waiting for her answer. Patiently. Over tacos.

Her sweet, mild-mannered, bespectacled, and yet still sexy as hell antiquities professor Griffin. And in that moment, she knew. He's worth the risk. He's the thing she never let herself admit she wanted.

So she said yes. Surprising not only herself, but her nearest and dearest.

"My mother will meet us there?" Savvy asks.

While Elle and Brie are on board with the marriage—they actually *like* Griffin—her mother is decidedly not. Savvy figures once the ceremony is over, her mother will just have to get over it. Eventually.

"Uh-huh," Brie says, evasively.

"She'll be there." Elle turns sideways so she can pat Savvy's knee. "I've got this."

"Shit!" Brie shouts suddenly, jamming on the brakes. "No! No! *No!*"

Savvy and Elle exchange a look. Savvy cranes her neck to see what's in front of them to merit this reaction, but Brie shouts, "Blindfold!"

Savvy feels the energy of the spell and suddenly she can't see anything. "Why?" Savvy asks, reaching up to adjust the cloth now covering her eyes.

Brie huffs. "I told Diego to make sure he got Griffin and the groomsmen here thirty minutes from now so we would *not* run into them. You can't see each other before the ceremony."

"Oh, come on, do we have to be that traditional?" Savvy asks.

"You can't see the face she's making right now, but I'm getting a big yes," Elle says in her calm way.

"He can't see her either!" Brie says, and Savvy hears her pound the steering wheel. "Why aren't they going inside?"

Elle interrupts Brie's dramatics. "I've conjured another blindfold. I'll put it on him."

Brie grumbles, but the car starts to move forward again.

Savvy guesses it's a good sign there are invisible butterflies fluttering inside and around her like a Disney witch at the thought Griffin is up ahead. *I'm going to marry him.*

No one is more surprised than her. Marriages are rare among witchkin—especially with men, or outsiders—if not entirely unheard of.

The car stops. "Wait here!" Brie barks. Her door opens and then slams shut. Elle gets out too.

Savvy waits until the back door opens and Elle reaches in to guide her out of the car. She hears the low honey of Griffin's voice protesting.

"Griffin?" she calls out.

"I take it you're blindfolded too?" Griffin sounds amused.

"Yes." Savvy laughs.

"You can thank me later, when you don't have bad luck!" Brie inserts.

"Keep talking so I can find you," Griffin says, closer now.

"I'm not sure—" Brie says.

Griffin's friend and best man, Diego, says, "Let it be, woman."

Savvy has to bite her lip to keep from laughing again. She can picture Brie with her hands on her hips, glaring at Diego, imagining hexing him.

"Marco," Savvy says, "I'm right over—"

"Polo." Griffin bumps into her.

She reaches out to find his hands with hers.

"There you are," he says.

"Here I am." Every nerve in her body sings at the contact between their fingers, at his nearness. He smells fresh out of the shower, one of her top three favorite Griffin states. Clean and woodsy.

"We're really doing this, huh?" she murmurs.

"We are," he murmurs back.

And then his lips find hers. There are cheers and also groans from their friends on either side, but Savvy blocks them out easily. Griffin fills her senses. His lips gently move against hers, teasing her lips open. He slides one hand around her back and she presses against him as close as she can without breaking contact. She deepens the kiss and . . .

"Okay, that's enough," Brie says right beside her. "Save something for later."

"We should've eloped," Savvy says, finishing the kiss with her palm on Griffin's cheek before dropping both of her hands into his again.

"You shouldn't be doing this at all," a frosty, feminine voice she recognizes too well says.

"Hi, Claudia," Griffin says as if he's unbothered. He's chosen to try to wear her mother down by simply being nice. He doesn't understand, because of course he can't. He doesn't know the truth about Savvy. He has no idea she's a witch.

And he never will.

"Mom," Savvy says, "we've been over this."

"I don't have to like it." Her mother sniffs. "And I won't."

Her mother, the mood killer. But Savvy refuses to let her disapproval be a hovering dark cloud over this occasion.

Savvy rests her forehead against Griffin's for a beat. "See you soon," she says.

"I can't wait." Griffin releases her hands with a reluctance she relates to.

Her friends each take an arm and steer her inside.

Savvy stands in front of the mirror in the preparatory suite. She wears The Dress, aka a tasteful off-the-shoulder beaded gown fitted to accentuate her curves. Her medium-length caramel curls are topped by the flower crown. She's in flats instead of heels, because she's plenty tall as is. She should feel entirely comfortable in this ensemble, which she chose.

She can't quite manage it.

It doesn't help that every witch Savvy knows has been around to ask her about one thing or another, some reprising Brie's and Elle's questions from before. *Is* her flower crown statement enough? Should it have more rue or maybe hemlock? How is she feeling? Because a quick spell, not even a spell, truly, just a *suggestion* of an incantation, can nix those nerves in a jiff, if she likes? And, oh, does she need more champagne? It's charmed, so it won't get her sloshed. But it'll take the edge off those nerves she *must* be feeling.

Still, Savvy knows this is an unusual occasion, not least because it involves her. Seemingly every witch located in the continental United States has traveled here to either celebrate or side-eye her decision. She's grateful that among all the gossipy strangers and, well, her mother, she also has Brie and Elle.

Or at least she is until Brie marches over with a flute of bubbly in one hand and considers Savvy's reflection. Brie's celestial-themed tattoo sleeves are a striking contrast with her slinky pale pink bridesmaid dress and fuchsia-highlighted hair.

She tsks. "I just think—look at this." She points at Savvy and casts a glamour. "It has more of a wow factor," she adds.

Brie is trying and failing to keep a straight face.

Savvy raises an eyebrow like a drawn arch. Because Brie has bestowed an entirely animated Jessica Rabbit look on her from head to toe, red gown and all. Yes, even her eyes resemble the cartoon sexpot's.

"Brie."

"Okay, so not that. . . . How about something *ethereal*. Like *the goddess* herself."

Savvy would protest that this fun is at her expense, but at least Brie isn't asking any more questions. And anyway, her friend has to get this out of her system first.

She gestures at Savvy, and her spell transforms Savvy back into 3D and the red cartoon dress into a flowing nightgown-esque garment. She hesitates, then nods to give Savvy knee-length Lady Godiva hair.

"I look like I'm about to start a cult," Savvy says. She puts her hands on her hips. "Stop trolling me."

She waves at her reflection, restoring the chosen look that she doesn't feel entirely comfortable in, which Brie *knows*.

"I'm nervous enough as it is," she says. "No more mockery. I think it might be suspicious if I show up to my own wedding in glamour."

"Let me live," Brie whines.

And, of course, this would be the moment when her mother reenters the fray. She's been lingering over by the champagne, tossing back one after another.

Savvy braces as she struts over in her low-cut, diamond-studded rose-colored jumpsuit. She's always embraced Dolly Parton as her style guru. But her personality is less Dolly's sweet sass and more murderous "bless your heart." C.R.O.N.E. and Savvy are her entire life—she can't understand why Savvy wants anything besides the job and their community in her own.

Savvy has always looked up to her mother, the famous Claudia, one of the leaders of this, what might be the most powerful C.R.O.N.E. chapter in the world. She wishes her mom would approve of the wedding, but has given up. Claudia has too much baggage about men and about love being a distraction from their mission.

"I was just playing around," Brie says. "This *is* a once-in-a-lifetime thing."

Claudia snorts. "We'll see about that."

Savvy may have to murder someone before the day is out.

Except Brie's right. This *is* a special day. And she's pretty sure there's no murder on wedding days. (Well, unless it's a TV show and George R. R. Martin is in charge.)

She imagines Griffin witnessing the magic dress-the-bridezilla shenanigans that just happened and has to press down guilt.

There's a reason she doesn't find Brie's antics funny. She's getting married as Savannah Wilde, which is who she is, but also as a respectable, non-witch citizen, which she most definitely is not.

C.R.O.N.E. operatives can't break their covers, not even for their spouses. So as far as Griffin knows she's a public relations consultant. He believes one of her biggest clients happens to be an animal rescue located at the Farmhouse that a lot of her friends and her mother are involved in. That's how it will stay. It's remarkable how much travel the PR gig covers for, and she's absorbed enough marketing speak over the years to sell the ruse. She's glamoured when she's actually working, so even if he did see her doing something with her powers, he wouldn't know he had.

He'll never find out who he's really marrying. That feels unfair. But there's nothing she can do about it, except be a good wife and a better operative. Witches have always had to live with a reality that can't accept them for who they are. She'd like to think Griffin is different, but the rules are the rules on this one. No testing that premise.

Elle comes bustling into the suite, carrying a tablet. The first warning sign is how she avoids Savvy and heads over to whisper to the table of bridesmaids (and fellow operatives) drinking champagne. There are gasps. Her mother, sensing gossip, immediately gravitates back to that end of the large room with the slanted wood-beamed ceiling.

"You really hated the red, even in theory?" Brie asks. "I bet Griffin would like it. I seem to remember you wearing a red dress when you met."

Not exactly. But the heat in the memory the statement conjures puts a flush in Savvy's cheeks.

"I don't want to be glamoured today. Or ever around Griffin, if I can help it." Savvy shakes her head. "You wear red."

"Blasphemy." Brie fluffs her hair. She's so fond of pink, it's basically the limit of her wardrobe. That's the reason Savvy agreed to have it be the color scheme for today.

"What?!" Her mother's shock is audible across the room. When she catches Savvy and Brie paying attention, she lowers her voice and turns away from them.

Savvy exchanges a look with her best friend and they stalk across the room. "Mom, what's going on?" she asks.

"Well . . ." Her mother evasively pours champagne. "I don't want to say I told you so."

This is a lie. Her mother *loves* saying that phrase. "Why would you be saying it?"

The others are silent.

"Seriously, what's up? Did Griffin pull a runner?" She gives it a teasing note, but she finds she's bracing for the response.

"No, nothing like that," her mother says. "Though you'd be better off . . ."

"Mom, stop it. Now, someone tell me what's going on. Right now." Savvy is using her means-business voice. It tends to be effective.

The group exchanges troubled glances. Elle finally says, "The Butcher of Salem is here."

"What do you mean?" Savvy is halfway to conjuring up an enchanted crossbow when Elle adds, "He's on the groom's side."

"Wait." Savvy isn't sure she heard correctly. "Come again?"

"The Butcher of Salem is downstairs, sitting on the groom's side."

Savvy can't believe this is happening. "How do we know it's him?"

"Apparently Mother Circe recognized him," her mother says.

That's confirmation, all right.

The Butcher of Salem is their oldest enemy. He presides

over an organization that C.R.O.N.E. avoids in the field when it can—when it can't, the two inevitably clash—and still uses glamours to avoid detection. For centuries, the Butcher and his men were in open conflict with the witches, the battles razing villages and forests as they hunted down her kind. Eventually, Mother Circe made a show of force with her coven that convinced the Butcher to agree to an armistice . . . of sorts. Whatever scuffles they have must stay out of the public eye, to keep the supernatural world secret.

The Butcher and Circe faced one another down hundreds of years ago—they're both long-lived through means not exactly natural, because he's a hypocrite—and for the two of them to be anywhere in public, let alone at the same event, is . . .

Savvy was surprised when Mother Circe RSVP'd to begin with; she rarely visits Atlanta these days. Savvy hasn't seen her since her C.R.O.N.E. induction at eighteen, and from what she understands Mother Circe declines to attend them these days.

"It has to just be a terrible coincidence," Savvy says. "You've all met Griffin."

There are some murmurs of agreement. A snort from her mother.

But whoever Griffin is, he's no Butcher of Salem, for goddess's sake.

"The question is, what do we do?" Brie asks.

Savvy frowns. "What do you mean?"

"You're going to let him stay? At your wedding?" She sounds skeptical. "He would kill every single one of us if he could get away with it."

"And hold trials first to drag it out," her mother says. "When Brie puts it that way, you can't mean to let him enjoy this day. That's not my daughter. Some company your husband-to-be keeps."

Savvy bristles. She has a reputation and it's not for coward-
ice. She puts dragons back to sleep without tucking them in.
She keeps demons from releasing poison into water supplies.
She isn't known for backing down.

An evil man has strolled onto *their* turf to witness her marriage. She wants to march downstairs and show him to the door
with a passel of hissing poisonous snakes at his heels, while
asking him if he enjoyed hunting down her lost sisters . . .

But it would blow her cover and potentially put them all at
risk.

"Back off, y'all." Elle gives a no-nonsense head shake and
holds up her hand. "I have planned this wedding meticulously,
but it's Savvy's day. The call is hers to make."

Brie presses. "What if he's here for us?"

A fair point. But . . . that would result in the kind of conflict
that might blow up the accords. Mutually assured destruction.

None of that matters, though. Not right now.

"Griffin can't find out about me," she says. "No, this has to
be random. There's no way Griffin knows who he really is. We
do the ceremony. We'll figure the rest out later. Can Cretin follow the Butcher afterward?" Her mother's familiar is a grumpy
raven worthy of her name. Some of the others' familiars are
nearby, hidden outside in the woods. Not Savvy's. Hers is back
at her and Griffin's house. But her mother doesn't go anywhere
without Cretin staying close.

Claudia catches her eye, nods. "Of course."

Savvy can tell that Claudia wants to say something more, so
she plows ahead. "Good. Then it's final. Let's do this."

She goes back to the mirror to give one more subtle adjust-
ment to the flower crown, the only armor she gets to wear into
this battlefield. She reminds herself: *Griffin is worth it.*

If the Butcher stays out of their way, she'll stay out of his.
For now.

2

✦ ✦ ✦

Griffin

Griffin can't wait to lay eyes on Savvy. Not just because he knows she'll be stunning in her dress—hell, she's stunning in anything (or, even better, nothing). She strolled into his thoroughly organized life and turned it upside down and he can't find it in him to care, not one bit.

Even that brief taste of her outside while sporting her friends' hastily tied blindfold made him all the more anxious to get on with marrying the woman he desperately wants to spend the rest of his life with.

His best man, Diego, is still grumbling about Savvy's friend Brie getting in his face because they arrived early. That part was Griffin's fault, though he was happy to let Diego take the heat.

Most of the men gathered around him in this medium-sized room set aside for the groom's party don't get why he's in such a hurry to exchange vows—and he doesn't care about that either. He loves his brothers and colleagues, but when he thinks of Savvy any concerns they voice about the wedding seem like they're coming out of the mouth of Charlie Brown's teacher. "Blah wah blah wah blah wah" is what he hears.

Diego snaps his fingers in front of Griffin's face. "Hey, listen to me, this is actually important, okay?"

"If you did the background check you suggested on Savvy, I will kill you." Griffin says it gently as he straightens the bow tie of his tux. His black-rimmed glasses are part of his cover.

He doesn't need them, but he has to keep wearing them with Savvy anyway.

"I still think that was a mistake," Diego says. "No, I'm doing one last check-in to make sure you want to go through with this. It'll change your whole life. Keeping what we do secret, it's not going to be easy."

"I've managed so far," Griffin says.

Not that he feels great about it.

Being an agent of H.U.N.T.E.R. (aka Humans Undertaking Nocturnal Terror and Evil Reduction) isn't an ordinary job. He's not the antiquities professor that Savvy believes he is. *But* there's a long tradition of keeping these sorts of things from your family. See every CIA agent ever. The work H.U.N.T.E.R. does these days is far more classified than anything a traditional government agency might tackle. They help keep the entire world safe from supernatural threats that would upend consensus reality if people knew about them. The work is sacred. Sure, the way they started out was bloodier by necessity—that largely involved protecting the world from the then-unchecked powers of witches—but what they do is still crucial.

Griffin is exceptional at it, and he's a steadying influence on his colleagues. He *is* a scholar, it's just that the kind of antiquities he knows about span far more than the usual human experience. He teaches a class at the local university and the arrangement allows him copious time in the field. That's how he and Savvy first encountered each other.

He shakes his head, remembering. They met traveling abroad, under odd circumstances. He was suspicious at first, part of his training, and then she charmed him completely. He'd thought he might never see her again, but fate threw them back together. Not that he believes in things as untestable as fate. . . .

The rest of their yearlong relationship is history in a whirl-wind. Why would he wait for some arbitrary amount of time to pass when he knows this is what he wants?

"So you're sure?" Diego prods.

"Positive," Griffin says, and stares at Diego in a "let it go, now" manner.

"All right, if you're sure, brother," Diego says, and claps him on the back. "You got the vows and stuff?"

"Yes." He wrote them down on a crib sheet tucked in his tux's right jacket pocket, though he's 99 percent positive he won't need it. He likes to be prepared. "You got the ring?"

Diego nods.

"We're ready then," Griffin says.

"You're ready," Diego says. "I'm losing my best wingman."

Griffin laughs, because it's true and the real source of Diego's objection. Griffin's vibe is less intimidating than his cut friend, who could be mistaken for a telenovela star. Women approach and talk to Griffin strictly to get close to Diego—or Griffin's brothers, Jacob and Quinn. Not that Griffin wasn't doing fine before Savvy. He was. But romance hasn't been a priority. He has responsibilities he can't afford to phone in.

Savvy, well, he can't phone in anything with her. Not even if he wanted to.

"She is a badass," Diego allows.

"You have no idea. Never try to take the last slice of pizza if you want to live." Griffin turns to the rest of the space they're using as a staging area. His dad's over in the corner with his brothers and a few other groomsmen. They're talking a little too excitedly for Griffin's taste.

The only reason they'd be this amped up is a new situation in the field.

He walks over. "What's up? Who's on emergency duty to-day anyway?"

They all go quiet. His father, Roman, has close-cropped silver hair and is still as buff as the job demands. The rest of the guys are in tuxes and study their feet. His clean-shaven, tidy, stylish brother Quinn shrugs, and his other brother, the burly, bearded, always-needs-a-haircut Jacob, elbows him in the ribs.

"Okay, what is happening? And don't say nothing, I won't believe you." Griffin is known for his instincts. Right now they're screaming the guys are hiding something.

Jacob nods to their dad.

"Fine. Don't overreact," Roman says. "But Mother Circe is downstairs."

Griffin thinks he misheard for a moment, the name echoing through the group. "Are you sure?"

Mother Circe is the most powerful witch they've ever faced, the head of C.R.O.N.E., which H.U.N.T.E.R. tries to avoid because it never goes well when they encounter each other. Way before Griffin's time, their work involved hunting witches, who used their powers with abandon, threatening community after community. H.U.N.T.E.R. doesn't focus on that anymore, obviously. Hasn't in hundreds of years, since the witches agreed to the Butcher's terms at the accords, both sides promising to keep incidents between them quiet and contained from the public eye. But to say there's continued bad blood between those witches and his organization would be a massive understatement.

"Maybe Savvy is their PR rep?" Diego offers.

"Secret agencies don't have PR reps," Griffin says, reeling. "Are you *sure* it's Circe?" he asks his dad again. "How do we know?"

Witches are famous for their ability to wear glamours.

"This came from the Butcher," his dad says. "You know he's here today."

Then it's legitimate. Those two went head-to-head in the old days—the 1600s, to be precise—and while they did serious damage to each other, and the witches took out villages across New

England, eventually the Butcher showed enough force for Circe to come to the table. The accords have held, inviolable. Without them, *all* their secrets would be public knowledge before long.

Griffin has heard legends about the Butcher since he was old enough to keep a secret. But he's mostly a figurehead now, a largely unseen leader. Their day-to-day at the Atlanta headquarters of H.U.N.T.E.R.—the agency itself is international—is run by people like his dad and, well, himself. The Butcher is only here because weddings are considered important by him, a way to carry on the sacred mission through generations—assuming that the kids are boys, and, oh, yes, that the spouses are kept in the dark. Griffin has the utmost respect for the Butcher, but privately he believes those particular rules are outdated.

But it's live with them or the *world* goes to darkness.

"What do you think is going on?" Griffin asks with a frown. "Is she challenging the peace?"

Roman shrugs. "Let's hope not. And it doesn't matter, you're getting married."

Griffin doesn't buy the casual attitude for a second. "But what about *her*?"

"We're all here, and I've got a nullifier with me. It's probably nothing to be concerned about," Roman says. "Odds are it's a complete coincidence."

"You believe that?" Griffin asks. This is beyond statistically improbable.

"What's the alternative?" Roman asks. "That Savvy knows about her and invited her?"

"When he puts it like that, if you *did* want an excuse to postpone . . ." Diego says.

No. No way. Griffin got so caught up in the drama of the infamous Mother Circe being here and what it might mean that he almost forgot why he is.

"Dad's right. Savvy is the furthest thing from a witch. It's nothing to go nuclear over right now . . . Just keep tabs on Circe until she leaves. Today is the day I marry the woman I love." Diego's mouth is open to protest again and Griffin says, "It's almost time. Discussion over."

The unsettling news has sobered the mood. Griffin doesn't mind that. He's a calm, steady type, even under pressure. *Especially* under it. The loud questioning of his choices from his brothers and Diego is something he's content to do without.

His dad pulls him aside as the others leave to set up for the processional.

"Nervous?" his father asks.

"Nope," Griffin answers honestly.

Roman grins. "I wasn't when I married your mother either."

Griffin's parents have an excellent marriage, and that's despite the secrets kept from his mother. That means it is possible to do this. His optimism about making it work long-term comes from watching the two of them.

"I don't make decisions lightly," Griffin says.

"Believe me, after getting a letter from your second-grade teacher about the fact you needed to undertake a study to answer what your favorite color was . . . I know."

"Hey, that's a surprisingly difficult question." *Not anymore. It's the sea green of Savvy's eyes.*

"Uh-huh. I'm happy for you, son."

Griffin's throat tightens. "I'm happy for me too."

They nod at each other in the way of manly men who would rather hug but then they might shed actual tears and it isn't the right time for that.

Griffin swallows. "You have a pet theory why Circe is here?"

Roman's mouth tightens. "I wish she weren't. But I trust your gut as much as I trust mine—as long as she doesn't make trouble, neither will we."

Griffin nods. He wishes he weren't going to get married in front of their oldest enemy, but he's used to dealing with surprises.

Diego pokes his head in from the main floor of the barn. "You're up in a sec," he says.

"See you out there," Roman says, and follows Diego out to be escorted to his seat.

Griffin's left alone in the vestibule to gather his thoughts— for all of thirty seconds. Then Diego pokes his head back in. "She even *looks* like a witch."

Whatever that means. Warts? Full hag style? Cackling? He's not going to encourage Diego by asking, despite his curiosity.

Griffin stays practical. "Don't tell me where she is, I'll want to look. She'll notice."

"Trust me, you can't miss her. The old crone radiates power, Griff."

"Behave, Diego," Griffin says. Though he isn't a fan of the idea of a witch observing his wedding.

Just then, there's a gentle knock on the wood paneling behind Diego. It's followed by the entrance of the officiant who's marrying them, slipping past his friend. Savvy's auntie Simone. She's chosen a long jewel-hued robe for the occasion.

"Is this one causing trouble?" she asks, eyebrows up.

Diego smiles, a picture of innocence, and she rolls her eyes.

"Ready?" she asks Griffin.

"More than."

"Good answer."

Savvy and her auntie Simone are close. Satisfied, Simone leaves to go take her place.

Music starts out in the main part of the venue, and, as rehearsed, he walks out and continues up the aisle flanked by rows of chairs. Circular tables are set up outside for the post-wedding meal. Savvy's friends and relatives watch him closely.

On the groom's side there's some restlessness, but his dad gives him a thumbs-up and his mother beams at him. They happen to be seated next to the Butcher in the front row. It's been a few years since Griffin has seen the man, and he's aged in that time—nothing like his actual age, obviously, but his black hair has gone gray, his eyebrows are thin, and his skin is grooved with wrinkles.

Griffin takes his position up front next to Simone, watching the bridesmaids and groomsmen come up the aisle. Diego is first, paired with smart-mouthed Brie, his favorite of Savvy's friends. Griffin smiles at her, but she has her eyes narrowed at him.

That's weird. She can't still be mad about Savvy and Griffin *almost* seeing each other, can she?

The rest of the wedding party marches out on cue, but there's none of the joking around or smiles between the pairs like at the rehearsal dinner. Griffin forces himself not to search the crowd for Mother Circe. He focuses straight down the center.

The wedding march begins, and the crowd stands.

The motion distracts him.

Damn it. Griffin does, in fact, spot her right away.

Mother Circe is standing in the front row of the bride's section, a silver-haired elderly woman in a high-necked deep green dress. She's staring across the aisle at the Butcher. Who's doing the same back. That . . . not good.

But it should keep her on her best behavior, being face-to-face with the man who stopped witches from leaving carnage in their wake. Who made her bargain with them.

Griffin relaxes. A fraction.

Savvy emerges. A few gasps come from the crowd at her beauty. Her mother's arm is linked through hers to escort her, since she doesn't have a father in the picture. His worries recede even further.

Whatever Griffin expected Savvy to look like, this surpasses it, because it's the reality. Where Savvy's concerned, the reality is always better than the fantasy.

She's in a long cream gown, and her hair's down with a flower crown holding her veil on. He's glad she decided not to wear it over her face. She smiles at him, and lifts one hand away from the bouquet in her hands to give him a small wave.

He smiles and returns the tiny wave. *Nothing could be more right than this.*

The sound of a cough from his side interrupts the moment. Make that, of coughing. Continuing on. And on. He looks over to find that the source of the noise is the Butcher. The man is bent double, hacking so loud he can be easily heard over the music.

His groomsmen are looking at Mother Circe, the serenely smiling Mother Circe.

Shit.

What if she's making him cough? For that matter, what if she tries to kill him? Maybe that's why she showed up here. It's not such an outlandish idea.

Griffin wills her to knock it off and everyone to stay put. If only *he* had magic powers.

But he doesn't. He has to hope instead.

3

Savvy

Any doubt Savvy has evaporates at the sight of Griffin, takes-her-breath-away handsome in his tux, waiting for her at the end of the aisle. How can he be so hot and kind at the same time? You can see it in his smile and his eyes, how sharp and thoughtful he is. He's built for a professor, too, especially given that she sees him reading far more often than working out.

But that's just another of the contradictions that make Griffin who he is. *Hers.*

She grins at him and adds a tiny wave. He returns the gesture, his eyes locked appreciatively on her. So what if they've been living together for a while? Their wedding night is going to be unforgettable. She'll make up for the lies she has to tell every day for the rest of their lives.

A loud cough sounds in the crowd, and her mother's hand tightens on her arm. Savvy expects to see someone leaving the ceremony, headed outside with their cold or whatever. Or maybe feel the force, like a swift breeze, of a witch casting a small healing or a silencing spell to make it stop.

But then she understands the person who's coughing must be the Butcher himself. She and her mother reach the aisle he's in, at the front. He's thin with pale, gnarled skin and, bent double hacking away, he resembles nothing so much as an ancient birch tree. Griffin's father gives her a worried but supportive nod while he tries to help steady the old devil.

She and her mother stop where they're supposed to, even though there's a seasick feeling, as if things might be on the verge of careening out of control.

Savvy's auntie Simone steps forward. She's the witch everyone comes to with their problems to get advice, to learn to deal with their emotions as kids, or to be gently coached out of bad situations as adults. She's unusually solemn.

"I believe an elder of the community will be asking the question," she says.

This isn't what they rehearsed. Auntie Simone is supposed to do the asking. Savvy looks around and finds Elle in the corner, tight-lipped.

The coughing continues.

Mother Circe stands, and Savvy's surprised to see her hair has gone completely silver. Somehow she never expected the woman to age. She holds her wrinkled hands out. Her eyes are vibrant, still, the right blue and the left brown. "Who gives permission for this daughter to be wed?" she asks, her voice deep and strong despite her aged appearance.

That's not quite the practiced wording either and that can't be an accident. Mother Circe must not want her being "given away" to Griffin, even ceremonially. *Why?* Savvy frowns at Elle.

Elle shrugs, as if to say, *What are you going to do? It's Circe.*

"I do," her mother says.

The Butcher is still coughing. Is he here to cause a disruption? This is pretty weak as far as that goes. Or so she thinks until . . .

"Someone has to stop her," Diego whisper-shouts to Griffin from the line of groomsmen.

In an instant, Savvy's senses are as heightened as they would be on a mission. Her mother releases her hand. What does Diego mean?

"Still all right, hon?" Claudia asks Savvy, low.

Savvy says, "Yes," but she's no longer certain.

She walks the rest of the way to Griffin. Diego is practically bouncing on his toes, and she can feel restless energy boiling in her bridal party.

She forgets to give Griffin her hands, or maybe he forgets to take them. They stand, staring at each other. The coughing fades, so that's something. Griffin's face is his, even if there's a shadow of worry on it. She knows its shape so well. The finest of lines at the corners that crinkle adorably when he smiles at her. The glasses he takes off when they go to bed . . . his kind hazel eyes. His thick black hair that resists being tamed by product, though he tries. All familiar.

But Savvy feels a weird sensation as they look at each other. She can't identify it, she just knows something is different than when they exchanged tiny waves moments before.

"Griffin, Savvy, friends of the bride and groom, thank you . . . all for joining us here today." Auntie Simone is clearly rattled. When they rehearsed, she used Savvy's full name, and the hesitation before "all" was telling. If the rock of their community is already shaken, this isn't going well. "Savvy and Griffin are here to be joined in the institution of holy matrimony."

That's when Auntie Simone notices they aren't holding hands. "Griffin, could you take Savvy—Savannah's hands?"

He hesitates.

What the hell?

Savvy holds her hands out, and he finally slips them into his own. Her heart thumps like it's between her ears instead of her brain: beating loud, fast. She takes a slow breath.

It doesn't help.

The coughing begins again, and it's so much louder in the absence of music. She follows Griffin's gaze over his shoulder to the Butcher.

She and Griffin look at each other one more time. He tugs her over as if to shield her. "Stay behind me," he says.

She doesn't know how to react.

"Can anyone make her stop?" Griffin says, loud, facing out to the venue.

She could pretend not to understand. She should.

"He *said* make the witch stop," Diego says. "Before she kills him! You make her stop or we will."

"I'm handling this," Griffin says to him.

Savvy and Auntie Simone exchange a look. Not one of them can *make* Mother Circe do anything. From what Savvy can tell, when she casts out her senses, Circe isn't doing anything. And how does Diego know she's a witch?

Mother Circe stands. She confirms Savvy's read on the situation. "I assure you this is no working of mine. The suggestion is an insult."

Uh-oh. An insulted Mother Circe is a precursor to something much worse than a coughing fit.

Savvy steps up beside Griffin, thinking she might warn him. But . . .

"Please," Griffin says, trying to push Savvy behind him again, entreating the crowd. "Can't you do something?"

That's when Savvy understands what's going on here. The Butcher and Mother Circe being at this wedding on either side isn't a coincidence. It's something far, far worse. Did Griffin trick her on purpose?

"Who are you?" she steps away and asks Griffin. "Really?"

He stares at her, then at Mother Circe, and around the rows of chairs set up in the barn. He focuses on her guests. But *they* aren't guests. They belong here. This is their territory. She's beginning to understand. It's the people he's brought here who don't belong.

"Did you know she's a witch?" he asks.

"Did you know he's the Butcher?" she volleys back.

Griffin gapes at her.

Savvy should behave. She truly should. This is not the thing to do, but Mother Circe says, "Go on, child, they have insulted us, when I did nothing," and it's permission.

The Butcher manages to straighten and through a cough says, "Good people are allergic to witches, so it doesn't matter if you meant to do anything or not."

"Go on," Mother Circe urges.

Savvy doesn't need to hear it again. Not anymore.

The way witchcraft behaves is in tune with nature. The larger the use, the more risk of upsetting the balance, and the more it takes out of the witch. But Savvy isn't content with a small demonstration at the moment.

Not a medium one either. She's on their home ground, at her strongest. These interlopers won't sense the magic here, since it's masked by spells. But it eddies around her, under her feet, meeting her own.

Did Savvy know Mother Circe was a witch? Oh, yes, Griffin. She absolutely knew.

Savvy lowers her hands and summons the element of wind to her, watching as the gust sweeps up the groom's side until it reaches its destination. She batters the Butcher and the groomsmen and Griffin with the wind, watching to see how he reacts.

The crowd erupts. The groom's side is fighting the strong wind, and the witch's side is filled with chatter. Magic is thick in the air. Mother Circe cackles, high-pitched, an attack cry.

Griffin is struggling to stay upright and looking at Savvy like she's a monster, a harpy from myth. To be fair, that's what she feels like. She wants to bring a tempest here. Raze the Butcher and the man who apparently played her for a fool to the ground with it.

"You lied to me," she says loudly, to be heard over the howling wind. She isn't sure exactly what Griffin is up to, but she knows one thing for certain. "You are a liar."

As Griffin's mother gapes in confusion, his father, Roman, lifts his hands overhead then cracks two halves of a device together. The wind's effect begins to recede. He must be using some kind of gadget that absorbs magic to blunt its impact. She knows who has countermeasures like that. This is the last piece of confirmation she needs.

"You're a *hunter.*" She spits the word.

"Yeah, I'm feeling a little betrayed myself here, babe," Griffin says, sarcasm heavy.

"You brought him here," Savvy says, and points at the Butcher. "You risked us all."

The wind renews its whip around them as Savvy calls on it again. She'll test the strength of their defenses. Her veil flies off, petals from the flowers whirling through the air around her.

Brie, behind her, restless, says, "Should we call our familiars? What's our next move here?"

"You don't have one," Diego says, but the wind nearly swallows his words.

Savvy raises her hands and lets the hunters reap the whirlwind.

"*You're a witch,*" Griffin says, not with wonder. Like it's the worst thing.

"I can't believe I was going to marry you!" Savvy has always been grateful for her power. Grateful for her sisters. The implication she should feel otherwise from the man she thought she loved—the man who is a member of *H.U.N.T.E.R.*—is too much insult for her.

She shoves Griffin backward using her power and he nearly falls. He's back up in no time.

Everyone's on their feet, in fact. This must be what it's like when all hell breaks loose.

Diego heads toward Mother Circe, and Brie whammies him with a spell, giving him giant fluffy boxing gloves. He flails trying to get them off. It wouldn't matter anyway.

Her mother is holding a protective circle around Mother Circe. Though with her cackling cry and powers, she can certainly handle herself.

The Butcher's voice calls out: "We leave this place to the hags. Retreat."

"No, we should stay," Griffin says. "Hold our ground. Like you did back then."

She's never heard that in his voice before. It takes a moment to interpret it. Anger. At her.

He has no idea. He has no *right*. Savvy's rage is pure, justified.

"No," she says, stalking toward him. "He's right. You *should* go. This is one fight you can't win. You've taken too much from us—from me—and you won't take a thing more."

"I haven't taken *anything* from you," he says. He hesitates, then, "You made me love you."

He says it as if she used a spell *on him*. It was only one time. Only a small spell. It's not why he loves—loved—her. She would never do that. And she didn't *have* to.

People say that love and hate are similar emotions, that there's not much distance between the two. Savvy never understood that. They're night and day, good and evil. Now she gets it.

What was love gathers into a mass of betrayal that burns so hot the air heats around her. And not only her—around Griffin.

He writhes in it, and she sees a nasty line of blisters forming on his neck above his collar. She suspects they aren't the only injuries. She eases up, the smallest amount, though she couldn't explain why.

"This," the Butcher shouts. "This is why we avoid witches. Creatures of emotion. They're dangerous and out of control. Retreat."

"Retreat," Griffin echoes. "Retreat!"

Mother Circe rises up into the air, hovering above the Butcher. "We are dangerous, true. But never out of control. You will never join one of yours with one of mine."

Circe gestures to Savvy, and Savvy feels her add her own call to the element. Brie steps beside Savvy, and her mother's there too, and Auntie Simone, and Elle. Their power forms a focused tornado, and they force the Butcher and his men and their accompanying wives and dates out of the barn.

Savvy's sense of betrayal feeds on the satisfaction of watching Griffin scramble backward, the disgust in how he said the word "witch" in her ears.

When it's only witches left in the barn, the double doors slam closed under the wind's surge. Savvy slumps with the weight of letting go of her power. And her dreams of a life together.

"I can't believe he 'Clark Kent'ed you," Brie says.

"That would imply he's Superman, not a lying *hunter*," Savvy says, and she clings to her rage because it's the only thing that will get her through this.

"Oh no," Brie says in horror. Savvy can't imagine what could provoke that response now. "You're crying," Brie says, accusing. She turns to the others. "She's crying! What do we do?"

"I'm not," Savvy says.

Savvy doesn't cry. Ever. And if she does, it's definitely not in front of anyone.

So when she reaches up and feels something damp on her cheek and realizes Brie is right, it's then that she knows she can never forgive the man who reduced her to tears.

"I'll kill him."

"Yes," Mother Circe says, landing softly. "They must be terminated. They know too much. They've all seen our true faces. We must make him an example. This is your assignment."

Savvy does what she would in the field. She flips the switch inside herself, turns on the lights that eliminate distractions and illuminate the immediate priority.

"Don't worry," she says. "I've got it."

4

Griffin

The scene outside the barn is nearly as chaotic as the one inside. Griffin's mother is huddled with several other women. He removes his jacket and tosses it aside, then limps in their direction as his father heads to her and puts his hand on her arm. Roman tells her something and she nods, and turns to gather the others.

Roman waves Griffin, his brothers, and Diego toward his giant SUV, clicking the doors unlocked. They pile in, Griffin wincing at the throb from his injuries. He's in the front, the rest in the back.

His dad peels out and speeds away from the remains of what was supposed to be the rest of Griffin's life. What the hell just happened?

"He needs medical attention," Diego says. "We should hit HQ."

Griffin wants to protest, but his arm feels like he stuck it into a furnace. He slowly undoes the buttons of his shirt cuff and pulls up the sleeve. He already ripped off his bow tie to get the cloth away from the wounded spot on his neck. The skin of his forearm—just this one, randomly, spookily—is angry red with what has to be a second-degree burn, maybe third. Savvy did that. With her *powers. Her witchcraft.* He almost married a witch. Savvy is a *witch*.

"I need to go home and get my stuff before she can," he says. "Imagine what she can do with all that."

"No," his father says without looking away from the road, "first we need to make sure you'll be okay. You got the brunt of the heat. And we don't know what—what the—"

"Magic," Griffin supplies.

"Might mean for the injury." His dad checks the rearview. "There's a giant raven following us."

A familiar, he means. Griffin shakes his head. He's in a nightmare.

"I can't believe this," Diego says. Then, "I told you, man."

Griffin doesn't point out the contradiction. Or that Diego didn't tell him jack shit, except that getting married was a mistake. He certainly never guessed the truth about Savvy. She acted as surprised as Griffin back there, but that has to be pretend, right? It can't be real. She must have known what she was doing this whole time. Did the witches actively decide to blow up the accords?

Why did she have to pick Griffin? Witches always have their reasons, they've all been taught that. Did she think he was weak? An easy target?

She has another think coming.

The Butcher tossing around words like "hag" sure pissed them off. He's already headed to actual higher ground, via the helicopter that was waiting outside for him. Griffin figures that's his prerogative, after several hundred years of being on the front lines. Though it would've been nice to have some direction from the top on how to deal with this mess.

It's not a mess, it's your life. No, Griffin is too precise for that. He revises. *It's both.*

"At least you found out before you went through with it," his brother Quinn offers from the back. His suit is still perfect, as usual.

"I liked Savvy," Jacob says with a scrub to his beard.

"I didn't," Diego says, flexing his fingers. The puffy gloves disintegrated when they got outside. "I knew it would never work."

"Yes, you did like her and no, you didn't know that." Griffin grits the words out. Part of him desperately wants to defend her, but he can't. Savvy is a witch, *and* apparently an operative of C.R.O.N.E. And Griffin didn't just like her. He also loved her. His heart might as well be seared like his arm. She made a fool of him.

"Guys, back off," his dad says. "What happened back there was intense. Practically unprecedented."

Griffin is the historian and scholar here, and he has no idea what his dad is referring to. "Practically?"

"*Romeo and Juliet* was based on a similar situation," Quinn says.

Griffin blinks. "That's our version of an urban legend."

"Is it? You never were particularly interested in literature. Or romance."

"What did you tell Mom?" Griffin asks, wondering what she must think after witnessing everything.

"That I'd explain what I can later, and to get everyone to go home in the meantime."

"This is a disaster." Griffin, stating the obvious.

His dad jerks the wheel and they turn onto a road that's completely covered by a canopy of trees. "Getting away from the familiar."

Diego's tapping out a message into his phone. "Big Rob will be waiting when we get there."

"I still think we should go home first." Except it isn't his home anymore.

"No," they say in chorus, so Griffin sighs and closes his eyes and doesn't bother arguing. He sees Savvy behind them, as she looked emerging in her wedding gown. Stunning. Bewitching, even. He opens them, hisses with the pain of his injuries, and stares out the window at the passing trees instead.

Diego can't stay quiet for more than a few minutes at a time. Today is no exception. "She was kinda hot when she was attacking us though."

Griffin turns, despite the pain, and looks at Diego over his shoulder. Diego shrugs. "I'm just saying."

"Well, don't," Griffin says.

Jacob punches Diego in the arm. "Too soon, bro."

Diego shrugs again, but he actually shuts up for the rest of the drive.

Griffin goes back to watching, the fields and suburbs turning to tall buildings as they reenter the city. He wonders if he'll ever be able to close his eyes again without seeing Savvy's face.

Headquarters is hidden in plain sight. The three-story complex far off the campus of the prestigious university it's affiliated with, courtesy of a former provost and operative, is officially referred to as the Experimental Sciences Building. Whispers about top-secret government contracts have kept others from prying into the details.

His dad enters the basement parking garage with a card and a retinal scan. The sliding door closes behind them. The lot is nearly empty, save their fleet of vehicles, offering a variety of choices, from the fast to the huge and slow, the nondescript to the distinctive. His dad parks and makes it around the side of the car to support Griffin before the others can. For his part, Griffin leans on his dad and holds his injured arm out at an awkward angle.

Big Rob dashes out to meet them, his shadow that of a giant. He's not quite *that* oversized, but he earned his nickname the honest way. You wouldn't blink twice if he did live at the top of a beanstalk. Which is an odd as fuck thing to think, so maybe Griffin *is* losing it.

"Hey, brother," Big Rob says, "you mind?"

He doesn't wait for Griffin's answer before sweeping a light over his arm to check it out. Then, the beam travels up to his neck.

"Hmm," Big Rob murmurs. Before Griffin can ask a question or protest, Big Rob scoops him up into his arms, careful not to touch the blistered arm.

"I'm not a child. I can walk," Griffin grumbles as Rob starts moving.

"Yeah, but we need to get some meds on that burn stat and you'll be too slow." Big Rob says it breezily. "Sorry about what happened."

"You already heard?"

Rob glances at Diego as they advance through the garage.

Griffin groans. "Diego, how many people have you texted about this?"

"Not that many," Diego says. "I mean, most of the people we know were there."

"Well, stop it." Griffin considers. "Jacob, take his phone."

"Over my dead body," Diego says, and then, "Hey, no."

The sound of their scuffle as Big Rob carries him through the doors and toward the med bay makes Griffin wonder how they ever got the best of the witches in the first place. The motion-activated lights above click on, timed with their passing.

Until this morning, he'd have thought H.U.N.T.E.R. capable of whatever was thrown at it, that they were more advanced now than way back when. Their dustups since the accords have gone both ways, with each side winning some and losing others. But the way Savvy called that wind and her clear fury . . . that's nothing to sniff at.

Big Rob brings Griffin into one of the shiny medical suites, outfitted with technology that might as well be magic.

H.U.N.T.E.R. uses equipment and gadgets that work to counteract and absorb the stuff, as well as deploy it in necessary combat situations. When fighting supernatural forces, magic is a necessity, although they try not to rely on it.

Diego crashes through the door behind them. "Did you really have to tell him to take my phone?"

"Out, you, all of you. Everyone except the patient." Big Rob gives a look that brooks no argument.

Griffin watches as Roman nods, puts his hand on Diego's shoulder, and extracts him from the room.

"Thanks," Griffin says.

"Thought you might want some quiet time." Big Rob busies himself at the counter nearby. "Shirt off."

"You're a good man." He strips his worse-for-wear dress shirt off as carefully as possible.

Big Rob turns back with a wince and a pair of long, glowing bandages. "Plus, this is going to sting."

"Aw, shit." Griffin can't catch a break. When Rob says you're going to feel anything at all, that means it'll hurt like hell. "Go on. Get it over with."

"You really had no idea?" Big Rob says, positioning Griffin's arm for better access.

The question hurts like a stab, or maybe, he realizes, that's what the bandage feels like. "What is that?"

"Bioluminescent cocktail, should kill any germs and accelerate the healing process."

He motions and Griffin tilts his head to give him access to his throat.

"You've been tinkering again?" Griffin asks.

Big Rob ducks his head, almost bashful. "A little."

"Feels better already," Griffin says, lying. He pushes up from the table.

"No, no." Big Rob's big hands stop his legs before they hit

# # #

the floor. "You need a breath. Take a minute to think. You just went through a trauma." He pauses. "And the bandages need sixty seconds to be effective."

The minute crawls by. Griffin remembers Savvy as he first saw her, and the lightning strike of the second time. He remembers the night he asked her to marry him. He tries to figure out what he missed, why he didn't see it . . . or, better yet, *feel* that she was tricking him. Every step along the way, he got in deeper. Even though he knew it was a risk. If that's what witches are capable of . . .

Again, he wonders how his organization will ever be a match for them. *But we were. We always have been.* They brought the witches under control in the first place. If they have to, they'll do it again.

He thinks of one specific day, a random day, a normal day. It was the day he decided he wanted to marry her. At least in his conscious brain.

Savvy showed up at home earlier than expected. He'd just barely gotten changed after a mission. She had a leftover piece of cake from some lunch birthday thing at her work at the firm and she didn't even ask him if he wanted a bite, didn't need to. She sailed through the bedroom door as he stashed his dirty clothes with a fork holding a bite in her hand and she put it to his lips.

No other cake in the world made him think of weddings. That one did. And the kiss she bestowed as she pushed him back onto the bed after.

Now he goes over it again. The firm, huh? The cake might have been spelled or something, to make him pop the question.

Even as he considers it, he rejects it. Griffin asked because he fell for *her*. The woman, not the witch, though.

"It's been three minutes," Big Rob says gently. "I'm opening the door."

They learned the lore about witches from the time they were

little boys. Their greatest and most powerful enemies. The accords were their first major victory in making the world safer.

Griffin hears the med door click open after Rob unlocks it. He waits.

Nothing happens.

That can't be good.

He levers up and onto his feet. His arm and neck are a dull throb of pain instead of a loud scream now.

Big Rob gives him a baffled look. "Where are they?"

"They've got bad news."

"How do you know?"

"They had to debate who gets to tell me."

His dad walks through at last, trailed by his brothers and Diego. "We've got bad news, son," Roman says.

Griffin looks at Big Rob. *See?*

"Well, I'm full up over here, seeing as how I almost married a witch."

"About that," Roman says, and hesitates.

"Diego texted too many people," Jacob says pointedly. "The Butcher thinks it makes us look weak if we don't respond. There's an assignment. For you, specifically."

Griffin isn't surprised by the logic. "What is it?"

"I'm sorry, I really am," Diego says.

Griffin believes him. This must be bad. Worse than bad, given the day so far. He reaches out to take the phone his father is offering. On it, there's a picture of Savvy and him that their wedding photographer took a few weeks ago.

In it, Savvy laughs like there's not a care in her world. Her smile used to be the brightest thing in his.

Now an order has been added below it:

TERMINATE IMMEDIATELY.

One Year Ago

✦✦✦

5

The Goddess and the Professor

On the sidewalk, Savvy wraps her sweater more tightly around her and knots the belt against the blustery wind blowing up off the Thames.

London is Savvy's favorite city to visit. She wouldn't want to live here, but only because too much familiarity might rub away at the charm. Great Britain is the first foreign country she ever got sent to on assignment, and the combination of excitement and nerves that tumble around in her whenever she lands at Heathrow is part memory of when she was a wide-eyed newly-sent-into-the-field witch. Although at this point Savvy is a seasoned operative, she gets a thrill from being here. Usually.

She wouldn't admit it to anyone, but she's been feeling off lately. She has a sense that something is missing from her life and she suspects it might be the one thing she absolutely shouldn't want: love. She is devoted to her job, obviously. Distractions are dangerous, that's what she's been taught. And so she jumped at the chance to come on this particular assignment. It'll remind her that this is all she needs.

London teems with magic, more than even older cities. There's an undercurrent of danger, of historical battles lost and won, and, of course, plenty of excellent strong tea. Jobs here are always interesting.

The first alert about the situation she's been sent to defuse reportedly came in from a mudlark friend of someone in the co-ven. London's mudlarks are people who haunt the foreshore of the mighty Thames river as a hobby or a lifestyle, tracking and charting its tides meticulously so they can comb through the treasure and trash it briefly deposits each day and then sweeps back out again.

Even now, Savvy sees a woman below her at the side of the river, picking at the wide swath of freshly revealed mud. She might be looking for ancient Roman coins or antique glass bottles . . . or something as normal as a cell phone dropped into the water. No metal detectors are allowed at this particular portion of the river, by regulation of the Port of London Authority, which issues mudlarking permits. Searching here is what's known as "eyes only." That's because everyday treasure hunters are discouraged from overly disturbing the Vauxhall site, since it has turned up some of the most ancient artifacts discovered in the Thames. Prehistoric structures—and items. Like the wooden mask that has washed up and resulted in the tiniest problem of inspiring the formation of a cult.

The river itself is a muddy green today. Savvy checked in with the local C.R.O.N.E. chapter house earlier for a briefing. She's here to do reconnaissance in prep for dealing with the acolytes, to gauge whether there's a continued risk from the mask's magic in these waters. The cult has set up shop in a flat across town, and she'll have to decouple their attachment to the item in question at that location. Otherwise, there's the real risk of resurrecting a dark-spirited god that will do nothing good after sleeping for centuries only to fully awaken in the modern day.

She hasn't bothered with donning a glamour yet. But now she draws on her power to transform her features as she cuts across the pavement to a set of stone steps leading down to the riverside. Soon she'll look like a different person, specifically a petite random tourist complete with camera hanging off her neck, on a visit to the foreshore. . . .

Except something stalls the simple spell, and she's left as is.

She reaches inside herself again, weaving the basic disguise and casting it over herself. . . .

She stares down at her hands, reaches up to her hair to confirm that the strangest thing is happening.

Which is nothing. The glamour is refusing to take hold.

Could it be the residual power of the item that brought her here? A troubling and unprecedented development, no matter what's causing it.

But Savvy can't just leave now, even if she's wearing her true face. And for all the mudlark knows, she reassures herself, she's still any old tourist.

She completes the journey down the stairs, keeping her distance from the woman. Once on the shore, she casts her senses wide. It's not a flashy spell, nothing that would draw anyone's notice. She needs an idea of how complicated the retrieval might prove to be, given this latest hiccup. Anyone watching will have no clue she's sweeping for a trace of the object in question's magic.

She'll hurry with her recon and then get out of here. That's the plan, until she hears the shouts from above and drops the search.

Shit, shit, shit.

The other thing about Vauxhall is that it has an inconvenient building located above the shoreline. The headquarters of MI6—the UK's Secret Intelligence Service—perches above her, a building filled with spies. One of the rules an operative has to follow is to stay out of the way of regular law-enforcement agencies. Avoiding their notice is sometimes tricky, but essential. Now the lack of glamour is more of a liability. She doesn't want her face on MI6's radar.

When she turns, there's a burst of activity above and people in suits headed her way. A man and a woman. MI6 officers, aka secret agents, she'd bet everything on it. That's the way her luck is running. Security guards would be in uniform.

One of C.R.O.N.E.'s most important duties is to keep human authorities far, far away from supernatural intrigue. They're to know nothing about the existence of anything beyond the norm. It's impossible to imagine they suspect what's really happening, but their presence is not something to be cavalier about either.

While she could spell herself hidden—assuming whatever prevented her from glamouring isn't powerful enough to halt that—they've already seen her. She could certainly take out her pocket broom and fly away, but that would hardly go unnoticed. No matter what, she can't do any sort of flashy magic in the open.

But she doesn't want to stay and chat with them either, not wearing her own face. What's her move here?

That's when she spots the man with the small motorboat tethered to the nearby bridge mooring. Her only pause is that he's wearing scuba gear and clearly just climbed out of the river.

Which seems, to be fake British about it, barking mad. But also convenient.

From where she stands, she can see he's built well, and when he pulls off his mask, changing out goggles for thick-rimmed glasses, his face strikes her as a good one. She heads for the shoreline, wading through the muddy bank, her impractical heeled boots sinking in.

The mudlark ignores the whole fuss, intent on the foreshore.

The man and woman in suits are walking more briskly down the steps now.

"Hey, honey," she calls to the man, "can you come get me over here?" She waves at him.

The man squints at her, and then at the engine on his boat. He's about to leave. She hurries to get closer.

He's looking over her shoulder at the likely intelligence officers heading toward her. From behind her, the male agent's voice shouts, "Hold! Wait there!"

"I've always wanted to go on a boat ride on the Thames," she says, a little more quietly, and puts her most charming smile on.

The man is staring at her. He's cute, in the big strong nerd sort of way. Black hair, intense eyes behind the glasses. "What?"

"I need a ride," she says. "I'm Savvy. I'll explain."

She hears the shouting to wait getting closer behind her, but refuses to look. That would be too suspicious.

Cute scuba man isn't buying it, though. "I don't know," he says, and she notices his accent isn't British. "I'm not looking for any trouble."

"Please?" She puts a plea into it, widening her eyes. No magic needed for this maneuver. It's one she tries not to use often, but the doe-eyed damsel-in-distress plays on the natural hero impulse of men. Nontoxic masculinity to the rescue? "Help me," she adds, mouthing the words.

He's got the motor running, and she must be losing her touch, because he sure seems like he's going to leave her there.

"Stop there!" the man in the suit calls again.

The woman adds, "We want a word with you!"

Savvy half turns and puts a hand to her heart as if she's surprised. "Me?"

She slides a pleading glance to the man with the boat. The suits are headed directly for her. Well, for both of them, actually. The man in glasses frowns.

Then the boat steers her way, stopping just short. The man reaches out a hand to her. Up close, the scuba suit shows off that "well-built" was understating it. His shoulders are perfectly shaped, the kind you could hold on to.

Get it together, Savvy orders herself. *There'll be time for ogling this guy later. Maybe.*

"What's this?" the man in his boring suit asks as he joins them. He's eyebrowless, but otherwise ordinary, and he steps carefully to avoid getting his loafers wet. "I'm SIS Officer Davids, and this is Officer Arnold." He nods to the woman, also in a boring suit and wearing thick glasses. The sun emerges briefly and its reflection obscures her eyes behind them. "There's no diving in this part of the river, sir, miss," Officer Davids says.

"Mudlarks have to have permits," Officer Arnold says in a thin reedy voice. "Do you?"

"Oh no. We didn't realize." The man is still reaching out to Savvy. "*Sweetheart*, we'd better get going."

"Yes," Savvy says, ignoring the rabbit of her pulse at the false endearment. She offers a ditzy smile to the spooks, scanning them for any traces of magic to worry about. She gets nothing back—and decides this encounter was inconvenient, but not the worst. "We're so sorry," she says, leaning on the sweet tea of her Southern accent. "American tourists. You know how we are."

The eyebrowless officer's expression says he does, and that Americans are way more annoying than they could possibly realize. The woman moves so Savvy finally glimpses her eyes. They are a striking blue, the right oddly a little more vibrant than the left, and narrowed, measuring.

Time to leave. *Stat.*

Savvy takes the hand of the man in the boat. When their fingers touch, his strong around hers, pulling her over and safely into the boat, Savvy's heart flutters in her chest. Again, ridiculous given the situation. She turns back to face the shore.

"Thank you for letting us go," Savvy says to the officers.

"Well . . ." Officer Davids hesitates.

"Take care while the two of you enjoy *our* city," Officer Arnold finishes.

"Oh, we will!" Savvy says. There's something of a tug on her attention and she desperately wants to be away from this place. Immediately.

Savvy's savior leans in close to her and speaks in her ear. "I'm Griffin. Life jacket under there." He nods toward a bench seat. "Put it on and then hang on tight." He raises his voice. "Yes! Thank you! Sorry!"

Griffin's low-voiced orders should make her prickly, but she finds she doesn't mind them. Her heart does that unfamiliar thing again. She does as he says, and he glances back to confirm that she has before he sends the boat out onto the choppy green water.

They both look back at the MI6 officers waiting on the foreshore with the oblivious mudlark. Then at each other.

"I could be anyone, you know," Griffin says. "You shouldn't trust people so easily."

Aw, he's worried for her. That's sweet. He doesn't know that a witch has nothing to fear from the creepy men of the world. They are easily dealt with. It's the best perk of being witchkin, Savvy often thinks. Not that Griffin seems creepy.

"Now, who are you and why'd you need the rescue?" he asks, revealing he's more suspicious of her than he's been letting on.

"Like I said, I wanted a boat ride." She retreats to her cover. "I do a lot of work for a charity back home—it's high-profile. I wouldn't want to get them in trouble because I was tromping around the wrong spot." She shrugs and points the questioning back his way. "You don't seem like the type who scubas illegally in the Thames."

"I didn't realize it wasn't allowed."

Fat chance. "You're American too?" she asks, though she already knows the answer. "Tourist?"

"Sort of. I'm a professor. I specialize in antiquities. I wanted to get a look at the ruins. . . ."

Ironic coincidence. The ruins hidden beneath the water are the remnants of a prehistoric witches' trading post. Part of the reason the artifact she's to neutralize washed up where it did. She does one last sweep with her senses while he watches her.

And that's when she catches it. The smallest hint of strong, old magic. Here in the boat.

"Is that all you did?" she asks.

He blinks. "Yes . . . other than rescuing you."

"Just checking." You can't be too careful. She gives him a dazzling smile to play it off.

Her working theory is that he's inadvertently been attracted to whatever holds the magic. Even fragments of some items will pull a civilian right in. *Especially items strong enough to somehow block a glamour. Or inspire a cult.* He may not even be aware he's taken it.

She'll have to drain whatever it is before it can affect him. Which makes the rest of this more delicate. He has to stay with her until she can.

"What about you—are you here on business or pleasure?" he asks. He's still wondering about her. Good.

Because the word "pleasure" coming from his mouth does something to Savvy. She presses her legs together. She could kill two problems with one solution tonight, if she's lucky: the artifact and her neglected sex life.

She gives an open smile. "Do I have to choose?"

Griffin's face goes pink in the cheeks. His hair is wet, mussed. His glasses frames are adorably dorky. "Oh, well, I . . ."

He's too cute when he rubs the back of his neck and stares ahead like steering the boat has suddenly gotten much more complicated. Savvy isn't sure what this is, and then she remembers. This is what fun is like. She's having *fun*.

Yes, she is.

Griffin knows it was a terrible idea to let this strange woman onto his boat. He could've been gone before MI6 reached the shore. But she also gave him a way to play the hapless tourist, in case it was him they were interested in. Which seems entirely likely.

And there's something about the way she asked him. Not to

mention, she's gorgeous in an unusual way. The bridge he was moored to has these grand bronze sculptures on the pylons—each one a woman symbolizing a different type of industry, one sporting a hammer and anvil, others an urn, a branch, a book. They appear to have stepped out of myth and frozen in place.

She could be one of them come to life. Tall and substantial, striking, with sharp, attentive eyes.

"Am I reading this wrong?" she asks. "I'm so sorry. I panicked back there. Sorry if I made you uncomfortable just now."

He doesn't want her to think he doesn't appreciate her obvious charms. He does, but this is unfamiliar territory for him—not to mention, he's wary of why she actually wanted to get away from the officers. And he has something he suspects holds dangerous magic in the boat, the small piece of wood he retrieved while diving. One of Big Rob's abnormal-energy-detecting gadgets pulled him right to it, and now he needs to do further testing to see if it holds the right kind of magic to account for what they've been detecting from a recent spike in London.

Griffin senses that this Savvy is not the shy, retiring flower she appears to be now, smiling innocently at him. He almost wondered if she was there for the same reason as him, but she has answered his questions believably and she's flirting way too much to be the enemy. . . .

"You don't seem like the panicking type," he says.

She smiles at him again, and he wonders if he's having sunstroke, then remembers he's in overcast London.

"I like an observant man." She looks behind them.

"No one's following us," he says, then realizes that's a weird thing for a professor to notice.

"Good," she says, and laughs. "I wasn't checking for that. Where are you staying? I owe you dinner, at least . . . if it's close to where I'm staying, anyway."

"So you only owe me dinner if it's convenient?" He's teasing, but it comes out serious. He shakes his head. "I rescued you."

"Let's say you helped me rescue myself and call it even," she counters. "So, dinner? Pleasure not business?"

"We'll see," he says.

This woman—this beautiful, flirting woman—is going to kill him. He can already tell.

The most disturbing thing of all is that he can't find it in himself to mind.

6

✦ ✦ ✦

The Goddess and the Professor

urns out they're both staying at the Savoy. That is too much
of a coincidence for Griffin's taste.

And so he *is* trying to extricate himself, though he doesn't
truly want to say goodbye to this odd woman yet. The cozy grandeur of the hotel lobby isn't helping his resolve. The black-and-white-checkerboard marble floors and golden chandelier lighting only make Savvy look more appealing. Who hurries to get away from a goddess?

People who remember goddesses can be dangerous.

"I bet you're starving," Savvy says. "Please, let me treat you."

He's not sure if she means it as a double entendre or if he simply hears everything that comes out of her mouth with a dual, seductive meaning. He's not great at flirting, never has been. Conversations? Yes. Banter? No.

He's managed to put off a real response to her invite. She came along as he returned the boat—a rental, so as to stay under the radar, for all the good it did—and got them a rideshare to the hotel.

"I am hungry," he says.

"Diving will do that."

"You dive?"

"Like a dolphin," Savvy says.

This woman is entirely too interesting.

They linger across from each other in the lobby. His decision to join her or not hangs between them. The smart thing would be to thank her and head upstairs, order room service, and examine the wood fragment in his scuba bag.

"Here's my proposal," she says. "Two Americans at the Savoy, who successfully fled security by boat, should stick together, right? Drinks in the American Bar, dinner at Kaspar's, and then . . . we'll go our separate ways."

Griffin can't help grinning at her determination. He does have to eat, and a few hours off won't make or break the mission.

"Okay, you convinced me," he says. "But I need to go upstairs and change."

"Me too."

"Why? You look perfect," he says, and then ducks his head. *Jesus, Griffin, you have zero game.* "That sounded fake. . . . But I meant it."

Savvy leans in and says, "I liked it. I think I like you." She sniffs him. "But you smell like the Thames. Take a shower too. I'll meet you back here in half an hour."

He nods and they stand awkwardly until Savvy says, "We both have to get on the elevator now."

Griffin gestures for her to cross the grand lobby first. "My kid brothers used to always jump between floors in elevators. It drove my parents crazy."

"How many brothers do you have?"

"Two," he says, and hesitates.

"That explains your big-brother energy," she says. "I can just picture little Griffin, the protector."

Ha, Griffin thinks, *hardly.* He was a thin, gawky kid who could barely protect himself. But he always did the assigned reading. The muscles came later.

"Are you calling me boring?" he murmurs to her as they board the elevator.

He presses his floor number and raises his brows for hers. "Same floor," she says.

Griffin is so screwed.

"What a coincidence," he says.

"A lucky one?"

"I don't believe in luck."

Her head tilts, caramel hair winding across her shoulder like a silky rope he wants to touch. "Huh. I guess I'll have to for the both of us."

The doors slide closed and he almost doesn't believe what she does. When the car starts to move, Savvy hops into the air, just like his kid brothers used to.

"It only works when you're going down," he says with a sidelong glance.

She shrugs one shoulder, attractively.

He cracks up and gives in to the urge to hop too. Then he forces his expression straight. It isn't easy. His cheeks want to slide back into a grin.

"You're a bad influence," he says.

"You have no idea," Savvy says.

He swallows the words "Prove it," but the grin returns. She gives him one back and it feels like a reward.

Yep. He's totally screwed.

Savvy is having the time of her recent life. When Griffin smiles it shows a surprisingly playful streak that, combined with his dorky glasses and seriousness otherwise, is apparently catnip to Savvy. He's a dish. Those broad shoulders tapering down into his narrow waist are delicious.

She didn't need to know about his brothers, but couldn't keep herself from asking. She barely managed to keep from pressing for more details. That isn't like her, unless it's part of a job. Her only job tonight is to keep him with her until she can neutralize the object he's carrying in his scuba bag—she had to use a tiny push of magic to get him to agree to dinner. She won't exert anything more on him than her wiles for the rest of the evening. It wouldn't be fair otherwise.

Hopefully, that'll be enough.

She needs a few minutes to cool off and update her own coven's headquarters. Technically she's still working, after all. It's not even a night off. She has to protect Griffin from whatever convinced him to take a little piece of magic from the site.

But there's nothing about the larger situation she's trouble-shooting that's so time sensitive she can't wait until tomorrow to tackle it. No, she can have tonight for herself. Spend it with Griffin and fix this one small problem.

She'll prove just what a bad influence she can be. This year has been so busy, it's been something of a dry spell for her—no pun intended. She lets herself into her room and pretends not to pay attention to which door Griffin goes to. Three down.

She deserves this little break. One night only. Then back to the real work.

She wants to see Griffin flustered. And, most of all, on top of her before the night is out.

The familiar she's also bringing back to the rescue charity—on paper—and to the Farmhouse—in reality—is curled up on her bed, striped tail wrapped around her like she's a cat. But she's not, she's a lemur Savvy nicknamed Leggy. Familiars tend to find the nearest coven when their senses awake. The Atlanta Farmhouse specializes in training difficult ones that don't match with any-one at that first place, and then finding them the right witches to pair with. The Paris chapter has been waiting for a few weeks for someone to fetch Leggy.

Savvy's only a little grumpy about the fact that she's not yet

found a familiar of her own. Maybe when she finally does, that
bond will fill the missing-something space.

She sits on the edge of the bed in the quietly elegant room,
and Leggy opens one sleepy eye, then closes it. "Good girl,"
Savvy says.

Then Savvy calls Brie using her secure talisman, a locket
she wears on a chain around her neck. The small silver globe
contains a mixture of herbs to boost its powers of communication. Like that, her friend's face hovers in the air above her, the
phantom version of FaceTime.

"Reporting in," Savvy says. "Got the lemur. A sweetie,
but no bond with me. She'll make someone a great familiar
though." She considers mentioning the problem with her glamour earlier, but she's got the situation in hand. It must have to
do with the mask. "I should be able to visit the flat the object's
in early tomorrow and neutralize it. Then home."

Brie's head tilts this way and then that. "Wait, you're not taking care of draining it tonight and hopping on the red-eye?" She
pauses. "Tell me it's because you met a hot royal or something."

"Or something," Savvy says, but she must have a tell.

"Come on," Brie says. "Spit it out."

"I identified one small piece that is in other hands, and I'll be
getting access to drain it tonight."

Brie's brows lift. "Whose hands?"

"A professor. We met at the river." Deciding not to mention the MI6 encounter or that she wasn't wearing her glamour
during it is definitely the right call. Brie would never let that go.

Brie's eyes widen. "Is he or she or them a cute professor?"

She won't let this go either. Savvy tries to poker-face her way
through. "I guess he's okay."

Brie claps. "That's a yes. Shag his brains out, friend. You
need to get lucky in the worst way."

Her best friend, always putting things so delicately.

"Don't make it sound like I'm hard up."

Brie snorts. "Babe, you're wound up so tight lately that I keep waiting for something to pull your grenade pin and turn you into *WandaVision*. Have fun. What are you wearing?"

Savvy sniffs. "*He* said I looked perfect in this sweater."

Brie starts to object, but Savvy beats her to it. She could use her magic, but instead she walks over to her suitcase and holds up a red dress with one shoulder and a fit so snug it could've been made for her.

"Good girl," Brie says. "Don't forget to use condoms and—"

"And suppress my powers so my orgasm doesn't blow him away. I'm not a teenager." Savvy recalls jumping in the elevator and wonders how true that is. Something about today is making her feel younger than usual.

A knock at the door interrupts.

"One second," she calls out, and nearly drops the dress.

"You're nervous!" Brie says, accusing.

"I am not and goodbye." Savvy ends the call. She peers at the door and the dress and then spirit-fingers her hands down her body to don the garment in an instant. She adds some matching red lipstick. Marilyn Monroe used to hang out in the bar they're going to, so it seems appropriate.

Ready, she hesitates at the door. She smooths her hair with butterfly hands.

She *is* nervous. Curse Brie and her annoying ability to accurately read Savvy's emotions, something Savvy herself isn't always great at.

Savvy takes a deep breath, releases it, and opens the door. Not wide, just in case Leggy gets curious. But Griffin still gets a peek at her dress.

"Damn," Griffin says, and then, "Sorry, I just. Wow."

"I didn't mind that either. And damn wow back."

She says it a little breathlessly because Griffin has arrived in a tuxedo. It's so Cary Grant in *Bringing Up Baby* that she can hardly stand to step out into the hall to join him. The sleek black lines and crisp white shirt beneath make him even more attractive than the scuba suit did. She wants to just tug him into her orbit. Except her orbit contains a lemur it might be hard to explain.

And the anticipation is part of what makes a one-night stand worth it. If her brain balks at thinking of him that way, she dismisses it. One night off. She'll never see him again.

She *deserves* this. And she is still working; she has to protect him from the object he took.

She's practically a hero for going to dinner with him. Imagining Brie's reaction to that statement makes her want to laugh.

Both she and Griffin are quiet on the walk to the elevator, and Savvy definitely gets caught sneaking looks at him. She doesn't mind, because she catches him sneaking a long look at her as they board the elevator. There's an older gentleman at the back.

"I don't usually do this kind of thing," Griffin says, for her ears only, as they descend. There's heat in his eyes as they rake down her dress.

"Oh? Fancy dinners in hotels? Then why did you pack that tux?"

His eyes meet hers. They're a gold-brown she could climb into. "Go to dinner in hotels with strange women, I meant." He says it lightly.

"We just met and here you're calling me strange."

Griffin shakes his head. "I'm beginning to think you're too quick for me to keep up with."

He doesn't sound bothered by it. Savvy grins at him, the most dazzling one she has, as the elevator stops. "You'll never know unless you keep trying."

My goddess, she didn't realize how much she missed flirting.

Missed someone looking at her this way. Like he's dying to know everything about her *and* to touch her.

Has she ever really had that? She's beginning to doubt it.

"Excuse me," the older man says, and slides past them to exit. "We've stopped, by the way. Good luck, friend," he tells Griffin as he gets off the elevator.

"See, he knows I'm going to need it," Griffin says with a suddenly shy grin.

He's so damn cute. And charming. He takes her elbow as they emerge into the lobby and navigate to the American Bar, so called because it was the first bar that served American cocktails in London—and Hollywood royalty tended to stay here and gravitate to it.

"Reservation for two, under Savannah," she tells the maître d'. No last name. She's already pushing how much Griffin knows about her.

"I don't see that," the immaculately attired host says.

"If you could just check again," Savvy says, and does a little magic.

"Oh, yes, sorry, madame, sir," he says, looking down. "Follow me."

There's no harm in small magics like these, and they upset no balance. Savvy doesn't usually jump lines. But this is too good an opportunity to pass up. She'd planned to come out tonight for the ambience, sit alone in her slinky dress, and try to rediscover her excitement at being in London.

Doing it with company—this company—is much better.

They sit at a glass-topped table and grin at each other until the curvy, vaguely punk server approaches.

"What'll we have this evening?" she asks.

"The Hanky Panky for me," Savvy says.

Griffin swallows. "A martini here."

"Traditional," she says as the waitress leaves.

"More of that big-brother energy you picked up on," he says. He leans in as if he's going to tell her a secret. He lingers close. "I feel like James Bond when I order one."

"What's your last name?" she asks. Then realizes she shouldn't have, because she ought not to reciprocate.

"Carter," he says, their gazes catching.

"Carter, Griffin Carter," she says. "It has a ring."

He rolls his eyes. "And yours?"

"Wilde," she says, even though it's true and she shouldn't.

"Fits," he says.

"Ha."

The bar isn't busy yet, and the server is already returning with their drinks in sparkling glasses. She sets Savvy's elegant red drink in front of her, nods to them both, and leaves.

Savvy takes a sip, then extends the coupe glass toward Griffin. "The Hanky Panky was created here," she says, not adding that the bartender who invented it, Ada Coleman, was also a witch. "It's a twist on a martini. You have to try it."

"I have to try the Hanky Panky," he says, and she does love that glazed look in his eye. She didn't order this drink by accident. Savvy might be out of practice at flirting, but she's no slouch.

Their fingers touch as he takes the glass. He sips, looking at her, and there's something unbelievably intimate about watching him drink from her glass. She's rethinking that whole not-just-pulling-him-into-her-room decision. She could've hidden Leggy in the bathroom.

"Mm," he says. "It's a little sweet."

She takes it back from him, touching his fingers again. "You like it?"

"Too much," he says.

The atmosphere around them is heavy and loaded. It takes

her a moment longer than it typically would to recognize when the threat arrives.

The man nods to her. Griffin swivels and receives a nod from him too.

The male MI6 officer from earlier stalks across the bar toward them as if he owns the place.

7

✦ ✦ ✦

The Goddess and the Professor

The man waves and stops at their table. Savvy's afraid to look over at Griffin, afraid her alarm bells will show. She slides her hand over his instead.

Solidarity. They played married earlier and they have to keep at it.

Griffin gives her fingers a squeeze back and she's reassured he understands—if not the reason this is such a treacherous development for her.

"Well, hello there, Officer Davids," he says, "fancy meeting you here."

His tone of voice is light. Savvy is grateful for that too. "Yes," Savvy says, "what a small world."

"Mind if I join you?" he asks.

Savvy does cut a look at Griffin then. She says, apologetically, "We are having a date night. . . ."

"But certainly," Griffin says with a shrug. "For a few minutes."

Officer Davids gestures and their server brings over a third chair to the table. She lingers, clearly interested in what's going on here.

"Can we buy you a drink?" Savvy asks him.

She's already thinking of different ways to head off the potential threat he poses. If the issue is forced, she'll act. A cocktail would give her something to subtly spell his attention away. Otherwise, she'll have to get more creative.

"I'm meeting someone here," he says. "So no need. How was the rest of your boat trip?"

He's meeting someone here. . . . Savvy doesn't buy it for a second. There's no such thing as a coincidence of *this* magnitude.

"Tell us about you," Savvy says, and props her chin on her hand to achieve peak nonthreatening status. "Your job must be way more exciting than running off tourists."

Griffin takes the hint and tips his martini toward the officer. "Yes, we were just talking about James Bond. Impress away."

"Were you?" The intelligence officer puts his elbows on the table. As if he intends to stay awhile. Bad manners that mean Savvy likes him less by the second.

"How interesting," he continues. "Those original novels by Fleming were a lot darker than people seem to remember."

"They are noir," Savvy says. "It's not that surprising."

"You've read them?" Griffin asks. He covers. "I didn't realize."

"Of course I have." Savvy sips her drink. When she sets it down, she gives her most flirtatious glance to Officer Davids. "Come on. Tell us one story from your James Bond résumé," she begs. "Please, you have to."

His face is unreadable, but then he looks across the bar. His face relaxes as he raises a hand and waves someone over. Savvy follows his gesture and finds Officer Arnold striding toward them.

Well, this isn't good.

"You two are joined at the hip," Griffin observes.

"We're partners," Officer Davids says as Officer Arnold arrives, bringing her own chair to the table to join them without asking. "These two were just asking me to tell them a story from work."

"You should," Officer Arnold says.

Officer Davids nods. His eyes dart back and forth between

Griffin and Savvy like a little mouse's. "There was this day. Typical overcast weather out, and Officer Arnold and I were at our desks analyzing information, when we were interrupted. A security guard came to us."

"Yes?" Savvy risks a glance at Griffin and finds him watching Officer Davids with a steely energy.

"He tells us there's some suspicious activity down by the Thames. Can we come take a look? So we do, and there's one of our usual mudlarks. But there's a couple down by the shoreline and something feels off. . . . We didn't feel we'd resolved the issue after we talked to them. We were still worried they might have taken something from or left something in the river, since they had a boat and one was seen diving. Or perhaps they were attempting to get a view of our building."

"Are you accusing us of something?" Griffin asks it levelly.

Savvy's dossier did point out that the proximity of MI6 has meant officers interrupting television shows filming and archaeologists investigating the ruins—afraid of some sort of sneak attack or bomb being planted. She wishes she could communicate to Griffin that that's probably the kind of thing causing them concern. . . .

But she can't, obviously.

Officer Davids lifts his hands. "Anything to add, Officer Arnold?"

The woman leans forward, her oddly varied eyes skimming over Griffin and Savvy. "I just want to know why you were pretending to be a couple today when I've just confirmed with the hotel that you have separate rooms."

She drops it like a bomb and waits.

You're going to have to do better than that, ordinary spook, Savvy thinks.

"I suppose you followed us with all your spy cams and the

like—it's so—" Savvy pretends to search for a word, flustered. "—cool."

"Cool?" Officer Arnold says with disdain.

"All that BBC TV stuff." Savvy waves a hand.

"You mean CCTV, *hon*," Griffin says, amused or pretending to be.

"Anyway, it's flattering that you think we're so interesting, Officers," Savvy says. "You've certainly spiced up our trip."

The two of them clearly weren't expecting this particular reaction. Officer Davids's mouse eyes narrow beneath the hairless skin where his brows should be. "You want us to believe you haven't done anything wrong? That you are innocent?"

"That you're really *a couple*?" Officer Arnold finishes.

Griffin opens his mouth to speak, but Savvy returns her hand over his. He doesn't flip it to squeeze back this time, but he lets her talk first. "Well, this is embarrassing." Savvy makes a big deal of leaning even farther over the table than Officer Arnold did, and yes, she knows she's serving Officer Davids (and Officer Arnold, for that matter) a good look at her cleavage, but she'll use all the weapons at her disposal.

Officer Davids coughs.

"You see," Savvy says, and catches Griffin's gaze. There's a spark of intrigue. He's not sure what she's going to do.

The thing is, Savvy is excellent at maintaining her cover.

"Sometimes, when we travel, we like to pretend to be strangers." She swallows and flushes and puts her hand to her chest, as if she can't believe she said it out loud. "Like we just met . . . and . . . It's a role-play scenario."

Griffin slides his hand over and takes hers in it, and she's just glad he's game at this point. "Yes, you see?" Griffin asks. "It helps keeps things . . . fresh."

Officer Davids seems confused. "You pretend to be strangers?"

Savvy pushes back. "I'm not comfortable saying any more. Are you—were you really investigating *us*?"

Officer Davids exchanges a look with Officer Arnold. "I—"

"I think you should apologize to the lady," Griffin says. "Both of you."

Griffin is on his feet then and has his hand on the back of her chair, pulling it out as she rises, and it's more Bondesque than he probably realizes. She definitely likes him.

"I do apologize if we overstepped." Officer Davids slouches a hair, at last.

Officer Arnold doesn't sound sorry. "We have to rely on our intuition, you know, and I still question . . ."

"Your intuition was wrong," Savvy says. "We'll be going now. We should thank you for making our night more . . . exciting."

The officers exchange a glance and seem to agree to let the two of them leave.

Griffin holds his arm out and Savvy threads hers through. They exit the bar. Have they gotten away? She can't be sure yet.

"Quick thinking," Griffin says.

"*Did* you take something today?" Savvy asks, because it would look more suspicious if she didn't.

"I'm a scholar," Griffin answers.

She takes this to mean he doesn't even know he removed something from the river. As she suspected.

"I had to ask."

"Well, then I have to ask . . . Are you some noir-reading criminal?" he asks.

"I wish," she says. No need to linger over that question. "But I am famished—being in England always makes me want to use words like 'famished.' And I'd prefer our meal not be crashed again, so . . . room service?"

Griffin looks over her shoulder, a callback to that afternoon when they met. She knows without turning that the officers are still back there, watching them.

He trains his gaze back on her, leans forward, and says, "Your room or mine?"

"Yours," Savvy says.

When they get off the elevator onto their floor, she hesitates as they pass her room—because of the low thumps coming from inside. "I better go check on . . . my dog," she says.

"Do you actually have a dog or are you just trying to get out of this? It's okay, I understand," he says. So sweet and earnest, and also it's clear he's hoping that isn't the case.

"I'll be right there, I swear."

He nods, continues on, and lets himself into his room. Only then does she apply her key to the door and open it into absolute chaos. Leggy is swinging from the overhead light fixture or, rather, hanging from it, and causing the fixture to swing and tap the nearest wall. Savvy's clothing is strewn across the room, and the leaves she left for the lemur to eat are all gone.

"Having fun?" she asks.

The lemur's big eyes manage to look both defiant and sheepish. "I promise we'll go on a field trip, just give me a few hours, okay? And keep it down in here?"

The lemur hesitates, then begins to lower herself down. Leggy is going to make someone a great familiar.

For her part, Savvy straightens her dress, gives her hair a fluff, and heads out to sate her hunger. Both kinds.

Finish the job, and leave, before those two intelligence officers can get any nosier.

Griffin knows that quick thinking and a playful intellect are his turn-ons, but he's never met anyone who combined the two to this degree. He doesn't do one-night stands, not since college. But somehow it feels like he and Savvy have known each other longer than an afternoon. It *almost* feels like the fact that he's using his cover identity doesn't matter.

He wants to spend more time with her, and he hopes to get a night's worth. That's all he can have, so, fine. He can justify this because of the snooping officers, supporting the story they went with. There's no way those two know he took a magic-infused sliver of wood from the river. Regular law enforcement are clueless and so they shall remain.

He gets the feeling Savvy enjoys messing with people like them—he no longer suspects she's up to anything else.

Anyway, he gets tonight *if* Savvy shows back up. The dog story and peeling off into her room might be a bad sign. He lingers around the door, and yes, he's waiting. He wonders how long he will before he calls it. He should at least go sit down.

He's still thinking that when the knocking sounds on the door in sprightly raps.

He opens it, and she's standing there with a wide grin, holding a bottle of red wine. "I didn't think you were coming back," he says, and motions for her to enter. He leans in a little as she sails past him. "But I'm glad you did."

What is he doing? None of this is like him.

Even though he's solo and had no expectation anyone would be joining him, he's left out nothing related to his true work. The sliver is tucked away in a small zipper case in his diving bag in the bathroom, ready to be tested and nullified, if needed, with Big Rob's gadgets.

Savvy strides in and looks around, opening her arms with a whistle. "It's a good thing we chose your room," she says with a wry smile. She's like one of the legendary stars from the 1940s, striding around his room in that sexy-as-fuck long red dress and taking in his reading stack beside the bed. All dry texts about prehistoric artifacts and cultural research, so nothing should strike her as off.

"Why's that?" he asks.

"You're extremely tidy."

"Now why does that sound like a criticism?"

She drops a hand to the back of a chair that faces a table. "Because mine is a mess. My little dog monster. You'd think I've lived there for a week."

"How long have you been here?" he asks.

She flutters a hand dismissively and he thinks he'd do anything she asked. "Let's not get into all that boring stuff. Let's order food."

Griffin laughs. "Okay."

He brings the room service menu and places it in front of her. He bends slightly over her, their heads close together, as they study it.

He inhales the scent of her hair, trying not to be too obvious about it. Her perfume has an herbal note, and the phrase "goddess of the garden" comes to him, despite the fact that she couldn't be more glamorous. She's somehow both. Her air is earthy. This is not the usual bent of Griffin's thoughts. This woman is making his brain into scrambled eggs. He's aware of his heart beating faster, desire building.

"You know what," she breathes, and he leans in closer.

"No. What?" he asks.

She turns her head, and their faces are at most an inch apart. "I don't think I'm hungry for food . . . yet. What we said downstairs, that we role-play . . . how about we . . ."

Griffin doesn't need more invitation than that. He slides one hand to her cheek and then behind her neck and uses the other one to pull her to her feet, flush against him. Then, he claims her mouth.

The meeting of their lips is wild and wet, and frankly, the hottest thing he's ever experienced. He tastes her again and again, tongues licking into each other's mouths, and she seemingly can't get enough either. She lifts one thigh, and his hand loops around it to bring them even closer, and they both make a noise that is pure need as she grinds her hips into his. He drops a kiss, sucking at her neck, and she groans.

He pulls back, reluctantly, to make sure this isn't going too fast. He only meant to start with a kiss. He supposes that's all they did.

But what a kiss.

She smiles at him, lips wet. "Why, professor, you're good at that."

"You too," he says, and when she reaches for his tie to undo it, he moves her hands away only because he can get rid of it faster.

He wishes he'd gotten the MI6 officers' address so he could send them a thank-you note. Without them, he'd never have met Savvy, never have kissed her . . .

They do order room service after, and Savvy could not be more content. The man knows how to give an orgasm or three. And how to be both commanding and thoughtful in bed, a rare combination. He's fallen asleep, and she wants to do the same. Snuggle in next to him and go for round two in the morning. But she can't.

She doesn't believe the officers were a true threat, but she still needs to get going, finish the assignment, and head home. She says a quiet goodbye—"Sleep well, Carter, Griffin Carter"—and presses a gentle kiss to his forehead before putting her feet softly on the floor.

Her senses have already told her where the object is, and she heads into the enormous marble bathroom, toward the scuba bag there. She could take it with her, but he might notice.

Magic objects that call people to them aren't subtle. He might not have known he took it, but he also might. So best to make it not matter.

She unzips a case empty other than a small piece of wood—which is odd, but oh well—and places the fragment on the counter. Then she opens her locket, shakes out a handful of herbs into her palm, and clenches her hand around wood and concoction both. She chants the appropriate Latin phrases. When she was a girl she was so annoyed by having to learn all that Latin, but for the more powerful spells it does seem to work better for her. Not for every witch, but of course she'd be stuck with it. She always thinks it sounds pretentious.

But she whispers the words and she feels the herbs absorb the old magic. That settled, she puts the sliver of wood on the bathroom counter, carefully pours the herbs back into her locket and closes it, and then replaces the piece of wood in the bag where she found it.

When she leaves the bathroom, she finds Griffin standing, gorgeously naked, and blinking sleepily. "Savvy?" he asks. "Sneaking out on me?"

"I'm afraid I have to go check up on my dog again. She gets lonely."

"Will you come back this time?" The heat in his eyes says he'd like nothing more.

She wants to say yes. But . . . "Would you rather I lie?"

He nods.

"Then I'll definitely see you again soon."

No parting kiss, she can't risk it. She'll be too easy to talk back into bed.

She goes to her room, packs everything quickly, and sets the room to rights. It's better if she doesn't see Griffin again before she leaves. It would be too tempting to do something ridiculously stupid, like leave him her number. She shouldn't have let him know her real name. She shouldn't know his.

"Let's go to work," she tells Leggy, and glamours her into a small dog with scruffy fur. What makes some animals familiars and others not is that they have their own subtle magic. It allows them to glamour themselves once taught, or be glamoured at any time, to avoid detection. Legend holds that witch familiars are usually cats, sometimes dogs, occasionally birds. That's because those are the typical disguises for them, as much as the reality.

Savvy puts Leggy as purse dog in a bag over her shoulder, leaving her head to peek out. Leggy's forged pet paperwork is already in her bag, ready to present to the gate agent. She checks her hand luggage at the front desk and says she'll need a car to the airport in two hours, far before sunrise.

Then off they go. This time she's able to glamour herself without trouble, which she chalks up to having drained the fragment. Anyone who sees her will have an entirely different woman to describe.

The studio-style flat is across town, and when she and Leggy reach it, Savvy pauses at the door and then spells it open. Inside, she and Leggy find the entire cult, sleeping around the leader. He wears the half-intact fragment of the red deer priestess mask that washed up from the Thames. The carving makes the man look half monster. Dark power emanates across the room.

He wakes at the sound of them entering, sits up, and stares eerily over at Savvy.

"I'll just be relieving you of that mask," she says. Then, "Go get it," to Leggy.

The man attempts to make a stand against Savvy, trying to get around her and leave with the artifact. The other members are slowly coming awake.

"Stay where you are!" Savvy uses her power to put on a light show that stuns them in place.

Leggy, meanwhile, proves entirely useful, taking her real form, scampering over and leaping up to steal the mask off the leader's face. She brings it back to Savvy, who takes it gratefully.

The cultists gape, not sure what's happening. Meeting Griffin was fortuitous in more ways than one—she crouches, while the cult watches, draining the magic from the mask into her locket more easily when it senses part of it is already there.

Savvy lets the people in the apartment keep the now-powerless mask, setting it on the ground. "You should return that to the river or a museum," she says.

The man and his followers, all dazed as if awakening from the mask's spell—which they are—seem to be listening. The man nods. "Thank . . . thank you," he says.

Time to go. The matter is closed.

Savvy doesn't know it, but she's on a plane back home, Leggy sleeping in glamoured puppy form beneath the seat in front of her, before Griffin wakes up.

The fragment from the river showed no magic at all upon testing with Rob's gadget, and Griffin's phone call home told him that whatever magic signature had spiked in London is gone, as of this morning. He asks if they want him to follow up, but they say no. There's another situation, up in Kentucky, and he's needed there.

On his way back home to his next job, he has the driver take an out-of-the-way route over the Vauxhall Bridge. "Stop here," he says, and the driver frowns, but does as he says and pulls over into a wide spot at the end. Griffin gets out, and he tells himself he's not looking for Savvy, down below the bridge. He's not.

They had a night to remember and that's plenty.

And anyway, there's no one there. The tide hasn't revealed the foreshore yet. From the top of the bridge, he tosses the small piece of wood back into the water where it belongs. He doesn't allow himself to think about missing her.

That would be foolish, and Griffin is no fool.

Now

8

✦ ✦ ✦

Savvy

Over Savvy's objections, she, her mother, Brie, and Elle are headed to the actual Farmhouse for firepower—instead of straight to Savvy's house. Elle's familiar is a dapple-gray horse named Pegasus, Peggy for short, who tends to hang out in Elle's pockets glamoured as a frog. Savvy rides behind her friend, wedding skirts ripped in half, as they gallop across the fields. Brie and her mother are following in her mom's pickup truck.

Savvy has plenty of magical weapons secreted away at the home she and Griffin share. Not to mention that her sweetly fierce familiar is there and probably climbing the walls, feeling the tumult inside her bonded partner. *I'm coming, kitten,* she thinks, and tries to calm herself. The connection is nonverbal, but maybe it will be some comfort to her special black cat to sense Savvy's rage and shock easing.

Oh no. If Griffin goes back home first, Paris won't know what's happened. She might greet him as normal. Surely he'll assume the cat is a familiar now. . . . Paris could defend herself, but would she? Against him?

Oh goddess. Does Savvy believe Griffin is capable of hurting her cat? He wouldn't. Right? No matter what he is.

"We have to hurry," she says, and Elle spurs Pegasus on faster.

Mother Circe took flight as soon as they got outside, telling them she would stay nearby until the matter is settled. She's usually a yaga. Despite the old legends, most witches prefer to live near their communities. But some of the old ones, like Mother Circe, have safe huts located in woods and cities across the world, and keep their locations secret.

Pegasus's hooves thunder on packed dirt as they hit the road that cuts through the property. The Farmhouse itself— the source of the entire property's nickname—comes into view in all its turreted, ramshackle glory. A series of outbuildings and barns with various purposes surround it. The familiars are in an uproar—both the paired and the unpaired—rushing out into the yard to meet them. There's the trundling Captain Bear, Brie's capybara, typically glamoured as a fluffy white dog when they're out and about. A full-grown grizzly bear that doesn't have a witch yet. An excess of dogs and cats of various sizes. A militant ostrich named Orange no one would risk crossing, paired with Simone.

Auntie Simone had her pocket broom handy and has already arrived. As Pegasus pulls up short at the edge of the yard, she hurries out from the house to meet them.

Savvy and Elle hop down, and Pegasus trots off toward the stables for a drink. "Call the broomsquires," Savvy says.

"Already done." Auntie Simone gestures at the men and women approaching from one of the barns, still dressed up for the wedding.

The broomsquires craft different shapes and sizes and types of brooms for all sorts of situations. They are toting combat brooms with shapes like bristled swords, faster and quieter than other styles.

Auntie Simone looks at her. "Do you want a wand?"

They hardly ever risk using wands. Witches as experienced as Savvy can focus their will easily enough without one. The impact from a wand can easily be deadly.

And that's what you need right now, she thinks.

"Yes."

"Are you sure?" Auntie Simone asks, tilting her head in question. "Or is that the hurt talking?"

"You know what Mother Circe said. I don't have a choice."

"You always have a choice, my Savvy. Don't let anyone tell you otherwise."

Savvy gapes. "Are you telling me to forget about what happened back there? He tricked me!"

"I know, sweet girl," Auntie Simone says. "But don't you love him?"

So much. "I *did,* but that doesn't matter. I have my orders. The job is what's important."

Auntie Simone frowns.

Savvy's mother and Brie roar up then in the black truck and save Savvy from having to say more. She strides over to the closest broomsquire and holds out her hand. The woman places the wood in her palm, and there's a zing of connection as she takes the broom in her right hand.

She turns back to Auntie Simone as the others come over to get combat brooms of their own.

"Wand, please," Savvy says.

Auntie Simone's disapproval is clear, but she produces a glowing, vibrating length of deep purple alchemical metal twisted like a rope. "Use it with care," she says.

"Oh, I will," Savvy says. "Hate is a kind of care."

Brie pats her on the shoulder. "Good line, babe. We ready?"

"I'm going in alone, but you can tag along," she says. There's no use trying to prevent that. When Brie opens her mouth to argue, Savvy says, "You are staying outside. He's mine." *He* was *mine, at least.*

"You know he'll bring others." Brie smiles as Captain Bear comes over and extends his tongue to lick her knee. "Yeah, buddy, you're coming too. No one will hurt you."

"Come on, Peggy," Elle says, broom in her right hand, as she bends to extend her left palm. Peggy as frog hops into it.

"Look, it's Cretin," her mother says as the giant raven swoops down to land on her extended arm. "He must've lost them. Don't worry, pet," she says, "we think we know where they are going."

Home, the home they were meant to share together forever.

"You haven't said 'I told you so' yet," Savvy says to Claudia. "Want to get it out of the way?"

Savvy knows how deeply her mother hates hunters—she lost one of her closest friends to an encounter with one when she was about Savvy's age. She was in love with Savvy's absentee father at the time, and blamed herself for not being there.

"I would never rub salt in your wound," Claudia says. "I know how it must hurt. You're my girl."

Savvy's throat tightens. "Let's go," she manages, and launches herself into the air, holding on to her broom with one hand and the wand with the other. The wind whips around her, tattered ivory skirts billowing like sails. She goes higher, faster, and hears the others following, calling to her to wait for them. She's waiting for no one.

Griffin Carter, your time is almost up.

The others have caught up to Savvy by the time they reach her—and Griffin's, but it was hers first—neighborhood in Decatur. The street is quiet. There are no vehicles in the driveway in front of the medium-sized, two-story bungalow-style home that was her first major purchase and step out into her own life.

Like most witch operatives-in-training, she stayed at the Farmhouse until she was in her midtwenties and found her niche working for the organization. Not everyone can or wants to be a field agent, obviously—there are the academy teachers for young witches, and then C.R.O.N.E.'s familiar healers and trainers, the spell-preparation workers, the broomsquires, and the intelligence gatherers. But Savvy always knew what she wanted to be. As a girl, she was obsessed not just with witch lore, but with characters like Modesty Blaise and Emma Peel, perhaps the root of her love of London. She read every single spy novel she could get her hands on growing up, and still does—not just Fleming's Bond, but John le Carré and Robert Ludlum, and eventually, thankfully, some spy books by and featuring women-as-actual-spies, from Kate Quinn and Alma Katsu.

She still reads and watches all sorts of spy media, although now she knows her job is entirely more thrilling than the made-up exploits of the characters. That's good, because it's all she's got now. *It's enough. More than enough,* she tells herself.

It should sound more convincing.

They land on the tidy grass in front of the house.

"He's not here," she says, and hears her disappointment.

"It could be a trap," her mother puts in.

Brie pats Captain Bear in white fluffy pup form's head. "Probably is. We should go in together."

"No," Savvy says. "This is *my* home. Wait here and be ready for them to show up."

"What kind of protection spell should we do? Boundary or hiding from random passersby?" her mother asks.

They can't maintain more than one such large enchantment simultaneously.

"Hiding," Savvy says. Their cover has to be maintained.

"Are you positive?" Claudia presses. "We could keep them out until you're clear of the house."

"Let him come. That's part of why we're here."

"We're on it," Elle says, still in her suit, her calm resolve closing the debate.

Brie and Claudia grumble, but must see in the set of Savvy's shoulders that this is no time to test her. She hands her broomstick to her mother and raises her arm to slip the wand into the back of her dress, between her shoulder blades.

What if he's already been and gone? *Then I'll hunt him down.* He has to pay for what he did to her. She catches her hand rubbing against her chest, as if he plunged a dagger into her heart. That probably would be more pleasant to deal with than this.

Behind her, energy crackles as her mother, Brie, and Elle weave the spell that will prevent the rest of the neighborhood from taking any notice of them, no matter what battle royale ensues.

She doesn't see Griffin as the kind of coward to hide in the shadows and ambush her. But it's not like she knows him as well as she thought, is it? So Savvy approaches the door carefully.

She never uses a key. Only Griffin has to do that.

She tests the door to find it still locked, as expected, but it turns in her hand because it recognizes her touch.

Paris is waiting and lunges at her as gracefully as the leopard she is. Her black-on-gray spotted fur gleams with a healthy sheen, the relatively small ears on her big diamond-shaped head up and alert as she greets Savvy. Usually, she appears to be a scruffy cat. Even as a kitten, she was able to glamour herself for protection on the streets, whereas some familiars can only be glamoured by a witch. Paris and Savvy's connection was instant.

And it's another reminder of Griffin.

She rubs the side of Paris's face. "It's going to be okay. Griffin, he betrayed us. It's just going to be you and me."

Paris makes a disgruntled hiss.

"I know you don't like it. I'll explain later. He thinks we're evil."

Paris blinks nearly clear green eyes at her.

"I know. Wild, isn't it? He's a hunter. We're enemies."

Paris shakes her head.

Wait a second. When Griffin and she decided he would move

in with her, he made a big deal about doing some renovations. He did them mostly with the help of his buddies.

What has he hidden in this house? Is it even safe to be here? She remembers the wand tucked against her back.

Safe as houses, she thinks, a phrase that never made sense to her until now. A house is only as safe as its defenses. She stops. The others are more vulnerable here, despite everything. She needs to stay calm, to think clearly. If they can manage to go back to the Farmhouse before he comes, she can slip out on her own and come back, ensuring no one else gets hurt unnecessarily.

"Let's gather some things. I can convince them to go back to the Farmhouse to regroup." She's been acting on instinct. She needs to be smart. Cautious, even if it's not her way.

She heads past the basement stairs—Griffin's office is down there—and back to the bedroom. Paris pads along behind her.

She pulls out a suitcase and unlocks the hidden compartment in the wall with all her best spell supplies, keyed to her. She starts adding them to the case, along with a few of her favorite clothing items. When she comes across a particularly comfy gray T-shirt for the Baker Street Irregulars that Griffin bought her, she wads it up and then tosses it in the air and watches it burn.

"Petty," she admits to Paris. "But satisfying."

Paris purrs.

There's a sound so low she almost misses it. Almost.

The click of the back door closing. Sure, she just thought—hoped?—she might miss him. But this is why she came, isn't it? She shouldn't want to avoid the inevitable. Her friends and mother are plenty capable of fighting, if they need to.

"Daddy's home," she whispers to Paris. She takes the wand from her wrecked dress and she waits.

And waits.

She hears the sound of footsteps heading down the stairs. How did he get past her mother, Brie, and Elle's physical perimeter without them spotting him? They couldn't cast a boundary spell, but they would have been watching on high alert. She should've let everyone come inside. Maybe they could've sent all his undoubtedly hidden H.U.N.T.E.R. gear into the aether, their rarely used version of nuking something from orbit.

He must think he's awfully slick, as if he can just sneak in here and she won't notice. She should march out there and confront him. . . . But she hesitates. The idea of looking him in the face just became extremely real and does something strange to her insides.

He bursts through the bedroom door before she can manage to make her limbs move.

Startled, she unleashes a zap of purple light from the wand that leaves the wall beside the entrance to the room smoking.

Griffin comes farther inside, holding a metallic device that looks like a Taser. As if he's going to touch a witch like her with that.

"Hi, honey," he says, "I'm home."

"I already made that joke to Paris."

Paris has shifted back to her kitty-cat glamour, which is an interesting choice. Griffin looks at the cat and raises his hand to call her, "Here, Paris, sweet girl."

Paris stays put, glancing between them.

"You are *not* taking my cat," Savvy says.

Griffin's jaw takes on a stubborn set. "Your cat? She's ours."

"She's my familiar," Savvy informs him. "And don't you dare mistreat her the way you did me."

"How *I* mistreated *you*," he says.

He's still in what's left of his tux, the worse for wear like her dress, sleeves torn. There's a pale bandage on the side of his neck and another on his forearm. She always liked his forearms. His shoulders. His neck.

He stalks toward her.

"Stay back," she says.

He keeps coming. "Returning to the scene of your crimes?"

"My crimes?" Her eyes narrow. "That's rich coming from someone who would've murdered me a few hundred years ago without blinking. Who'd be happy to do it now."

Griffin goes still. The weight of what she's said hangs between them.

She has a sudden suspicion. "Why are you here?"

"Why are you?" he asks.

Mother Circe's directive was clear. What if the Butcher issued the same one?

There's a stack of thick books on Griffin's side of the bed, as normal, and she aims a shot from the wand at it. The books flare into flame instantly.

He gasps. Then, "You burned my books! Those are from the library!"

Savvy smiles coldly. "Sorry, not sorry."

"Two can play that game, goddess," he says.

That used to be an affectionate nickname.

Before she figures out his meaning, he goes for the built-in shelves along the top of the wall filled with her favorite spy novels. "How did I miss this?" he asks as he sweeps a hand along the spines, knocking the books onto the floor.

"You—why—you—" She takes dead aim with the wand.

He discharges the thing he's holding as he lunges out of the way of her strike. Tiny silver pins fly outward and settle on the floor in between her books, forming a rough circle around Griffin, pointing up like tines of a weird fork.

"This next one is going to hurt you more than me," she says.

"Try it." Griffin smiles and she can't figure out why. He must have been taught what a powerful witch with a wand is capable of—but the expression on his face is unbothered, the coldest she's ever seen.

Fine. She'll blast it off, then. She levels the wand in his direction and channels her distress into the blast . . . which breaks up into tiny arcs, captured by the metal tines.

She gapes. What the hell?

"Think lightning rod," Griffin says, smug. He presses the button on the part of the device still in his hand, and the metal prongs that sucked up the blast of wand return to it.

"I guess we'll just have to do this the old-fashioned way," Savvy says, grabbing a bottle filled with a potent poisonous concoction from her suitcase. Paris shadows her as she lunges for the door.

Once she's in the hall, she sprints to the kitchen, tucking the wand into the back of her dress and throwing open a drawer to pull out her favorite chef's knife. She unstoppers the bottle with her teeth and then pours the solution over the blade. It sizzles on contact.

Griffin stalks into the room, moving slowly, as if he's unbothered. Damn him, she still notices how handsome he is.

"Running so soon," he says. "I'm surprised. And a little disappointed, if I'm honest."

"I'm not running away from anything," she counters, gripping the knife. "You always were the dim type."

He reaches up, removes his glasses, and tosses them away. "You're the one who never noticed I didn't need these."

"Not really," Savvy says, preparing her grip, waiting for her opening. "I thought it was why you sucked at finding the right spot in bed."

Griffin has gotten closer than she intended. She hadn't planned to stab him—well, not *this* up close and personal—but they're practically nose-to-nose. Paris is staying out of it for now, though she growls a warning as Griffin nears.

"You never seemed to have any complaints about my sucking," Griffin says.

Heat floods through her. Anger, mixed with something else.

The nerve. And he's not wrong. She lifts her chin. "We've already established I'm a fantastic actor."

She takes a step back, heading toward the outer hallway and the front door. She doesn't want to notice what she sees then, a flash of emotion in Griffin's eyes. Is that hurt?

"Yes," he says, "we have, at that."

As she reaches the hallway, the front door crashes open and she continues backing away as Griffin follows. Griffin's friend Diego appears. She's caught between them.

Brie is visible behind Diego, floating, an avenging pink-clad angel with her hair whipping around her head.

"Company," Savvy says, "but you weren't invited, Diego."

Griffin takes her arm, and Savvy throws him off and backs up so she has some range.

"She's mine," Griffin tells Diego. "Remember."

"No, she's not," Savvy says, and finally lets her poison blade fly.

9

✦ ✦ ✦

Griffin

Griffin isn't surprised Savvy beat him here—or that she's feeling murderous. From every account in H.U.N.T.E.R.'s archives, that's the latent state of most witches. It certainly is for most of the other freelance magic beings or users he's ever encountered. He never personally ran into a member of C.R.O.N.E.—that he knew of—before Savvy, but he's learned what they're capable of doing. There've been at least three operatives lost in conflicts since he's been active. That's why the rule is to defend yourself first when in a direct confrontation, as fiercely as possible, if you want to survive.

He dodges Savvy's thrown blade, strides over to the door, and shoves Diego back toward a protesting, hovering Brie. He slams the door closed so hard the hinges rattle and locks it, shutting them outside. And him and Savvy in.

"What are you doing?" Savvy asks.

The knife she threw is on the floor off to the right and he fully expects her to go for it. The wand bomb he has holds the juice from her blast, but it can't absorb another one. Big Rob warned him about that. He's supposed to use it to finish her off—redirecting her own power back at her.

He knows what he's been assigned to do, but he's still wrapping his head around it. Is it so easy for Savvy to imagine taking him out?

"This is between us," he says.

"There's nothing between us, not anymore."

"I'm curious," he says. Because he can't agree. He wants answers. "Why me? Why did you set me up that day on the Thames? Were you and those MI6 officers in it together?"

Savvy shakes her head like he's being idiotic. "I could ask you the same thing. I should've known when I found that fragment of mask in your bag."

"What mask?" Griffin asks. And then, "So you admit it, you knew who I was."

"No," Savvy says, "I thought you were a dumb tourist lured in by the thing's magic. It happens all the time."

"Well, I was lured in by yours all right," Griffin says, advancing. "As you know. You must've *loved* that. Manipulating me."

"Fuck off," she says. "I didn't do that."

"I'm supposed to believe that?"

She stalks a step closer and throws up her hands. "You think I don't feel stupid for falling for you and your good-Boy-Scout act?"

They're practically nose-to-nose again. Both breathing heavier than normal. He can smell the hint of florals and herbs, Savvy's perfume—probably some kind of spell all its own. Her dress is tattered, as if it's been dragged along the ground. Her hair tangled.

She looks fierce and . . . beautiful. He wants to grab her, but he's no longer sure what he'd do after catching her.

No, Griffin tells himself, *she's not for you. She's a trap. The enemy.*

"It's not an act. I *am* the good guy here."

Savvy's gorgeous mouth drops open. She doesn't speak for a long moment. He doesn't know what he expects, but it's not her pointing her finger and poking him in the chest with it.

"You actually believe that."

He also doesn't expect the sweep of her leg as she takes his out from under him. She's running again then, back to the kitchen.

"Very mature," he says as he gets up. "Can't we talk about this?"

"What's there to talk about?" She picks up the knife and turns to face him. "You have never been the good guys. You're like the so-called good guys who mess with women's heads and think rom-com stalking is sexy and who are actually the villains. In every story. The problem. The ones who need taking down. We're supposed to keep away from each other, as much as we can. Why did *you* target *me*?"

"You must know I learned the truth today." He holds out his arms. "And, really, *we're* the bad guys? You and your kind almost destroyed the world. You tortured people. Destroyed villages. If it wasn't for the accords . . . I've seen what magic can do, the harm it can cause, and it's not pretty." Every job he works is to keep the regular world safe from it.

She squints. "You are deluded."

"Pot, kettle."

Savvy raises her hands then. He watches as the knives float out of the open drawer in the kitchen and point in his direction.

Well, hell.

He dives behind the living room wall as she lets them fly. He hears them puncture it. *Thunk. Thunk. Thunk.*

"Come on, *professor*," she says, "let me make this quick."

He peeks out around the wall and the knives are withdrawing. She has them arrayed in the air again in moments, and it reminds him of the way the flowers of her crown swirled around her at the church.

Diego wasn't entirely wrong.

It was hot.

Someone help him, this is too. *She's still messing with your head. Take her out, Griffin. You're here to take her out.*

A mighty roar sounds and Griffin goggles at the fact that

there's suddenly a black leopard in the room with them. An unhappy one.

"Move, Paris," Savvy orders.

The leopard pads over and stands in front of him.

"That's Paris?" He looks at the large gleaming black-and-gray-spotted predator with her back to him. She makes a growling noise at Savvy.

"I mean it, this isn't funny," Savvy says.

"You said she was your cat. You meant . . . But she's *a cat.*"

"Yes," Savvy says, "a big one. Who is being a real pain right now."

Paris holds her ground.

"Maybe she wants to go with me," Griffin says.

Paris shakes her head again, back and forth. A no.

Wait. What. She seems to be responding to him. "Can she understand me?" he asks.

"See, he's surprised how smart you are. I know you thought you liked him. So did I." Savvy is talking to the cat, ignoring him. "But we didn't know the truth."

He could send the blast from the wand back at her.

He should.

He takes the wand bomb from his pocket and prepares to detonate it.

Paris turns her gaze on him and shakes her giant diamond-shaped head again.

"Stop shaming me," he says to the leopard. "I have a job to do here."

"You do?" Savvy asks. "Funny, me too."

She's magnificent, the blades shining in the air around her, her magic holding them effortlessly in place. She's also exasperated with Paris. "Stop being a turncoat, Paris. Get out of the way."

"Good kitty," Griffin says.

Savvy closes her eyes for a breath, then opens them. The knives stay in place around her. "If we have the same job," Savvy says, "which one of us do you think leaves here alive?"

An arrow streaks past Savvy and pierces the kitchen cabinet behind her.

"How about neither of you?" a new voice says from the hallway.

Male. Unfamiliar. Griffin can't see him, but he must have come in the back door. What the fuck?

"Is this one of your friends?" Savvy asks Griffin. "I thought it was 'between us.' Cheater."

"He's not with me," Griffin says, frowning. He clearly isn't with Savvy either.

"How about none of the three of you leave?" Another interloper, only this one sashays into view from the hall, coming right toward them. A necromancer in a long black dress with hissing snakes for hair.

Griffin has crossed paths with her in the field before. She's powerful. And, as far as he can tell, bottomlessly evil. Living proof of what he said to Savvy—living proof of what women with magic can do. Are the two of them allies?

"Oh no," Savvy says.

Maybe not.

Paris yowls, loud enough that it shakes the walls. Griffin's and Savvy's eyes meet, and then they use Paris's distraction to dive in opposite directions. He toward the living room wall, she into the kitchen.

Griffin second-guesses it immediately. If these two are free-lancers who've suddenly shown up, he and Savvy should've gone for cover behind the kitchen island together. Freelance mercs specialize in various forms of magic or other useful supporting jobs for the darker side of the supernatural world.

Word of their conflict must be spreading, and others are trying to get in on the action. But why?

Paris is snarling at the necromancer, but when Savvy whistles, this time Paris heeds her and vanishes into the kitchen.

The man who came in first still hasn't revealed himself.

"Come on, Savannah Wilde, show yourself," the necromancer says, as if she's bored. The snakes of her hair are striking with potent snaps of their jaws. "I want the bragging rights of taking you down first." She winks at Griffin, who peeks around the wall at her. "He's cute," she says. "But falling for a hunter? Such bad form. Don't worry, though, hunter, you're still next."

Griffin feels the crackle of electricity as the snake-haired necromancer forms two balls of darkness on her palms. He's sure Savvy has a plan—she's still holding those knives in the air, after all—but he acts on pure instinct.

He detonates the wand bomb, right at the snake-haired woman. It explodes out with a charge even Griffin feels as the pins swirl around her. "The fuck—" she says, but that's all she gets out before the stored charge from the wand has her in its grip and she collapses, unconscious.

Savvy slowly rises from behind the counter, blinking at the downed necromancer. "I had that," she says.

"You're welcome," Griffin says.

But she ignores him, looking past him, and then saying "Get down" to him. Her wand is raised and there's an intensity in her expression as she sends a blast—to his right. A mercenary in gray fatigues careens forward and then goes flat, the crossbow he holds tumbling out of his slack grip.

"What the hell," Savvy asks, "is going on?"

"I don't know," Griffin says. "But I don't like it."

They are apparently going to ignore the fact that they just saved each other's lives. Savvy comes closer and they stand side by side as the door crashes in.

"We need to go," Diego says. "We have company."

"We noticed," Griffin says. "What's going on?"

"Um . . ." Diego is the worse for wear. Sleeves torn, suit tattered and dirty.

Brie barges in, similarly mussed. "Come on, there's mercs showing up out here."

"You don't say?" Savvy says. And nods at the examples on the floor.

Brie frowns at the necromancer. "Is that—?"

"Melissa the Gorgon?" Savvy says. "Yes."

"Friend?" Griffin asks. Witches and necromancers are supposed to be cut from the same cloth, so he's not surprised they'd turn on each other this fast.

"Obviously not," Savvy says quickly. Then she shakes her head. "Why am I talking to you about this? Forget I said anything."

"Too late. You were talking to me," Griffin says.

Brie's eyes narrow.

Diego doesn't even blink at the felled attackers. He's too busy gawking at Paris. "Is that your cat?"

A fluffy white dog prances through the front door then, straight over to Paris, and touches noses with her. As soon as they make contact, the dog changes into . . . a capybara. The chunky body angles in, snout still touching Paris's elegant black snoot.

Griffin can't help thinking a) that is cute and b) this is not how he envisioned today going. Not even after the big reveal about Savvy's true nature. Being attacked by freelance mercs and watching a dog-turned-capybara snuggle a cat-turned-leopard.

"Are you guys back together or something?" Brie asks.

"No," both Griffin and Savvy blurt out in unison.

Brie snorts. "We have to go. Get your stuff. You can kill each other later. Right now we need to keep you alive."

"What are you talking about?" Savvy demands, taking the words out of Griffin's mouth.

"Check your phones," she says.

"I'll cover you," Diego volunteers.

So Griffin does. Savvy's appears in her hand. There's an alert in his messages. She gasps.

The same thing must be in hers too.

Griffin and Savvy have both been terminated from their employment ties. There's now a large bounty on each of their heads.

Oh no. Mother Circe and the Butcher must have gotten tired of waiting—even though it's only been a couple of hours. The leaders seemingly don't trust either of them to clean up this mess without making it worse. Add the bragging rights to that and . . . this means it is now open season on the two of them.

"They ditched us that fast?" he says.

"Fuck," Savvy says.

"Yeah," Brie says, "about sums it up."

Griffin tries to figure out why the Butcher would do this. He has no idea how loyal Circe is, but it all feels like it's happening too quickly. The only justification he can come up with is that both leaders are afraid the accords will crumble because of Griffin and Savvy.

This way, H.U.N.T.E.R. and C.R.O.N.E. proper are out of the fight . . . except their friends and families aren't just going to abandon them.

Brie nods to Savvy. "Come on, let's go."

Savvy snaps her fingers, and Paris nudges against Griffin's leg for a second, then goes to her. Brie tugs on Savvy, pulling her out the door as the capybara and leopard follow them. Diego waves him out the same way.

On the lawn, Savvy's mother is motioning for Brie and Savvy to hurry. Elle's on her broom already. There's a giant raven swooping overhead, calling now and again. Two more freelancers are facedown on what used to be their quiet, well-maintained yard.

Griffin senses he and Savvy might agree on one thing: that *these* interlopers are the worst people in their world. Their only loyalty is to money and power.

Savvy picks up a sharp-looking broom off the ground. Diego is steering Griffin toward the SUV they brought here, waiting at the curb. His brother Jacob must already be inside. His dad and Quinn went home to check on his mother.

Griffin shakes off Diego.

He pauses, and Savvy faces him as if she feels the weight of his gaze. Their eyes lock for a long moment, and then he's watching as Paris shrinks back into her usual domestic-cat form, and leaps onto the broom in front of Savvy.

Savvy turns away, and then the broom rises, and she vanishes into the night sky like a shooting star.

To say they have unfinished business would be the understatement of the centuries—all of them. He wonders if he'll ever see her again.

And if either of them will make it out of this alive.

Ten Months Ago

10

✦ ✦ ✦

The Goddess and the Professor

Savvy is already glamoured today as she and a local witch guide head down a central Parisian street. She learned her lesson with that near slipup in England a couple of months back—never assume the magic involved in a supernatural incident won't prevent you from donning your disguise at the scene.

Even if it did work out pretty well in the end. The best one-night stand of her life. She almost wishes she'd gotten Griffin Carter's number. She hasn't let herself google him or do a location spell or any of the things she's considered late at night, remembering. . . . Besides, she let him know her last name, so he could've chosen to track her down and he hasn't. The missing-something-she-worries-is-love feeling didn't go away after London, but she's been successfully ignoring it for the past two months.

Even for Savvy, getting called out to Paris to prevent a zombie apocalypse is an unusual assignment. How no one experimenting with necromantic magic has ever attempted to reanimate the catacombs and their skeletons before beats her. It was bound to happen sooner or later.

What C.R.O.N.E. hasn't learned yet is who's behind this. But the chapter house here called the Farmhouse for an assist after multiple recent encounters with skeletons rambling about aboveground, including one that was hungry for flesh.

Her guide is Yvette, a dark-skinned witch with a lilt to her

French accent, and they're set to venture beneath the streets. Savvy will gorge herself on jambon beurre sandwiches later. Where they're entering the famous ossuaries below Paris is far from the public tours of a tiny slice of the catacombs that stretch beneath much of the city. There are no lines and tickets here. The street is deserted due to the effects of Yvette's subtle spell to keep people away.

She waves Savvy closer as she kneels in mud boots—which Savvy also wears—beside a manhole cover. She moves her hand over it, and the thick metal plate slides aside.

"You go first." She motions to Savvy.

Savvy lowers herself into the opening and finds the rungs of a ladder with her feet, then her fingers. She sends a slight glow through the metal as she starts down. Once she's far enough, Yvette begins her journey down the ladder, too, lifting one hand free to replace the cover. The ladder's light is the only illumination.

The air is cool and musty as they climb down and down and down. When Savvy finally checks over her shoulder and spots ground below, she hops off with relief, landing in the dirt.

Yvette joins her and nods. "This way."

Not such a talkative witch, not yet, anyway. Yvette removes a flashlight from her backpack. "Less noticeable," she says, frowning back toward the ladder. "We may still encounter others. Using magic for light is risky."

Fine, okay, making the ladder glow wasn't subtle, but no one saw. Yvette means cataphiles, the explorers who illegally poke around these tunnels for fun or danger or simply to map them. Savvy follows Yvette's lead this time.

The passage is dry and narrow, with graffiti covering the walls, and a couple of times Savvy has to turn sideways.

Finally, the flashlight's beam settles on bones stacked into a wall ahead. A skull is turned so the empty eyes stare out at Savvy.

"Up here," Yvette says.

They enter a roughly round chamber, the walls all made of more old bones. As the flashlight dances over the skeletal walls, Savvy understands what they're looking at. There are several places where bones are obviously missing. Enough of them that the walls are strangely uneven, but *something* is holding them in place, when they should have collapsed. She reaches a hand out toward the nearest absence and doesn't touch, but does search for the presence of magic.

She sucks in a breath as darkness floods through her. The magic that lingers in these bones, in these bodies, is recent, not old. It seethes and crawls, looking for a way into her too.

She gathers her energy and forces it away from her. "I've never felt anything quite like it," she says in French.

"Neither have we."

Savvy considers. "I worry about draining it—that might not be safe. We need to figure out how to destroy it instead."

"Yes."

Why did they call on her if they've already figured all this out? That's when she hears voices approaching.

Yvette gives her a look, illuminated by the flashlight. *See?*

Savvy's thinking is more along the lines of *What if it's the person responsible for this magic?* She doesn't have the right approach yet.

Another beam of light cuts through the darkness, and as three men come into view, she sees that it's from one of their headlamps. Savvy puts Yvette subtly behind her—but not subtly enough, because it earns an affronted breath, which she ignores. She sends out another tentative feeler, carefully, in the hopes it won't be detected if this *is* whoever's behind that dark magic.

She senses nothing, except three breathing humans.

"It's okay, I think," she mutters to Yvette.

"I know."

Savvy resists rolling her eyes as the men get close enough to see them. *"Bonjour,"* the one in front calls in American-accented French, and Savvy nearly faints.

She manages to keep herself from saying his name somehow. He wouldn't recognize her, not glamoured to be ten years older and four inches shorter, with dishwater-blond hair pulled back into a ponytail, in baggy wader overalls and mud boots.

But she recognizes him easily enough despite the darkness.

"Hello." Savvy wishes she could bite the word back. She should've used French, so she wouldn't be memorable in any way. She has to figure out what she's going to do . . . or not do.

Because the creator of the best memory she's had in years, Griffin Carter, is right in front of her.

Griffin had hoped that he and his associates wouldn't bump into anyone down here. He should've known better than to plan on it.

"Hello," the pale woman in the front says, and the word hangs in the air. There's nothing remarkable about her. So why does something tickle at the back of his mind?

"We were just going," she adds, switching from English to French.

The other, dark-skinned woman scoffs.

"We're not the authorities," Griffin says. "Don't worry."

"Well, not the Parisian authorities," Diego says from behind him. Griffin looks over his shoulder and is unsurprised to find his friend grinning at the women before them flirtatiously. You can't take him anywhere.

Griffin elbows him.

The third member of their party, Denis, is a local guide from H.U.N.T.E.R.'s European HQ. He steps forward and trains his headlamp on a wall of bones that's clearly missing a few in the middle. How is it still standing? This is what they came to see, but they can hardly examine or discuss it with an audience.

"You're not grave robbers, are you?" their guide asks in his perfectly accented French.

"Would we admit it if we were?" the pale woman says.

Griffin laughs. "Probably not."

"Like I said, we were just leaving," she says.

Her friend grumbles, but lets herself be towed into the passage going the opposite way.

"Should we stop them?" Diego asks.

"This is a popular entrance point for explorers. I doubt they realized what they were looking at, besides bones," Denis says.

"And what *are* we looking at besides bones?" Griffin asks.

"We've narrowed down this area—it's where the bone walkers have been coming from."

Griffin isn't sure there's a distinction between the terms "bone walkers" and "zombies." This whole situation is surreal, even for H.U.N.T.E.R. Back at the local base of operations, Denis showed them a pile of old bones arranged on a gurney, and the gadget from Big Rob they used to measure the magic was off the charts, despite the bones no longer being animated. Denis swore that the skeleton had been caught with its bony fingers closing around the throat of a homeless man nearby, and barely put down by their nullifiers.

"Could they be the bodies of witches or sorcerers?" Griffin asks, frowning.

"They could," Denis agrees. "But there's no way to know. We must act on the assumption something is reanimating them instead."

"Not something," Diego says.

His eyes and Griffin's lock. "Someone," Griffin says.

"We have pulled our files on everyone we know who is active and skilled at necromancy," Denis says.

"We'll want to review them for the likeliest suspects. In the meantime, let's leave a surprise here," Griffin says.

Denis frowns but watches as Griffin removes something that looks like an empty eye socket, lined around the edge with bone-colored plastic. He reaches into the nearest skull and presses it in. No one would notice it, not in a million years.

"Camera," he says. Big Rob has a knack for gadgets that blend in with the scenery. It's amazing how often old or supernatural creatures don't think about technology.

"They have ways to hide from those," Denis says.

Griffin doesn't mind the skepticism. The Parisian chapter tends to be a bit judgmental about the techniques of Americans. "But they might not bother, if they're not expecting one."

Denis murmurs half-hearted agreement.

"What do we do now?" Diego asks. "Go back to the hotel and get ready to party? It's my first time in Paris."

"*You* are going to go through the files with Denis and sort out the most promising ones. I'm going to check in with home base to discuss our options, then I'll meet you."

Diego pouts. "I could follow those two women, make sure they were innocent."

"Nice try," Griffin says dryly. The thought occurred to him, and he isn't going to explain it, but he has a gut feeling they aren't a problem. Denis's lack of concern bolsters it.

"We will find who is responsible before this escalates," Griffin says to him. "I promise you."

Denis nods. "We would never have summoned you if we believed otherwise. You personally came highly recommended."

A large bone—so to speak—coming from the Frenchman. "We're lucky to have your expertise," Griffin says.

"Don't let this one out of your sight," he says under his breath to Denis, with a glance to Diego.

"*Oui,*" Denis says.

They leave the way they came and Griffin stands for a moment, watching Denis and Diego head off into the Parisian twilight. He's restless. He needs to call home, but he'd rather take a stroll by the Seine. He justifies heading that way by promising he'll use the time to consider their problem and how they can flush out the person or people behind these attacks. They have the feeling of someone testing, trying, to see if they can get away with it. Which means the end goal is something larger.

When he sees the river, a boat chugging past with tourists, the old buildings flanking it, he tells himself it's just the idyllic scene that calls her to mind. The most beautiful woman he's ever met, so he'll probably think of her every time he sees beauty in the world. For the rest of his life.

He should look her up.

Except, no, you shouldn't. You made the wise decision.

Griffin and wise decisions, it's what he does. He doesn't usually regret them. This one, he regrets at least once daily. Though it makes him feel faintly silly.

He spots her in the distance—well, he thinks he does. *Great, I'm escalating to hallucinations now.* A tall silhouette he'll never forget. Curves that could kill a man. Long tangle of caramel-blond hair. That smart mouth.

Okay, now he's truly losing it. He blinks at the woman approaching, fully prepared to be disappointed by her being just *a* beautiful woman, and not the one he wishes she were.

Except as she gets closer, he stops walking. A tourist couple runs into him, and it barely fazes him. The woman stops at a book stall, turning toward it to browse.

He should be able to gather his wits. Instead he heads closer to her. The table of used books is filled with paperback spy thrillers and vintage mysteries and other well-worn volumes. He looks down at them, barely breathing, and doesn't manage to catch a single title. The woman picks up a book and asks, in French, how much it is.

The bookseller, beret and all, making the most of this exchange, answers in English and refers to her as "a woman of fine taste."

She laughs and says, "In that case, I'll take it. I hope you're right."

She passes over money, and Griffin is frozen. He can't believe this is happening. This *can't* be happening. She takes her book and motions for the man running the stall to keep the change. The bookseller puts a hand to his heart. "Beautiful and kind," he says.

And then she turns and . . . walks on up the sidewalk. She hasn't seen him.

"Savvy," he calls, hurrying to catch her, dumbstruck.

She stops and faces him. Her face splits in a smile so bright he feels like she's dealt him a blow. "I thought you were pretending we'd never met."

"It's you." He breathes the words.

"And you," she says.

He acts on pure instinct, which is a very un-Griffin-like thing to do. He is pulled to her, a sensation stronger than gravity, and when he reaches her, he puts one hand on the side of her face and—when she doesn't protest—his other on her opposite cheek.

"Well," she says.

He captures her lips with his, and she laughs gently against his lips and slides her arms around him.

Light applause sounds nearby, and he almost ignores it. But when they pull apart, both of them breathless, it's the bookseller.

"Lucky man!" he says.

"He doesn't believe in luck," Savvy says.

She remembered. The capriciousness of what he wants in this moment goes against the heart of who he is. He's rational.

He believes in statistics. Facts. Knowledge. Even in the defeat of chaotic magical threats, it is a method he turns to in order to counter madness.

He grins wide. "The luckiest man in Paris."

"Doesn't that depend on whether I'm happy to see you?" Savvy asks, coy.

Good god, how could he have missed someone he spent part of one day and half a night with this much? How can he recover if she wants to go their separate ways, right here, right now? Even if it's impossible for them to ever truly be together?

"Yes," he says, "yes, it does."

"Excellent," Savvy says, "because I find that I am. Very happy." She leans in and kisses him again. Her lips are soft and inviting.

And damn it. Just like that.

Griffin has to believe in luck after all.

11

✦ ✦ ✦

The Goddess and the Professor

Savvy would be lying if she didn't admit to second-guessing her decision to let Griffin see her. The reasons she should have done anything other than drop her glamour and change into a more flattering, casual number far outnumber the reason she did: she wanted to.

What are the odds reality would throw them together again? Surprisingly, witches tend to be practical about such matters. No one on their side does love spells these days, because it removes the ability to consent. It's a violation. And, also, most of the requesters operated from the premise that there's one right human for each person. A soulmate.

But, if that were true, love potions would never have become popular. They wouldn't have been needed. Fate wouldn't be so cruel as to leave people who were supposed to be together in places they'd never meet. And Savvy can't imagine anything more evil than stealing someone's choice of who to love.

Not that she loves Griffin. She barely knows him. And she's not in the market for a soulmate, never has been. Her mother has warned her about how romantic relationships end up, particularly for operatives. Spoiler alert: badly.

But she can admit to herself—hand tucked into his, heat radiating through her from that one place of touch—part of her *wants* to know him inside and out. The sheer ease with which their lips fit together in that moment on the street, the effortless rightness of it . . . the way the missing-something feeling evaporated.

She shakes her head as they amble alongside each other. "What are you doing here?" she asks.

"I'm in town for a conference," he says. "You?"

She imagines admitting she's here to hunt someone making skeletal zombies. "Does anyone need a reason to be in Paris?"

"Good point."

"Have you done any sightseeing so far?" She isn't necessarily going to bring up the catacombs, but she is curious about his interest. He's in jeans and a turtleneck, hiking boots. Nothing that would give away his recent visit beneath the city. She wonders where his companions went.

"A sight that takes my breath away." Griffin ducks his head.

Savvy catches an almost blush and sends it away before it can color her cheeks. "Nice line."

"It's not a line," he says, and tilts his head at her. "How is your face better?"

She stops in a mostly mock protest. "What?"

"I mean, than my memory of it. . . . Which is an excellent memory. Why do I feel like I've been hit in the head when I look at you?"

"Another good line, and I couldn't tell you why. The description I get most is: tall." He laughs and she enjoys the rich sound of it. "No, I'm serious. If someone is telling you how to find me, they'll say, 'Look for the tall one.' I'm 'the tall one.'"

Sometimes men are made uncomfortable by her height. Not men whose opinion she cares about, but it used to sting when she was younger. She's got an inch or two on Griffin, she guesses, in flats, and she regrets bringing it up for a second.

Until he bends his knees so he has to gaze up at her. "I like it. It makes you easier for me to spot—across a—a crowded city."

"You're *definitely* improving."

"I figured I'd better up my game."

She catches him checking his watch. "I'm so sorry," she says. "You probably have somewhere to be. So do I."

They stare at each other for a deeply held moment. Griffin straightens. They're almost eye to eye. Definitely standing toe to toe. The wise thing for her to do is make her excuses and peel off. She needs to strategize about the situation, both the zombies and this dangerous attraction. Yvette obviously thinks the American consult on the first only semi-necessary at best. But that dark magic down there, it can't be allowed to linger. . . .

"I don't care," Griffin says.

"Me neither."

Which should disturb Savvy. It really, truly should. She puts her job first, always.

"Catch up over dinner?" Griffin asks. "In my room?"

"He shoots, he scores." She grins at him. She'll figure out a way to buy some more time.

"I will never be able to keep up with you."

It hangs there between them. The "I never thought we'd see each other again" underlying this entire conversation has transformed quick as alchemy from the context of his using that single word now. The "never," which includes "ever," which is a time frame, which implies something besides their past meeting and this one. It implies their next meeting. She should run screaming. Definitely.

You're here to prevent a zombie apocalypse.

He smiles at her, sweet and soft and hot as a fire she can't wait to stick her hand into.

The dead can wait, she thinks.

They're not at the same hotel—if they had been again, that might've been too much of a coincidence for Griffin's suspicious nature to roll with. But they're not staying too far apart. By mutual agreement, they head toward Griffin's, the quietly posh Hôtel d'Aubusson in the Latin Quarter. The concierge's family has a few members in their organization.

As they walk, Savvy fires off a text to make an excuse to someone. Griffin wants to ask who, wants to know who she texts with, not because he's interested in controlling it, but because he's curious about her life. The details of it. The people who get to be in it. . . .

He recognizes the danger of this line of thinking. And still doesn't care.

He sends a text of his own, letting Diego know he's going radio silent for a few hours and *not* inviting questions about it. Then, he dashes off a quick note back to headquarters, letting them know the camera is in place and to ping immediately if anything or anyone notable shows up on it. Following which, he says a silent prayer that the catacombs remain quiet for the rest of the night.

Griffin nods to the doorman, who manages not to raise an eyebrow at his returning with a goddess—bless the French and their famous discretion.

"Nice digs," Savvy says. She pauses. A pause that stretches out, makes itself comfortable, and Griffin uncomfortable. "We're making a mistake, aren't we?" she asks at last.

"What do you mean?" He manages to say it levelly and disregard the sudden panic he is definitely not going to acknowledge feeling at the question.

He steers Savvy toward the elevator gently. "That is . . . how do you mean?"

Savvy doesn't quite look at him. "We have that perfect jewel of an evening to remember. Are we just going to mess it up? We can't . . ."

She doesn't finish the thought, but she's sincerely troubled. He can see that.

He turns them from the elevator and crooks his head toward the jazz bar in the opposite corner of the lobby. She nods in grateful agreement and they cross to it.

They settle in at a table at the back of a semi-full barroom where a man with dreads is playing the piano, accompanied by a woman with a smoky voice. It's a cozy spot with a vibrant, romantic soundtrack in the world capital of love. He can't screw this up, right? And what does it matter if he does? Griffin isn't looking for anything serious.

He doesn't think.

Maybe Savvy has done them a favor slowing things down.

"Want to eat down here?" he asks.

She nods, and he summons the waiter, who rushes over and supplies them with menus.

He orders himself a martini and raises a brow at her. "The same," she says.

Once the waiter leaves, Savvy looks a little embarrassed. "I freaked without warning. I'm sorry." She checks her phone, seems undisturbed by what she finds there. She finally looks at him.

The music and engaged audience mean they have plenty of privacy here at their small circular table. He still would rather be here than anywhere else he can think of.

"Not at all," he says. "I get it."

"You do? Can you explain it to me, then?"

Griffin sets a hand on the table, palm up. An offering. She hesitates, then slips hers into it.

"I don't do that—one-night stands," Griffin says. "Except with you."

"And this would be a two-night stand," Savvy says. "You probably don't do those either."

"I don't think there's anything usual about me and you." He pauses. "But I hear you. How about this? Let's treat this dinner like a normal date." Griffin says it but silently adds *as much as possible,* given all the oddities and his cover. "Let's see if it gets awkward. If it does, we'll call it. Say goodbye."

She nods again, seeming less skittish already. "Solid plan."

The waiter, bless him, returns with their drinks and sets them on the table. They both go simple, steak frites, rare. Savvy sips her drink, then says, "Okay, so tell me all about you. Did you always want to be a scandalously sexy professor?"

Griffin barks a surprised laugh. "How come you can recover your composure so quickly?" He considers her question and answers as truthfully as he can. "I always loved facts. Books. Museums and figuring out the stories behind objects, the context . . . what gives them their power. And I don't think I've ever been accused of being scandalously hot before. Definitely not by my brothers."

"Brothers tend to be like that."

"Do you have them?"

"No," she says, with a small smile, "only child of a ferocious single mom. But we have a big community back home."

"Where's that?" he asks, and takes a drink of his martini.

"Atlanta," she says, after a beat.

He nearly spits gin onto the table. He coughs as he swallows.

"What is it?" she asks.

"Me too," he says. "I live in Atlanta."

"Damn," she says.

He doesn't know if that's a good "damn" or a bad "damn" or both. He echoes it. But there's something else underneath it for him. A whisper in his subconscious: *This is meant to be.*

An entirely schmaltzy thought, not Griffin's typical variety.

"I have an idea," he says.

"What's that?"

He can see in her eyes that the revelation spooked her, hear it in the slow skepticism of her question.

He speaks gently. "How about, no matter what we decide at the end of this meal or night or whatever, we make a deal, so the future isn't hanging over us. . . ."

"I'm listening." She leans in. He catches a hint of her scent, mingling with the bite of their cocktails. He wants to press his lips to her neck, and if things go well, hopefully he'll be able to do that before long. But this is important business to take care of.

"How about we make an agreement to meet up if we're interested in seeing the other person again—a month from now, at seven o'clock, at a bookstore back home."

Savvy considers. Then, "Little Shop of Stories."

"My favorite." Griffin finds it has become true since the name came out of her mouth, though before that he preferred a used bookstore that occasionally turned up obscure volumes for him.

"Mine too," she says with a touch of skepticism. "I know it's a kids' store, but I have such good memories going back so far. I still go in at least once a month."

"Imagine," he says. "We could have met there."

"No," she says. "That would have been too boring."

Griffin shrugs. "Boring is nice sometimes."

"Not for us, though," she says. She gives him a more relaxed smile then, and scoots around the table, closer, and speaks softly against his neck. "Deal."

He turns his head and their eyes lock. He gambles. "Have the food sent to my room?"

"Good idea," she says. "You're full of those tonight."

He's already signaling the waiter, and she laughs.

Savvy doesn't like to use magic to do things like slow her heartbeat. But she's pretty sure she would have had a panic attack in the lobby if she didn't.

Savvy doesn't get the doubts. She has the gut instincts of, well, someone who often has the weight of the world on her shoulders. The realization that she has chosen, even momentarily, to neglect work for Griffin scared the shit out of her, to put it bluntly. Both Yvette and Brie assured her when she texted them that a few hours away were fine, that they would keep at the problem.

But the fact that she's willing to do that, that she *is* capable of neglecting her work, means something she can barely wrap her head around. She could really fall for Griffin.

She has developed a case of feelings.

This isn't part of her plan. *He* isn't part of it. Flings and fun are what romance has always meant to her, but this doesn't seem like either anymore. Even though, logically, it should. Her mother would be apoplectic. She would ask if she's taught Savvy nothing.

And yet. Her panic eased away somewhat when he was patient. When he touched her, it became a distant echo, and that scares her too. She almost ran at the news that they live in the same city. It's too much.

But his proposal, taking the weight of deciding to see each other again or not out of tonight and putting it in their future selves' hands, was so good. She relaxes into the idea that this could be the last time they see each other.

Even as the back of her brain screams the hope that it isn't.

How the fuck has she gotten herself into this situation?

Griffin smiles at her and her mind shorts out.

"I'd say penny for your thoughts, but we're in Paris, and I suspect we're both doing too much thinking."

"Fair," Savvy says. She glances sidelong at him as he opens his hotel room door. It's a roomy setup, a big bed and a nice table and chairs in the corner. She heads there, avoiding the elephant-sized mattress in the room.

"I'm sorry I'm being weird," she says. "I don't usually startle easy. And you should know, I also don't do commitment."

"This is a weird situation," Griffin says. "And seriously, no pressure. We're not talking about commitment. We can just have dinner."

The fact that her saying the C-word doesn't have him running for the hills is telling. But he's probably being truthful, and the pressure is in her mind. She can have this, just this, and go back to normal back home.

He has pushed up the sleeves of his shirt, revealing those delicious forearms. The room smells like him, masculine and wonderful. She doesn't know what she wants from tonight anymore, but dinner is the beginning.

Savvy owes him an explanation for how strange she's acting. "It's just that I don't even know you yet," she says, "but when I saw you, I felt like someone I've been waiting for just showed up. I felt like I do know you. It sounds over-the-top, I know."

"Not to me." Griffin sidles over and takes the seat across from her. He puts those forearms right on the table, as if they're not temptation all by themselves. "What would make you more comfortable?"

Understanding my reactions to you and feeling in control of them. . . .

"I'm not uncomfortable," she says. "It's just . . . when you do know someone, you can read them. You know what their gestures mean, what they're thinking by the expression on their face." Savvy realizes the irony here, of course, is that he can never know exactly what she's thinking. She has too many secrets to keep.

"Well," Griffin says, "I get that. Those things take time."

"Do they?" Savvy asks without meaning to, curious because she's never allowed herself to give anyone that time.

"Yes," Griffin says. "At least, that's what my dad would say. He and Mom are my idea of relationship goals."

"Really?" Savvy thinks of her mother's one relationship, with her father, and how she blamed it for what happened to her best friend in the field. *Never again,* her mother always said. *Distraction is a killer.* "Tell me about them."

They keep talking over dinner. Griffin tells her the story of how his parents met in college, and if you leave out the part where his father has a secret-agent life his mom doesn't know about, it's straight-up swoonworthy. His father dotes on his mom, and vice versa. And they challenge each other.

Savvy laughs at all the right moments, and he can sense it when she starts to relax. She gets up, checking her phone again, and sits on the bed. "Is this okay?" she asks.

"Of course."

Griffin doesn't want to risk her freaking again, so he goes to the other side and sits down. An expanse of milky duvet separates them. She rolls onto her side facing him. "I thought about looking you up," she says.

He slides down so he's on his side too. "Me too."

"But we didn't," Savvy says.

Griffin is quiet for a long moment, to give her time to say something else. When she doesn't, he whispers conspiratorially, "I think we might be idiots."

She laughs, and it's such a good sound. "You have a point."

She sounds drowsy. They talk for a while longer, about meaningless things—Atlanta traffic, downtowns called uptowns—and important ones—favorite foods (tacos!), books, music—and essential ones—first crushes, first losses, first everything-normals. When Savvy's eyes slip closed, he takes it as a positive sign that she's relaxed enough to fall asleep. He closes his own eyes, just for two seconds. . . .

He wakes up later to the sound of his phone buzzing, and then a knock at the door. Savvy is nestled against him, and she doesn't wake when he stirs. He slides his shoulder gently out from under her and goes to the door.

Diego is outside. He starts to barrel in and instead Griffin steps out into the hallway, forcing him back. "What is it?" Griffin asks while checking his phone.

Diego gives him a look. "You have someone in there."

"None of your business. Why are you here?"

"You do! You dog! Who is it? Some French girl?" Diego looks around him at the door. "I'd tell you."

"Even though I wouldn't want to know. Now shut up and tell me what you're doing here."

"That," Diego says, nodding at the phone in Griffin's hand.

Griffin pulls up the message that just came through from HQ. A video attachment. He opens it and pushes play.

A woman's figure appears on-screen. She wears a long dark skirt, hair whirling around her head—wait, that's not hair, those are snakes. She has two men in long cloaks with her. But it's how she lifts her hands and their specific motions toward the bones that give her away. There's only one type of person who makes gestures like that. A practitioner of the darkest type of magic.

"Necromancer," Diego says. "She was in the files. Calls herself Melissa the Gorgon."

The timing is what it is. Griffin closes out of the image. "We need to get there."

Diego nods. "I've got the gear ready."

"I'll meet you downstairs." Diego starts to protest, and Griffin says, "I mean, it Diego."

Diego knows better than to argue for once.

Griffin lets himself back into the room after this rude awakening by his real world. What's he going to tell her? There's an antiquities emergency? Yes, that's exactly what he's going to tell her. What other option is there?

He puts some gear into his pockets and dons boots, then

goes to Savvy's side and gently touches her shoulder. She opens her eyes. "What's up?" she asks, blinking awake. "Besides you. Oh, you're dressed too."

"I have to go," he says.

"What—you have an antiquities emergency?" She sounds skeptical and a little disappointed.

"Yes, actually." Griffin touches the side of her cheek, brushes back a stray lock of hair. "A piece that is extremely rare and will only be available for me to see while this particular curator is drunk." A shadow of hurt flares in her eyes, but it's gone quickly and she nods.

"I should get going anyway," she says.

"Let me leave first," Griffin says.

She frowns.

"My friend, who's here with me, he's nosy. It's for your privacy."

He can see her calculating all the ways this request could be taken and deciding to go with face value. "Thanks."

He hesitates, but then he leans in and gives her a slow, lingering kiss. "I hope to see you in a month," he says. "No hard feelings if not."

"Same," she says, and flops back on the bed. "Except I'll secretly hate you forever, obviously. I'll give you ten minutes, then I'm leaving."

He goes to work. Work, something they talked about only in terms of how important it is to both of them. He shouldn't have indulged tonight. He should've been on the case.

Griffin and Diego leave the hotel and venture back to the catacombs. Denis meets them there.

The Frenchman sets a lantern down to illuminate the scene.

The three necromancers have animated two skeletons, moving in jerky motions.

The necromancer, Melissa the Gorgon, turns to them, her snakes hissing.

"You go for the skeletons," Griffin orders Diego, who removes one of Big Rob's magic-draining gadgets and heads into the breach.

"Oh, big bad hunters, I see," Melissa says, and mock-yawns. "At least you're not those C.R.O.N.E. harpies."

"You wish," Griffin counters. "You probably get along great with them."

"I don't—you're at least honest about being assholes." The necromancer holds her hands up and conjures two dark balls of shadow above them. "Unlike the two-faced witches, who pretend they're better than the rest of us."

Diego has the first skeleton down, and Denis has felled one of the other necromancers. Each of them moves on to his next target.

"While I'd love to hear more about your feelings," Griffin says, removing a shock gun designed specially for magic users, "it's time this plot of yours ended."

Melissa opens her mouth and he deploys the weapon before she can speak. It sucks up the darkness she's conjuring and eventually brings her to her knees. She scowls up at him.

"I'll give you twelve hours to leave the country. Your necromancy-for-hire days are over."

"Fine," she says with an eye roll. "Asshole."

"We'll hunt you down if you try anything like this again," he assures her.

Denis and Diego have subdued everyone else by then, and it's time for cleanup and escorting these necromancers to flights out of the country.

Once Griffin is finally able to escape back to the hotel, he hopes Savvy will be waiting.

The room is empty. No note. No nothing. He'll just have to wait and see.

Savvy isn't sure whether to believe Griffin's story about a 3 A.M. artifact opportunity or not. Though it seems like he'd be able to come up with a more convincing lie, so maybe it was true. She only knows she had the deepest sleep in months in those hours in his bed, at least part of it in his arms. That despite access to the best potions in creation from Auntie Simone.

Later the next day, Savvy and Yvette return to the catacombs site and find bones littered on the ground and other signs of an altercation. "What has happened?" Yvette asks.

"Someone got here before us and took care of business." It happens. There's no sense of overwhelming darkness at work, and the bone wall has collapsed inward, as it would on its own.

Savvy shrugs and begins to clear the site of magic residue, weaving a spell to banish the faint traces left of the negative energy she initially detected. It's weak enough, she can do it easily.

She should be more curious about the precise answer to Yvette's question, is surprised that she isn't. But instead her mind circles back again and again to a month from now and whether she will show up, despite knowing she shouldn't.

And, if she does, whether Griffin will be there too.

Now

12

✦ ✦ ✦

Griffin

Griffin has to fight the impulse to expel his brother Jacob from behind the wheel, take over, and turn the SUV around. Savvy isn't even back there anyway. She flew off.

"You realize you shouldn't be associating with me either, not anymore," he says.

"Brother," Diego says, hurt.

"And he's not even your real one," Jacob adds.

Griffin's jaw feels tight enough to snap in two, so he forces a deep breath. Then, "Let me rephrase—you shouldn't be *seen* associating with me. It's too dangerous right now."

Jacob scrubs one hand over his beard, the other on the top of the SUV's steering wheel. "Dad texted. He's going to attempt to appeal to the Butcher's better sense. We just need you to lay low until then."

Griffin didn't realize. His reaction to this information surprises him. The first thought that occurred to him was that he's no longer sure the Butcher has a better nature. But he can't say that out loud. Not to mention, he has no evidence for it.

Only Savvy's insistence they're not the good guys . . . and the Butcher and Circe turning on two loyal operatives, making them prey to mercenary wolves. . . .

Jacob returns both hands to the wheel and jerks the car onto an interstate on-ramp—suddenly, to throw off anyone tailing them—and Griffin thinks back to Savvy's saying he was deluded.

"Isn't it odd that Mother Circe isn't backing up Savvy?" he asks.

"Witches, please," Diego says. "Who knows? We're going to my cabin, right? It's the obvious choice of hideout. Not even y'all have been there."

Jacob and Griffin exchange a look.

"You mean that place is real?" Griffin asks slowly.

Diego has always claimed that when his parents died they left him a cabin on a lake and that he goes there to meditate. None of them can picture Diego quietly communing with nature. . . . They always assumed it was a cover story for when his hookups lasted more than one day.

"You guys doubted the cabin." Diego shakes his head. "*For shame*. You'll see. I have hidden depths." He tilts his chin up.

Another look between brothers is exchanged, but they keep quiet on the believability of Diego's claims.

"Just tell me how to get there," Jacob says.

Diego *hmmph*s. "You're going the right way."

Griffin wants to speculate more out loud about the speed with which the Butcher and Mother Circe changed their minds— but something makes him hold back. It all still seems too fast. This entire day. The speed with which his life and relationship changed . . .

Were upended.

And might be ended altogether?

The car is quiet as Jacob drives, even Diego speaking only to give directions. They make good time out of town, and the "cabin" seems to be only about forty-five minutes away, somewhere around Lake Lanier.

Diego is confident in the direction-giving. Almost like this isn't a trip to an imaginary locale.

Griffin wonders what would have happened if the interlopers hadn't shown up. Savvy clearly thought she'd be the only one leaving. Could she have gone through with it? Does she hate him that much, simply for being a hunter?

Not that he can blame her. It's not as if his first emotions today were to stop and understand her viewpoint. They both got blindsided, he can sense the truth of that more and more, and they both reacted badly. It's not as if he refused the Butcher's command to take her out, while it still existed, before it was turned on him. . . .

But it's not like he couldn't have tried harder to execute it. The same must be true for Savvy.

When the outside threats arrived, he moved instinctively to protect her, and he isn't sorry. He doesn't know what to do next, which is an unfamiliar state for Griffin. He doesn't like uncertainty.

"Up here, then left," Diego says. "How we doing back there, Griff?"

"Oh, you know. Eager to see the cabin."

"Smart-ass," Diego mutters. "Keep your feelings to yourself. That's fine with us, isn't it, Jacob?"

"No," Jacob says, "bottling things up is dangerous. As we've seen."

"I wasn't bottling things up," Griffin says. "I was maintaining my cover."

Jacob sighs. "That's not what I meant and you know it."

"Do I? My entire life is in shambles. You two are supposed to be after the bounty on my head like everyone else. The woman I lo—was supposed to marry is a witch who apparently hates me now and would kill me without a thought." Except she didn't. She didn't try all that hard, despite the knives floating in the air. Does that give him pause or hope?

"We won't let it happen," Jacob says, but he sounds unsure.

Could Savvy really do it? Because the more Griffin thinks on it, the more he's becoming convinced that he couldn't take her out. Not really. Is he angry at the situation? Yes. But he craves the ability to talk to Savvy about it. Openly, for once.

Even though it's insanity to consider it. It's not happening. Their cat is a fucking leopard, for chrissakes. She fled with her friends riding a broomstick. *Flying.*

"Up here on the right, the one with the bottle tree," Diego says.

Griffin leans forward in the back seat and squints through the windshield. He and Jacob look at each other and Jacob turns onto the driveway of a robin's-egg-blue cabin with, yes, a bottle tree, for capturing spirits in the yard. An old tradition for protecting a home and making it safe. Blue glass shimmers from the branches, artful.

"My idea," Diego says. "My mom and I worked on it together."

Shit. Turns out maybe Griffin hasn't known anything important about anyone in his life. Diego might honestly have hidden depths.

Jacob parks.

"Come on," Diego says, and hops out.

He crosses the yard quickly and leaps up the steps. The cabin is . . . nice. Well-maintained, as is much of the rest of the neighborhood. Far tidier than Diego's actual apartment.

"How often do you come here?" Griffin asks. He's still not sure that this isn't someone else's house they're about to break into. Diego would do that to save face.

Diego pulls his keys out of his pocket. "Every few weeks. It quiets my mind."

He unlocks the door.

The inside is even more fascinating than the outside. Griffin never met Diego's parents. They died a few years before Diego joined the organization. The décor is brightly colored and there are photos of Diego at various ages with people who must be his parents and cousins and friends. Diego's apartment in town looks like something from a men's design catalogue. Cold. This feels like seeing into his heart.

"There's a view of the lake out back," his friend says, and scrubs his neck. "Guest room's that way. You two can share."

"Diego . . ." Griffin hesitates. "This is a really nice place."

"Yeah, I know," Diego says. "It was my mom's favorite spot on Earth."

"Thanks for inviting us to your hidden depths," Jacob says. Then, "Do you have a beer?"

"Don't push it," Diego says, but seems to relax. "Negra Modelo in the fridge."

"I need something stronger," Griffin says.

"Bourbon's in the cabinet. I'll go out for groceries. There's a security cam that Big Rob set up for me. I'll send you the link. I imagine Griffin could use some of the time he's in hiding to think."

"I'm not hiding," Griffin says. "I'm regrouping. Hence, the bourbon."

"Hence." Diego's expression says he isn't buying it. "Sure. I'll be back in a bit." He lifts his hand and Jacob tosses the keys over. He catches them, then hesitates. "Give me your phone."

He's talking to Griffin. "You're asking *me* for my phone? I don't think so."

Diego holds his hand out. "Bourbon and regrouping can result in bad decisions. Trust me, I know."

Griffin sighs but hands it over. What's he going to do with it anyway? Look for updates on the bounty on his and Savvy's heads?

Diego turns to leave. "You'll thank me later. Now drink up."

Griffin rummages in the cabinet and finds a bottle of Willett, pours himself two fingers in a glass. Then he wanders through the cozy living room and toward the back sliding doors. He wonders if they're the *only* ones of Diego's friends who've ever been here. Maybe everyone has a universe of secrets inside them, which they choose to share willingly or only when they have to. Maybe he should've asked more questions. . . .

Not just of Savvy, but himself.

He hopes she's okay, somewhere safe like this.

He lets himself out the sliding doors and stares at the water. Lakes, rivers, ponds, even the ocean, they all remind him of her now. Of that day on the Thames. And then meeting her again by the Seine.

If she's telling the truth about not having ensnared him purposely, they must have met by chance. They could've been on the same case, the magic signature in London. That would explain why it disappeared around the same time she left him. But . . . don't C.R.O.N.E. witches create problems? They're not supposed to be solving them. He has so many questions.

He remembers how gun-shy Savvy got the second time they met. She didn't act like someone setting a trap at all. He was the one who proposed meeting up back home.

What are the odds the universe would bring them together and then push them apart?

Meant to be, those words that he's only ever thought about one woman in his life, sound in the back of his subconscious again. The water is calm in contrast to his roiling emotions. He downs the bourbon in one long swallow.

Jacob comes to the sliding doors. "Dad called."

Griffin doesn't want to know. But he asks, "More good news, I take it?"

Jacob walks out to join him. "Not the worst, at least on the surface. The Butcher says he might be willing to reconsider your termination—if, uh, you finish Savvy off soon."

Something inside Griffin howls with outrage. "And Mother Circe, any chance she'll back off?"

Jacob shakes his head. "Not likely. What are you going to do?"

Griffin studies the water, still shimmering as sunset falls. What a day.

There's the distant noise of people partying out on boats or in yards, having their normal continue like always. Whatever he does now may determine whether he has even the abnormal he's used to again.

"I need to see her. Can you loan me your phone?"

Jacob hesitates. "I get it, but I don't think that's a good idea. Diego was right for once."

"She probably wouldn't take my call anyway." Griffin lets his brother believe he's caving.

"There's too much chance you might do something . . ." His brother searches for the least offensive word.

"Stupid?"

"I was going to say 'rash,' maybe even 'brave,' but then realized I have no idea what I'd do in your place. 'Good luck' is about all I have to say."

Luck, which Griffin believes in only because of Savvy in the first place. "What about more bourbon?"

"That I can do," his brother says, and claps him on the shoulder. He lets himself be steered back into the kitchen, to the table.

After a while, Diego returns with two bags of groceries and takes in the bottle and the glass waiting for him. "I see we've reached the copious alcohol part of the day. Deal me in."

Griffin manages to keep watering down his drink in the bathroom, so they won't notice. Meanwhile, he keeps pouring. And pouring.

They're eager to commiserate, and Griffin's practice at playing slightly drunk goes back to college and promising his mother he'd keep an eye on his brothers, but without them necessarily realizing it.

Finally, it starts to get late enough for his noises about going to sleep to land on ears that want to hear them. "I think I'm going to bed," he says with a scrub of his face. "More updates have to come overnight. I need to decide if I'm going to take up the exit strategy Dad is trying to negotiate with the Butcher. . . ." Diego's mouth opens, but Griffin cuts him off. "I need to sleep on it."

Diego and Jacob are both obviously exhausted too and approve. "I get it," Diego says, though Griffin isn't aware of him ever having a relationship with any of his women.

"I'll take the couch, so you can have the guest bed," Jacob nobly volunteers.

This absolutely will make what Griffin has planned harder, but to protest would look extremely weird.

"Thanks, Jake." Griffin pats his brother on the shoulder and heads up the hall to Diego's guest room. His friend has left out some sweats, which is frankly thoughtful enough to give him pause. He does trust them both. He should tell them what he's planning.

But they'll only try to talk him out of it. What he told his dad just this morning—seemingly ages ago—is true. He doesn't make decisions lightly. His mind is set.

He stares at the ceiling for as long as he can stand it. Then he changes into the sweats, just to be out of his tattered wedding tux. *RIP, best suit.* Their training includes all manner of techniques for sneaking into and out of places, so transitioning to stealth mode comes naturally.

And he's not going to get caught by monsters—just by Diego or Jacob. That's not such a big deal, right? He creeps down the hallway, and the familiar buzz of Jacob's snoring emanates from the living room.

Griffin pauses when he sees the kitchen light on.

Diego sits at the table. Griffin's phone is in the center of it.

"You really think I'm going to miss you pretending to be hammered?" Diego's words are soft, a little slurred, because his drinks were real. "You didn't get me *that* wasted. Tell me what you're doing."

Griffin finishes his journey and slides into a chair beside Diego. "I have to talk to her—before I can decide anything."

"You did that already, remember?"

"No, we were venting at each other. We need to talk."

"What if she doesn't want to?" Diego asks it with a tinge of regret in his voice.

"Entirely possible. But I won't know if I don't give her the chance."

"For the record, I'm half on your side here, half on the side of smashing your phone and calling your dad on mine."

Griffin could absolutely get his phone before Diego could do any such thing. But he doesn't want to fight with his friend. He understands that the protectiveness comes from a place of real caring. "I appreciate you bringing us here. Keeping me safe." He sighs. "But it's not going to go well if you try to stop me. I didn't want to put you in that position."

"At least you had time to think it over. Go on, call her. I'm going to get some sleep." Diego nods toward the phone.

Griffin waits until he's gone and picks it up. Jacob's still snoring away, so he heads out the sliding doors into the cool night. The stars are more visible here than in the midst of the city lights. The lake reflects a thumbnail moon. He imagines seeing a witch fly across it on a broom and finds that the image doesn't threaten him. It brings a wry smile.

Interesting.

Maybe he is about to do something dumb. He should put the phone back and get some sleep, see how he feels in the morning. He should at least have a conversation with his father.

He stands, staring at the phone, undecided, for the longest time.

13

✦ ✦ ✦

Savvy

Savvy wishes she could keep flying forever. She doesn't want to process what just happened or the fact that she's been disavowed by Mother Circe and what that means. She certainly doesn't want to think about Griffin discharging that power bomb to save her. He could've used it against her. . . .

But he didn't.

She could've taken him out, but *she* didn't. When it counted, she protected him. And the thing is, she's pretty sure she'd do the same thing again.

Her mother flies parallel to her. "Where will you go?" Claudia asks. "I'll contact Circe. Reason with her."

Right. She can't turn and go back home. And she can't go to the Farmhouse now either.

Brie flies up along her other side, Elle on her flank. "She can come to my place," Brie says. "People forget it exists."

It's not an ideal solution. But Brie does still spend so much time at the Farmhouse that she's rarely at her own apartment, which Savvy has nicknamed . . .

"The pink palace it is," she says.

"This has got to be a mistake. I'll fix it." Claudia tosses out the words and peels off, heading in the opposite direction.

If anyone can troubleshoot this nightmare, it's her mother, but Savvy doesn't hold out a lot of hope for Mother Circe's flexibility. Savvy has too many feelings and thoughts racing around in her head. It's not as if the situation with Griffin isn't disaster enough. But it's also a nightmare to be the center of a bounty hunt involving the entire supernatural world, H.U.N.T.E.R., and likely even some of her own kind. . . .

Savvy has always done her duty to witchkin and in protecting humankind. She only ever, *ever* put the job second for Griffin. Even that is barely true. And *this* is how she's repaid? The turn happened so quick.

Almost too quick, she thinks. Though she isn't sure exactly what about that bothers her.

Brie guides Elle and Savvy through the night sky to the duplex she rents half of. The other half belongs to a camera technician who works on various TV shows that film in and around Atlanta. He's nice, Captain Bear likes him, and he's none the wiser that he lives next to a witch and her capybara familiar.

Which means they pause high above the house, hidden by clouds, as Brie works a spell that will hide their landing.

Once she's done, they set down on the tiny front yard. Captain Bear and Paris jump off their brooms to immediately zip off around the back of the house. Elle steps off her broom, lets down Peggy, and peers after them.

"They're looking for intruders," Savvy says.

"Or going to the bathroom," Brie says.

"Both," Elle says. "Almost certainly both."

Even the familiars are in on the danger. Savvy hates it.

"Paris put herself between me and Griffin back there," she says.

Brie's mouth makes a small O of surprise. "Is that why he came out of there alive?" She says it breezily, but Savvy knows her friend well enough to hear the serious tone below.

Savvy isn't going to lie. "No, I don't think it is."

"Understandable," Elle says. "You two would be married by now if my masterfully planned event had taken place."

Brie sighs. "Y'all want a drink?"

"Yes, please," Savvy and Elle say in unison.

The familiars careen back from around the side of the house as Brie unlocks her door and lets them all in. The pink palace gets its name from the obvious. There are dozens, maybe hundreds, of shades of pink represented here, as if a pretty-princess party threw up. But then there are the punk design choices to offset it—like a pillow with safety pins for fringe. Images of iconic punk records and screen-printed show posters dot the walls, in a variety of pink frames.

Brie is nothing if not a contradiction, aesthetically and otherwise. She crosses to a pale pink vintage bar cart and pauses. "Requests?"

"Strong," Savvy says.

Elle nods.

"Strong, it is," Brie confirms. She plucks down three martini glasses from the hanging rack and then taps the edges to fill them with . . . whatever bracing concoction she's chosen.

She carries the drinks over and hands them to Elle and Savvy, then goes back for her own. Savvy stares down at a perfectly garnished martini.

Shit. Martinis make her think of Griffin.

"You'll get through this," Brie says. "One way or another."

She lifts her glass to clink, and Savvy and Elle both indulge her. "One way or another, in the immortal words of Debbie Harry," Savvy says. She takes a healthy quaff of the cocktail. Then she sets it down on a deep magenta side table. "I'm going to lose it just sitting around here."

"Do you want to talk about it?" Elle asks, and smooths a hand down her tailored, still wrinkle-free trousers.

Savvy watches Paris and fluffy white Captain Bear, still in their glamoured forms. They roll around on the floor, playing, and then seem to launch into a game of hide-and-seek, disappearing into the next room. Peggy sits next to Elle, her throat rhythmically puffing in and out.

"Of course she doesn't," Brie says.

"You don't know that," Elle says.

They look at Savvy, waiting for the verdict.

Savvy lets the question rattle around inside her. She does. But not to her friends.

"Mother Circe made her decision fast," she says finally.

Brie makes a face and drinks deep. "Your mother will set her straight."

The three of them look at one another. None of them entirely believes it. There's something . . . off about this whole situation. Besides the obvious. It keeps bothering Savvy. What is she missing? She needs to move. To think.

"Should we fortify your defenses?" she asks.

"They're impeccable," Brie says. "But sure, it'll give us something to do. I hate waiting around."

"I know you do. And I hate it even more."

"Savvy—" Brie hesitates. "—whatever happens, we're your friends."

Elle nods, agreeing. "You can count on us."

Savvy swallows. "Thank you. And same. I just want to be alone for a while. All right?"

"Obviously," Brie says. "And if you change your mind . . ."

"Thanks. I'll do the upstairs," Savvy says, and stands.

Which leaves Brie and Elle the down. One of the benefits of living in the Atlanta suburbs is that the duplex is pricey in rent, but also sizable.

Savvy heads up the steps, chanting while holding her locket. The energy of Brie's protection spells responds to her. The sensation is like standing in an ocean among gentle waves. *We're here,* the enchantments practically whisper, *ready and waiting.*

Brie's magic is friendly to her because they're friends. What they said to each other downstairs is true. They're sisters of a sort, the three of them. It's a tangible reminder that she has people in her corner still. But she doesn't like the idea of them being endangered because of her.

Griffin's in danger too.

She wonders where he is right now. Who's protecting *him*? Certainly not the Butcher, that's clear. But his brothers and Diego must be. His father. They're probably downing bourbon and cursing her name.

Despite some of the things they said to each other back at the house, she can't imagine Griffin joining in. But how well does she know him?

And how well did she let him know her?

Her mother doesn't have to say "I told you so." Because she did tell Savvy, frequently and in triplicate. But Savvy wanted love, despite everything she'd been taught. And she was convinced she'd found it. That she'd found everything she secretly needed, even though she wasn't supposed to.

She wanders the rooms upstairs, reinforcing the spells. First, through Brie's small sewing room, with cabinets of artfully arranged spell supplies. After that, she visits Brie's bedroom with its fuchsia comforter and turntable in the corner. The guest room with a fold-out couch, where Savvy has never spent the night before, because why wouldn't they stay at the comfortable Farmhouse with its never-ending guest rooms instead?

Paris scampers up beside her as she looks out the window into the night. The yard is dark and deserted. There's no sound from the neighbor next door either. He's probably on a night shoot. Paris drops her glamour, growing big enough to nudge against Savvy's hip. Savvy scratches behind her silky ear.

"What was that back there? Getting in between us?" Savvy murmurs.

Paris purrs. Something most black leopards don't do—Savvy presumes it's an artifact of her also having a natural glamour of domestic cat.

"You still trust him?" Savvy gazes down into Paris's nearly glowing eyes.

Paris's head bobs up and down. She understands language more and more all the time, a relatively rare trait for a familiar.

"I could find where he's gone. Probably. Unless he's hiding even from me," she muses out loud and realizes it's true.

She refuses to think before she acts, once the notion occurs.

Paris trails her as she heads back to the sewing room and quickly selects the right ingredients from the colorful bottles and vials on Brie's shelves, then helps herself to a gray marble mortar and pestle. A little rue for remembering, salt from the sea for travel, ground glass for seeing. She chants the Latin under her breath, sending out the will to look, to find. It feels good to act, to sink into the spellwork. And then, the final step, to imagine Griffin as if he's standing in front of her.

After a moment, she sees him as clearly as if he is. He's by a lake, staring up at the sky. His head tilts down to his phone and then he seems to look straight back at her.

A ghostly finger of sensation runs down Savvy's spine, and her heart aches. His face reflects conflict. Worry. There's a light purple bruise forming on his cheekbone. No glasses, which reminds her he's not who she thought. . . . But she isn't who he thought either. He keeps staring ahead at her.

He doesn't see her. He can't. But she wants to reach out to him. And *she* could. All she has to do now to complete the spell is follow this thread to wherever he is.

But is it a good idea? They were sent to kill each other. Both of them are in mortal jeopardy from basically everyone except their closest friends and family. And those people may suffer for backing them.

Then she revisits what happened at the house. . . . He protected her, while she had knives in the air, pointed at him. And she did the same, moved to keep him alive, without thinking. She'd do it again too. And again.

He's a hunter, yes, but she's beginning to think maybe *he* doesn't understand what that means to her. He obviously doesn't understand what her job as a C.R.O.N.E. witch is— was?—about.

Could he still be worth a chance? Her gut says yes.

Wherever he is, Griffin peers down at his phone for a long moment, and then he taps out a message to someone. He closes his eyes, then hits send without looking.

Her phone buzzes and she pulls it out of a small pocket hidden in the lining of her tattered dress.

Nosy Paris comes over and nudges her.

"Yes, I know. I'm going to look at it."

She considers dropping the spell. It's intrusive to keep watching his reaction as she reads whatever he's just sent her, and decides whether to respond. But though she might be considering an open line of communication, she's no saint. She's a spy at heart. And she wants every last piece of information available to her. So she leaves the spell up as she takes out her phone and reads.

Can we meet? Neutral location. Just us. No one else.

Brie will be pissed if she says yes, while Elle will likely think it's romantic. But that's *if they find out*. Savvy will have to either sneak out or fudge the truth to get past her friends' questions.

There's also the fact that this could be a trap. A setup. She needs reassurance that it isn't. So she types back: *Is that a good idea?*

The way Griffin's broad shoulders give a little in relief at her response, before he even reads it, does something low in her belly. He doesn't hesitate before typing back.

She reads it immediately this time: *It's the only good idea I have right now.*

She may be the most foolish witch under the stars, but she believes him. Goddess help her.

"Where?" she whispers as she types the same word.

He ticks his head to the side. She really should stop watching him. She doesn't want to.

The square, he sends back.

He doesn't need to be any more specific. The old courthouse square in Decatur. A public place. But it's nearly midnight, so by the time she gets there it'll be deserted except for people out drinking in the bars or heading home from the same. They won't stick out there. A couple fighting in public.

Or possibly not fighting?

It's also where the bookstore they set up their first meeting in Atlanta is. The first time they saw each other not far from home, but in some semblance of their real lives.

Savvy drops the location spell, letting her sight of him go. *One hour,* she types back. And then she rummages through Brie's closet for a pocket broom, conjures it to full size, and presses open the window.

She turns her head to Paris. "I'll be back. You stay here so they know that."

Paris nods and turns to pad from the room, presumably buying Savvy some time and distraction.

14

✦ ✦ ✦

Griffin

Griffin is surprised but tentatively hopeful that Savvy agreed to meet. He managed to nick Diego's keys and take off in his friend's vehicle without having to explain himself. . . . Hopefully, he won't end up regretting that decision.

He takes a circuitous route when he gets close to Decatur just to verify no one is following him, and parks a few blocks away from the square in an empty spot on a quiet street. This will give him another chance to spot anyone tailing him. The last thing he wants is to compromise Savvy's safety.

She must be wondering if this is a trap. He would be. Yes, it has occurred to him that she could be using this as an ambush too. He's willing to risk it. And he wouldn't judge her, not for that. They're up against the longest odds he can imagine.

He's still not sure what to say. Or what she might say to him. But he needs to see this through. Their relationship might have been built on a pair of big lies, but being together felt right and true anyway, and it might still now that he's had a chance to cool off and begin to take in this new revelation. Also, he's not sure how they get through this without each other.

Downtown Decatur is mostly quiet, a few late-night weekend revelers out. Drunken calls echo back and forth on outdoor patios, and he hears laughter from street seating as he nears the square. No one's following him that he can spot, so he chances it, crossing the street onto the broad lawn around the hulking old historic courthouse.

He heads around the far side, anticipating where he'll find her. If he's right, and she is there, that'll be a good sign.

He almost holds his breath when he takes the last turn and the other side of the lawn comes into view. At first, he doesn't spot anyone waiting. No familiar tall, curvy silhouette among the big old trees.

The strength of the disappointment that washes over him nearly brings him to his knees. Him, a warrior. He takes a deep breath and finds his center, steeling himself as he's done so many times over the course of his life. Except, this time, it refuses to work.

But then, she shows.

She materializes, getting more solid as she walks toward him. She's releasing a masking spell of some kind, he guesses. It's probably meant to rub it in his nose that she has magic. Or . . . knowing Savvy, and he thinks he does . . . is this a test to see how he reacts?

He stays as still as possible.

All he knows for sure is that his heart beats faster as she approaches. That his spine finds itself. He was right to come here.

She pauses a half dozen steps away from him and glances back over her shoulder at the quiet, dark storefront of Little Shop of Stories.

He waits for her. He took the step of contacting her. It's her turn to reach out now.

She walks closer. "So it isn't a trap," she says.

She stops near enough that he can take in the familiar, lovely planes of her face. She's not smiling now, but he can recall her dimples just so when she does. And how her warm, soft skin feels under his fingers . . .

He fists his hands to stop himself from touching her.

"I'm glad you came," he says.

"Should we walk? Moving targets are less easily hit." Savvy

hugs her arms around herself, then seems to catch the tell that she's nervous and drops them.

"Good point."

They settle into a comfortable pace side by side, but not touching. Once more, Griffin waits her out.

"I think I told you that I never imagined my wedding as a kid. Never thought I'd get married." Savvy's tone is dry. "Seems like I nailed that one."

"Savvy," Griffin says, "neither of us could have predicted this, right?"

She pauses in midstride and gives him a sidelong look. "If that's a roundabout way of asking if I knew, I didn't. I would never knowingly date a hunter."

The word "never" echoes between them.

"Why is that?" This is the crux of it, isn't it? Griffin needs to understand. "Is it just because we were the ones who limited your use of your powers?"

Savvy stops then and turns to him. "You keep saying that. Why?"

Griffin frowns. "Because it's what happened. . . . Back then, with the Butcher and your Mother Circe. The accords."

"She's not my anything, not after she tossed me to the men who hunt like wolves. And the necromancer." Savvy bites her lip. She seems to consider something. Then she says, "Griffin. That's not what happened then. We're far more powerful than you could ever be."

Griffin's skepticism must show.

She holds up her hand. "I don't mean it like that. Well, not exactly like that. Listen. Mother Circe led her original coven to make the Butcher back off. *That's* how the accords happened. The accords were meant to protect the rest of the world. To prevent something like mutually assured destruction, if the supernatural world was widely discovered. *We* live within specific tenets. We try not to disrupt the natural world beyond using our powers to keep it in balance. We fight only when we have to, for our lives, or to protect humanity."

Griffin tries to wrap his head around this complete revision of the history of witches he has been taught. He doesn't have a clue how to respond.

"Griffin . . ."

He likes her saying his name. Softly.

She goes on. "All the witch burning, all the deaths. They risked putting the world out of balance and they hurt us. They still hurt us, the memory. I won't lie—there are occasionally dark witches, of course, just like there are evil humans or anyone else. Yes, the covens fought your kind. . . . They fought back. But we were the ones who suffered most, and we were not at fault. C.R.O.N.E.—now—we're protectors."

He can't move. He lets what she's saying wash over him. If she's telling the truth, it makes a certain sort of sense. It also means that the Butcher isn't just *not* a hero. Not the legend who saved them all that Griffin grew up hearing about. No, if it's true then he's a certified villain. That doesn't feel right either. Why are their concepts of history so different, when their understanding of the accords' purpose—to stay under the world's radar—are largely the same?

Griffin protests, "But Mother Circe, we've been told how she threatened villages. She's supposed to have wiped the Roanoke settlers clear off the map."

"I know we've been blamed for a lot of things that we didn't do—Mother Circe is no different." Savvy pauses. "I'll admit, I don't know all the specifics of what took place back then. It's painful history. We tend to avoid rehashing it. Well, except my mother. She lost a friend . . . to one of you. A hunter."

"No wonder she hates me."

"She didn't know what you were."

"Right." Griffin isn't sure what to say to get Savvy to believe that this is all news to him.

She goes on. "I can tell you that we work to prevent harm. Not cause it."

Griffin seizes on this. Common ground. "Would you believe me if I said that's exactly how I'd describe what the operatives at H.U.N.T.E.R. do? We use knowledge and advanced technology to siphon away and counter harmful magic. We fight to protect humans too. I've always been told one of the things we protect them—and each other—from is witches. But I'm here. I'm listening."

"Hm."

He imagines this is as hard for Savvy to swallow as what she's just told him.

"Too bad we can't go back in time and see who's right," Griffin says.

Savvy's eyebrows gather together. "Actually, that's not a bad—"

Griffin hears the sudden electric buzz and flare of a souped-up Taser and dives onto Savvy, taking her down, to protect her, on pure instinct. The ground where they stood smokes from the impact.

He looks out in front of them to see Melissa the Gorgon, building a mass of black energy around her. The freelancer in gray fatigues is here too, holding the weird-ass Taser, something like Tesla coils popping between its points. His visual scan also finds some new entrants in the race to take out the two of them.

It *must* mean something that neither Griffin nor Savvy went for the kill back at the house. Since those two mercenaries are here. A termination order is a last resort for his organization, and it must be for Savvy's too. Griffin assumed Savvy would take hers out, but she didn't. But this lends credence to what she just told him. Maybe they are *both* the good guys. But, if that's true, why would the Butcher and Mother Circe behave as they have?

"This should be interesting," Savvy says.

"I can think of other words."

Griffin and Savvy get up and stand back-to-back, watching the interlopers approach from either side.

He hears a familiar voice behind him. "Don't move, brother."

Oh no. He turns to confirm it. Diego is here.

"You brought reinforcements?" Savvy says, whirling to face Griffin. Her hands begin to glow with pale light.

"I didn't tell anyone where I was going," Griffin says. "I promise."

Savvy squints. "I'm supposed to believe that?"

"Savvy, duck!" Griffin says.

She does, just in time to avoid the floating darkness Melissa the Gorgon is aiming toward them as she stalks closer. She holds on to the back of the shadow she weaves with both hands.

"Diego, you shouldn't be here," Griffin says. "Go. We've got this."

"No way." Diego shouts, "Jacob, hurry up!"

My brother's here too. Great.

"I didn't know they were coming," Griffin says. "I swear."

"I believe you," Savvy says, and her eyes are fierce.

Griffin would be relieved if he weren't distracted by a man with horns wearing a long cloak landing behind Melissa of the snake hair.

Griffin slides a glance to Savvy. "That's not one of mine. Yours?"

"No, I swear."

From the other direction, there's a man who looks like he must've been on the same training regimen as the heroes who get cast in Marvel movies. A barely human-sized Hulk. As he nears, Griffin sees that he's got scars crisscrossing his face.

"That's the Slasher," Savvy says. "He's an assassin. A good one."

She sends a blast of pale magic down to his feet, slowing him down. A little. His hands twirl twin blades, accelerating as he continues to approach. Melissa the Gorgon is still weaving her shadow.

Meanwhile, Diego and Jacob are setting up one of Rob's big-ass weapons on a tripod behind them. A nullifying mega-ray. Suddenly, Griffin isn't sorry they showed up.

"If he's so good," Diego calls, "what's up with his face?"

As if in answer, the assassin launches one of his blades. The steel spins through the air and Diego barely manages to dodge it, lunging behind the firepower Jacob's rushing to get active.

"He did it to himself," Savvy shouts.

"Oh," Diego calls back, still in hiding.

"We need to get out of here," Griffin says to Savvy. "The boys can handle this."

She huffs, conjuring another ball of light in her palm. "I'm not running."

"Get out of the way, brother," Diego says, creeping out and coming closer. "We got this."

"Notice how he didn't tell *me* to get out of the way," Savvy says, chin lifting. "Just you."

"You broke his heart," Diego says. "I'm mad at you."

"He broke mine."

"Come with me," Griffin says, his own heart pounding at her words, ignoring Diego and Jacob. "We're leaving them here."

Savvy is obviously torn. "I'm not sure they can handle this. But I—I can."

At that moment, Melissa, the Slasher, and the original merc decide to make their moves. The horned man in the cloak stands back to see how they do, and Griffin can't help admiring the strategy.

"Savvy, we do the same job—as we've just determined. We're not going to let you take on five—" Griffin looks out and corrects himself. "—six assassins by yourself."

"One of them's dead," Savvy says.

"What?"

Savvy nods toward Melissa the Gorgon, who grins and whose hair snakes seem to be grinning too. The merc with the Taser isn't moving as smoothly as before. How did Griffin miss it? The necromancer is controlling him.

"I left him alive," Savvy says.

"You're soft, and that's your problem." Melissa the Gorgon almost sings the words. "He was useful to me this way."

The merc rushes them then, and Savvy shoves Griffin aside as he protests. She sends a blaze of bright light cracking out from her palm and it smacks into the sprinting merc's chest. He staggers, then stumbles, then stops at Savvy's feet and gazes up at her. Griffin goes to help, but then the man says, "Thank you," and falls, dead.

This was pure cover for Melissa, whose darkness is now seeping into everyone else there to take out Griffin and Savvy, including the Slasher.

"Savvy," Griffin says, and she looks at him. "I know," she says. "If she infects them with death magic, she can control them even before they die."

"Deploy the ray," Griffin shouts to Diego and Jacob.

But then he sees the man in the cloak, the only one not being driven by Melissa the Gorgon, advancing on Jacob, as Diego comes toward them.

"We need to retreat," Griffin says, low.

Savvy turns her head and takes in the situation. Jacob is relatively new to the field. He grapples with the horned man, but then the nullifier is sparking as the man tosses Jake to the ground and begins destroying the weapon's controls. Clearly, he's tangled with hunters before.

"Let's get out of here," Griffin says. Meaning all of them.

"No," Savvy says. "Like you said, we need to talk. We're not done. Stay put."

Savvy's tone means she's serious, and so he manages to make himself wait. The infected assassins are mostly standing their ground, and Melissa is still grinning.

"I told you I wanted to be the one to take you," she says to Savvy.

"Come and get me," Savvy says, and grins, holding her hands out, palms up. "But make it fair. Just you and me."

Griffin doesn't like this, not one bit.

Especially when Melissa's grin widens. "I thought you'd never ask, my sweet."

"'My sweet'?" Griffin asks. As does Diego, who's standing next to him.

"Okay, so she went to witch school with me and maybe we dated in high school," Savvy says over her shoulder. "She didn't have the snakes for hair then."

A wave of dark shadow surrounds Melissa as she comes toward Savvy.

"You broke my heart. Prepare to die," Melissa says.

Savvy shakes her palms and they flare to life. She's a fiery sun goddess. He never knew how apt that name was for her until now. "You were hurting familiars. You didn't have a heart." Like when she called the wind in the barn, she seems to summon light, even in the darkness. Griffin gapes as she gets brighter and brighter and Melissa's grin turns into a grimace and her wide eyes into a squint and then there's the scream as she falls unconscious and the shadows around her dispel.

"I didn't kill her," Savvy says. "But we won't want to hang out here."

The assassins Melissa infected are, in fact, dazed and shaking off the aftereffects of the necromancer's control.

"That was so hot," Diego says.

Griffin holds out his hand to Savvy and says, "This way."

She slides her hand into his, no convincing necessary.

To Diego and Jacob, he says, "She saved your asses. Report back to HQ. Take that broken monstrosity with you. Get out of here now."

"I like it when you realize how wrong you are," Savvy says, "and start giving other people orders."

He doesn't linger to make sure they're following the orders. He can feel the shift in the energy between Savvy and him, the usual heat between them crackling to life. He stalks ahead, the sweet contact of Savvy's hand in his, and when they hit the street the SUV is parked on, he regrets that he has to release her to take out the key and unlock the doors.

She climbs in the passenger side, and he slips behind the wheel and wastes no time in getting them out of there. He accelerates, quickly leaving downtown behind. Residential neighborhoods with tall trees pop up instead of businesses, all quiet and dark this late. The air is still thick between them, heavy and full of possibility.

He finally slows down when he hears—it can't be, but it is—a laugh. Savvy is laughing.

He glances over at her. "Diego was right, for once. That was hot."

"It was?" Savvy says it innocently. Flirting. She's flirting with him.

Their eyes catch and she doesn't look away. It's an invitation.

He isn't about to let it pass.

He turns onto the next street, and finds it quiet; steers to the end of a cul-de-sac, where a new house is under construction; and carefully parks the SUV so it isn't under a streetlight.

Savvy grins at him.

Their eyes connect and hold, as solid as the touch of their hands earlier. He can read the dare on her face. She angles herself closer, propping her free hand onto the console, not looking away.

His magnificent witch. He just has to convince her that she is his again.

"Kiss me, already," she says.

He leans into her, wrapping his hand around her hair and tilting her head to position her mouth to meet his. He pours the fire in his heart into his kiss, lips gently commanding hers to part, and they do, and he tries to show her how astounding she was back there, to worship the strength of her, the bravery, and that he saw the way she acted to save them, when she could've used the situation to get rid of him and Diego and his brother.

She moans into his mouth. "More," she says.

He runs a hand down her neck to cup her breast and then rubs her hard nipple through the thin cloth, squeezes it lightly.

"More," she says again, almost a whimper.

Can he give it to her? Here, now?

He'll die trying. "Slide back."

15

✦ ✦ ✦

Savvy

A distant voice in Savvy's head tells her they should keep moving. But the flood of adrenaline from the powerful spell and from Griffin being on her side . . . the electricity between them sparking . . .

The sensible voice is not nearly as loud as the one saying *Stay, stay here,* with Griffin.

When he gives her the order—"Slide back"—she nearly loses her breath. She does as he says, vaulting backward over the console of the hulking SUV and into its spacious back seat. She stares out from the corner, diagonal to Griffin.

"You coming?" she asks when he pauses and stares at her like he's a bone-dry desert and she's the ocean he longs for.

He reaches over and lowers the seat he's in down flat, then slides into the back beside her.

Oh, damn. He's coming for her all right.

"Savvy," he says, "spread your legs."

She's still in the tatters of her wedding dress, and if she was wet before—she was, almost as soon as they kissed—now she is drowning.

"Okay," she says. The old, playing-with-Griffin Savvy would've said something like "Don't mind if I do," and maybe they'll be back at that place again. But this is no time for games.

This is about need. Pure, simple. All-consuming. She knows it's probably foolish and, right here, right now, she doesn't care.

She scoots lower and angles her body so he has access, skirt rucking up around her hips.

He growls when he sees the lacy-nothing panties she has on, a teaser for their wedding night. *This* is still technically their wedding night. Or the early morning after their wedding night. It makes her want to laugh.

But all thought is stolen when Griffin says, "These were for me," in a kind of wonder and then reaches for them. He rips them off her, the lace tearing like the tissue-thin fabric it is. And then he moves between her legs and he licks her.

Goddess.

Her knees drop wider to give him better access, and she's never been more grateful for anything than that apparently H.U.N.T.E.R. operatives drive vehicles as big as tanks. Griffin slides his arms under her legs and licks into her. She is boneless, helpless, when he adds two fingers, then three, pumping them in and out while he kisses her clit, first so gently, and then he sucks the nub and stars go off behind her eyes.

"Fuck me," Griffin says.

Don't mind if I do, Savvy should say. But still breathless, she only says, "Yes."

When she opens her eyes, she sees that the curse wasn't a command, but a reaction to her unrestrained orgasm. Shit, for the first time since she was a teenager playing around with sexuality, she forgot to mask. Pinpoints of light float through the car around them. She feels suddenly, unaccountably, shy.

Until he says, "You said yes. You making good on it?"

"Lie back," she says, taking over at giving the orders.

He opens his mouth and she thinks he might protest, but he just says, "Quickly. I'm dying."

They do need to hurry. The little voice comes back. The louder voice doesn't want to. It wants to linger here. Take all the time in the world.

Griffin inches back on the seat, and Savvy uses a light touch to pull his sweats down, uncovering his gorgeous thighs. She moves over him, sliding her hand up and down his cock as she tucks her legs around him, keeping him between her thighs.

Mine, she thinks. *He's mine. Griffin Carter is still mine.*

Even if he doesn't know it yet. He let her save him and his men back there. It was what she needed to know. The rest are all details they can figure out. She hopes. She prays. Or maybe she's simply lost her mind.

Slowly, painfully slowly, she slides down onto him, taking him fully inside her, holding nothing back.

"Fuck, Savvy," he says reaching up for her breasts, tracing his thumbs across her nipples. "Nothing feels like you. Nothing."

She rolls her hips. "You want this," she says, and glories in the thrust of him lifting his hips to fill her, all the way to the hilt, and then she lifts away, almost letting his cock free. Almost.

"Always," he says, and palms her ass under her skirt.

She slides back down.

"Fuck me, goddess," he says, and she does. Every other concern leaves her and they slam into each other and then press apart, together, apart. The sounds of their breathing and their skin are all she knows. Desert and ocean meeting, a flood, a devastation.

When they come, it's Savvy first. She leaves herself open, letting the orgasm fill her and pour out into Griffin. She lets him feel what she feels.

After they can speak, Griffin says, "I saw stars."

"I let both of us see them," Savvy says. "They've always been there."

"What?" Griffin asks, curious, not affronted.

"I guess you could say I've been holding back," she says. "But not anymore."

"Never hide from me." The intensity of the words again makes her want to linger. But they have to go.

"We still need to finish talking," Savvy says, though she wants to lie here, in his arms. She wants them to be naked together, here, anywhere. But after the power she's expended over the course of this insane day, she needs to rest.

"We need to get out of here," he says.

"Afraid so."

She almost says she loves him, but she hesitates, holds it back. This part has always been easy. The rest of it has only gotten more complicated. But she wants to. She feels like they're *together*, because they are.

The pendant of her necklace flares. At the same time, her phone starts to buzz.

She pulls back and straightens the shreds of her wedding dress as best she can. "We can go to Brie's. She just figured out I'm not there."

Savvy isn't sure how to prepare herself or Griffin for the oasis of pink and likely interrogation they're about to enter. In the passenger seat, as Griffin drives, a text comes through that she can't ignore like the rest.

I'm doing a summoning if you don't respond immediately.

"I have to take it," Savvy tells Griffin.

When her phone buzzes with Brie's next call, the latest in a nonstop barrage of texts and calls via both phone and necklace, Savvy picks up and says, "We're headed to you. We'll be there in a sec."

Brie's not on speaker, but she may as well be. "We? Who is *we?*"

Savvy clicks end rather than respond. Her eardrums can only take so much. She may have just saved them.

Griffin gives her a sidelong glance. "You just hung up on her?" He winces.

"Sometimes you just have to let people feel their feelings. She's going to have a lot of them in a sec." Savvy raises her hand and points ahead to the duplex.

Griffin pulls into the driveway and hasn't even gotten the SUV turned off before the front door flies open. Brie rushes out with Captain Bear trundling behind her.

"I forgot about the capybara," Griffin says, opening his door.

Savvy gets out as quickly as she can, to run interception.

"Oh, oh no, no no no," Brie says, stalking closer. "No, no, no. My eyes! Tell me I'm not seeing this!"

Paris and Elle appear in the door. Elle gives a tentative hand raise, but there's a furrow to her brow too.

Captain has this way of standing on his back feet and fluttering his paws when his mistress is upset. He does it now.

Griffin watches him. "That's . . ."

"Adorable, I know," Savvy says, standing beside him.

Brie stops with a hand to her chest. *What is happening?* She waves the hand between Savvy and Griffin.

So, sure, Savvy should have expected the strength of this reaction. The sex clouded her judgment. She realizes that. . . . As far as Brie knows, she's behaving rationally. Savvy is the one who isn't. And maybe she has a point.

Nothing about their larger situation has changed.

Savvy steps forward to meet Brie, and Griffin moves to stay beside her. The man has a death wish.

"Are you back together?" Brie practically shrieks the question.

"Yes," Griffin says confidently. Just as Savvy says, "No."

They look at each other.

"Not yet," Savvy says. She should've realized this earlier, but it's Brie's reaction that reminds her how much they have to deal with. Just because they still turn each other on, that doesn't mean this will all work out. She can't think with her emotions on this one. She was raised to never believe in fairy tales.

"We're working on it," Griffin says.

Brie lifts her eyebrows. So does Savvy. She doesn't hate hearing it, and that only means she has to guard against her own tendencies.

"How about if you bring this party inside?" Elle calls softly. "It's four A.M., Brie, your neighbor is home, remember."

Savvy turns her head and spots a light on upstairs next door.

Brie sighs, frustrated and still vibrating on a high frequency, but turns to tromp back inside. Captain Bear pads along behind her.

Savvy starts for the door, but Griffin catches her hand in his. "I thought we had an understanding back there."

She should remove her hand from his. "We still have a lot to figure out."

He can't argue with that, and he doesn't. But she lets him hold her hand as they approach the door. She's tired, and the touch keeps her going, awake at the contact. She stifles a yawn.

Paris is waiting just inside the door in leopard form and she rubs herself first against Savvy, then Griffin. Pleased.

"Don't you start," Savvy mutters.

Paris purrs loudly and Griffin pointedly scratches her head.

"Don't make yourself at home," Brie says to Griffin. "What did he do?" she asks Savvy. "Brainwash you?"

"Hi, Elle," Griffin says, and gingerly sits down on the maroon couch on the other side of Peggy. The frog croaks at him with disapproval.

He gets up and hovers, about as out of place as Savvy has ever seen him.

"I'm not on your side," Elle says to Griffin. "So you know."

"Explain," Brie says, and waves her hands around between the two of them. "This."

Savvy sits on a salmon-pink velvet settee and nods for Griffin to come beside her. He does, looking grateful. This is a delicate situation.

"We decided to meet. We were interrupted." Savvy folds her hands in her lap.

Brie's eyes go wide with shock. She sticks her hands out, palms facing them, at her sides. "Don't make me do something I'll regret. Tell me what happened."

Griffin pipes in. "Savvy faced down Melissa the Gorgon at the height of her powers and saved my ass, and also the asses of Diego and my brother Jacob. Then we took off and . . ."

Savvy doesn't miss the heat in his eyes at what he elides. They took off all right. Into the stratosphere. She needs to get back down to Mother Earth.

"Diego does have a nice ass. But he also *is* an ass. As are you. Have you forgotten these are hunters?" Brie asks Savvy.

"I can see you're trusting my judgment," she says dryly. "I'm not sure it's that simple."

Elle is eyeing her with open concern. "Are you all right? That couldn't have been an easy fight."

"I solared, but I'm recovering."

The girls go quiet. "You need to rest," Brie says. "Reenergize."

Griffin lifts his hand. "What does that mean? Are you okay?"

The concern is cute, she has to admit it to herself. But unnecessary. "I'm fine. I've just . . . used a lot of my power today. We're not endless wells of magic. We have to recharge."

"Don't tell him these things!" Brie puts her hands on her hips.

Griffin stands. "Then we're recharging you. Where can she sleep?" He has that demanding tone that Savvy should definitely hate but doesn't.

"Oh, you'd like that, wouldn't you—" Brie pauses and looks

between them. "Wait a second—I know what's going on." She strides forward and jabs a finger in the air toward Griffin.

Oh no, Savvy realizes.

Brie's not just pointing toward Griffin, but toward Griffin's crotch. *"Do you have a magic penis?"*

Griffin is taken aback, which, fair. "Ah . . ."

"He does not have a magic penis," Savvy says.

"He has bespelled you with his penis," Brie says, nodding.

"He has not."

"I, ah," Griffin says, and swallows, "never thought I'd have to say this, but I'm pretty sure it's just a normal penis."

Savvy takes pity on him. "Don't sell yourself short." Then, hearing what she said with horror: "So to speak. It's a saying."

Brie exchanges a look with Elle like, *Are you getting this?* She mouths: "Magic peen."

Griffin's cheeks are bright red and Savvy would be amused if she weren't suddenly so tired. "It's a good penis, that's all I meant."

Griffin is shaking his head and sinks back onto the settee, then jumps back to his feet as he visibly remembers what they were saying before Brie's accusation. "She needs to rest." He nods to Savvy. "And *you* distracted *me* from that," he says to Brie.

Brie makes an "I'm watching you" gesture to Griffin. "Says a master of distraction." She is giving Savvy a significant look that Savvy is suddenly too damn exhausted to deal with.

"I need to sleep, then we make a plan, and never talk about magic peen again," Savvy says. She already has the beginnings of an idea, though no one else is going to like it. That's all the more reason she needs to get her strength fully back by morning. She pauses and asks one of her questions anyway. "Why were you in England last year?" she asks Griffin.

He is clearly glad to be talking about anything else besides his not-magic-but-still-wonderful dick.

"Chasing a magic signature," Griffin says. "It vanished before I could find it—I'm guessing that was you?"

Savvy nods and tugs her lip, thinking.

"Can we have one second?" Brie asks her. "The master of distraction made me forget something."

The fact that she asks, rather than grabbing Savvy's arm and towing her out of the room, is concerning. Savvy follows her into the kitchen. Paris trails them, leaving Griffin alone in the other room with Elle.

"What is it?" Savvy asks.

"Melissa the Gorgon, again, huh?" Brie asks. "Did she offer to run away with you?"

"Ha ha." Savvy rolls her eyes. "What do you really want?"

"Your mother has been in touch. She sent Cretin."

For her mother to communicate through her raven and not show up or call is . . . worrying. To say the least. This can't be good news.

"And?"

"Mother Circe has said the only way you could be forgiven—her words, not mine—is if you slaughter the slaughterer."

"So she's really not letting go." It makes Savvy all the more eager to pursue the plan she's forming. But she's so tired. She desperately wants to close her eyes. "She—and the Butcher for that matter—must realize that if this goes on, it will eventually break the accords. There's too many people after us. . . . If what happened earlier took place during the day, we'd be on the news. I don't like this."

"And now you know how I feel." Brie tips her head toward the living room. "What are you doing with him? There's no way this works out. Magic penis or not."

Savvy hedges. "We're not done yet."

Brie nods slowly. "Promise me you won't sacrifice yourself for him."

"She won't," Griffin says, stepping into the pink kitchen, the design cheerful even in the dark before dawn. "I would never let her do that."

He has his hands in his pockets.

"It wouldn't be up to you," Savvy says, and yawns. She watches to make sure he understands that. He gives away nothing.

"She's got you there," Brie says. She narrows her eyes at him. "You hurt her again, you die."

Griffin seems unbothered. "I didn't mean to hurt her the first time."

"Yeah, well." Brie sniffs. Then growls, and says, "I hate it when people take the wind out of my sails."

"She really does," Savvy says, and the words sound like she's fading, even to her own ears.

Griffin is next to her, and before she can protest, he sweeps her up, his arm behind her knees. She can't help laying her head on his chest. He smells like them together.

"Upstairs," Brie says. "Second door on the right. Don't even think about leaving or contacting anyone. You get some sleep. Tomorrow there will be a reckoning."

Savvy wants to say that she fears Brie is right, and that what's coming is going to be worse than the rest, and maybe split them apart. All of them.

Not just her and Griffin.

But Griffin carries her up the stairs and she stays quiet. He lowers her onto the bed and moments later she feels the dip as he climbs in beside her.

And then she's asleep. The last thing she's aware of is Paris's head under her fingers, the big cat next to her side of the bed.

Nine Months Ago

16

✦ ✦ ✦

The Goddess and the Professor

S avvy alights on the sidewalk of a quiet block nearish the square in Decatur. Her pocket broom shrinks down to a spray of twigs and she stashes it in her skirt. Making sure no one is around to see her, she drops the spell that hides her from view and then fidget-smooths her casual black-and-white dress. Obviously, it has pockets—witches *must* have pockets. Where else does an everyday pocket broom go?

She decided not to go full-on dressed up, because then someone might ask what the occasion is and . . .

Griffin might not come. She probably shouldn't be here either.

She isn't used to being nervous in her own city. Honestly, she's not used to being nervous, period. She knows who she is. She likes her life. If that missing-something feeling thrums inside her, a chord plucked on strings, well, that's fine. She has what she needs: her community and her job. Her mother would lose it if she knew what Savvy was up to or that her idle daydreams in the past month have been about a certain sexy professor with black hair and glasses. And this night.

So if Griffin doesn't show, which she is training herself to expect, then it's no big deal. Him not coming means he will never be aware that *she* did show up. She can live with that. Because of course she can.

She's only spent time with the man twice. This evening can't be as important as its looming silhouette in her mind indicates. He'd probably just turn out to be another boring jerk once they tried to have an actual relationship. It'll be a *good* thing if he stands her up.

Right.

Savvy shakes her head and walks toward the store. As she gets closer, there's more sidewalk traffic, people out enjoying a mild winter evening. There's just enough noise that she almost misses the small, curious "Meow." She catches it, though, and turns to look for the source. Second nature.

She barely catches the shape in the shadow of the alley, but then the rail-thin black cat moves a fraction and the streetlight reflects on green eyes. She steps a little closer to get a better look.

The cat, young but not quite a kitten, stares up at her. "Meow," the cat says again, as if talking straight to Savvy.

Savvy hesitates. She's timed her arrival to be just at seven o'clock. Not early, not late. A stray cat being out here isn't that unusual. This could even be somebody's house cat that wandered too far.

She can give a nudge to send the cat home, if that's the case. When she moves closer and crouches so she's on the cat's level, it scampers back a bit.

"Don't be afraid," she whispers, and the cat continues to look at her, tilting its head a fraction. "Go away home now. Go on. Find your way home."

There. At least she's done a good deed for the night, no matter how the rest of it goes.

She stands and walks back out to the sidewalk and the rest of the way to Little Shop's door. She presses it open and spots the manager behind the counter. He nods to her. "Here for your book?"

"I'm going to look around first," she says.

He settles back down to the endless tasks of running a

busy bookstore. The size of the store is perfect. Each room has tall ceilings, and the overall space is small enough to feel cozy but large enough to feel like you can make discoveries. Kids'-book covers and art from picture books dot the bright, cheerful walls.

Savvy meanders toward a display table without actually taking in a single title on it, trying to subtly scan the rows of the store as best she can. There's a young couple with small kids who are racing around in barely contained excitement in one corner. A woman wearing a hippie skirt with a teen boy in tow in the graphic-novel section. And . . . Savvy.

No Griffin that she can see.

She tells herself she's not a fool. That she wanted to come, and she'd have regretted not knowing. Now she can move on. Whatever she may or may not be missing, it isn't Griffin Carter. For all she knows he's dead, killed in a tragic accident. Yes, that must be it, and she definitely won't google to find out what happened. Obviously *death* is the only thing that could keep a man away from *her.*

Growing up in a community of mostly women teaches you how to pep-talk yourself and kick an ex to the curb with style. She's only practicing what they'd tell her. In fact, maybe she'll call Brie and Elle and see if they're up for margaritas and karaoke. Not that Griffin is her ex, but just to put the nail in the coffin of the possibility.

Not that she's mentioned him to either of them since she talked to Brie the day she and Griffin met. She didn't want it getting back to her mother.

Damn. She really thought he would show.

"Meow."

A familiar one. The cat is inside the store? How?

She peers around the nearest bookshelf, and the black shape

whips around the corner of another. None of the other customers give any sign of noticing it.

Savvy heads in the cat's direction. What else is she going to do? She makes a little "psst pssst psst" noise, meaning "Come here." The little bony-legged cat must have followed her right in through the door.

"You were supposed to go home," she mutters.

"I was?"

She rounds the corner of another tall bookshelf, and her mouth drops open. Griffin stands in front of her, frowning in faint confusion. He's wearing a casual blazer over an open-throated button-down with jeans. His hair is neatly combed and she wants to mess it up. A nerdy tall drink of water.

Definitely not dead.

Which makes her wonder why he didn't greet her when she came in.

"Were you hiding from me?" She blurts the question without thinking.

"No!" Griffin says, and, yes, she made it even more awkward. He presses his glasses up, clearly embarrassed. "Maybe a little. I was early. Half an hour early. It's okay, you can wince."

Her heart flips over. Maybe tonight *is* important. Maybe Griffin will be good for her. It's worth a try. He's *here*.

"I'm not going to wince. Before, I was talking to a cat." He frowns at her again, this time like she's hallucinating.

"Ah, okay," he says. "Do you want to get out of here? I thought we could grab dinner."

"*Meow.*"

Savvy almost forgot that she's on the chase. "Did you—"

"Hear the cat meowing?" Griffin asks. "The one you were talking to, I take it? Store cat?"

"Pretty sure they don't have one," Savvy says. "I was telling it to go home. Before."

"Well," Griffin says, taking it in stride, "let's see if we can find her."

Savvy tilts her head. "How do you know it's a her?"

"I don't, I guess."

"*Meowwww.*"

"This way," Savvy says, and uses it as an excuse to take Griffin's arm and steer him along with her.

They pass by the couple with the young kids and she idly wonders if Griffin wants kids and then she wonders if she does and no way is she bringing that up. There's a little room in the back closed off by a beaded curtain and the next "*Meow*" leads them that way.

Griffin pushes aside the curtain. "After you."

Savvy heads inside, aware of Griffin's presence behind her. She looks around the room filled with a rack of costumes and masks and a small table with coloring books and comes up with no cat. *But* there's a small child-sized circus tent set up in one corner. The scrawny kitty has to be in there.

Griffin puts a hand on Savvy's shoulder and presses in front of her. "I can check. I wouldn't want you to get hurt. Feral cats can cause real damage."

Savvy raises her brows. "I think I can deal with a cat, feral or otherwise."

She steps in front of him and holds his gaze.

"Sorry," Griffin says finally, "I'm used to being in charge at work."

"Well, I'm not a student," Savvy points out, and shoos him. "And I do work with an animal rescue. They're local, even."

"I don't think there's room for both of us anyway," Griffin says, and goes over to take a post outside the curtain. "I'll keep watch over here, in case she tries to run back out."

"Good plan," Savvy says.

And then she goes over and lowers herself onto her knees. She pushes aside the opening of the tent and is glad she's blocking any possible view of Griffin's when she does. A leopard cub stares back at her. Green eyes, lightly spotted fur. A beauty.

"Oh," she says softly as she understands. The cat is a familiar.

She backs out, pulling the flaps tight behind her.

"What is it?" Griffin asks.

"Found her. I think I can coax her to come out. Will you wait in the store? I'll be right there."

Griffin nods and leaves, seeming not to think this is strange at all *or* not wanting to annoy Savvy by trying to take charge again. Good call on his part.

"Well, you're a tricky one," Savvy says, and releases the flaps. "Come on out."

She sits and waits. The leopard finally presses through the opening of the circus tent and rubs against her leg.

"I told you to go home."

The leopard stops moving and stares at her, as if to say, *Yes, catch up.*

Savvy blinks. *"I'm* home?"

The cat stares at her in a way that isn't a no. "Okay, well, we can't have him seeing you like this. I'll just . . ."

But the cub has already re-glamoured herself into a regular cat, before Savvy can. "You're a clever girl, aren't you?"

Because Griffin is right. There's no way this cat isn't a girl.

"Can I pick you up?"

The cat answers by climbing into Savvy's lap, purring loudly.

Savvy scoops the cat up to her heart and something clicks into place. The twining together of their energy. The bond between witch and familiar. At long last. The pairing isn't usually this fast, but she's heard stories of witches who locked eyes with their familiars and bonded immediately. She suspects the cat chose her. Tears sting her eyes and the purring of the cat feels like it's coming from her soul.

She swallows, takes a breath, and reemerges with her familiar caught to her chest to find Griffin.

He's waiting right outside the room and he smiles at her and the cat. She smiles back.

He follows her as she makes her way over to the counter. "Don't suppose you know this little girl?" she asks the manager, making it transparent she wants the answer to be anything except yes.

"Afraid not," the manager says. "She likes you. You should keep her."

"I'm thinking about it," Savvy says.

The men laugh when *her* cat familiar stretches in her arms and then settles back down, green eyes gazing up at her. She's waited years and years for the right creature to find her, and now it happened tonight. What timing.

"I don't think you have a choice," Griffin says, still smiling.

"Your special order," the manager says, and produces a book for her. Griffin leans in to check out the cover.

Savvy waits for his reaction. It's a spy thriller by Alma Katsu. *Red Widow.*

"You really do love spy novels?" he asks, sounding amused.

"Yes, I do." Savvy isn't ready to let go of the cat in her arms. "Can you reach my wallet—"

"Let me get it," Griffin says.

Savvy opens her mouth to protest as he pulls out a card and hands it over.

"He's cute too," the manager says, and glances between them. "First date?"

Savvy frowns. "Why do you ask?"

"Big first-date vibes."

"Technically, it's our third date," Griffin says, and Savvy could kiss him. If she weren't holding a cat. *Her* cat. "I'll carry the book," he says.

When they hit the door, she leans over and presses a kiss to his cheek. The cat in her arms purrs even louder.

Griffin has never been so happy about a stray cat in his life. Chasing it in the store gave him an excuse to get closer to Savvy—even if he almost messed up by trying to take over. They stand on the sidewalk outside the store, and he's not sure where the rest of the evening is headed anymore. Not that he would change anything. Savvy looks . . . happy.

He can't believe she ordered a spy novel. It's a sign. Of how perfect Savvy could be for him. He wishes he could tell her the truth, but he can't. He can help her with her new plus-one, though.

"I didn't know if you'd come," she says, and then peers down into the cat's face.

"Yes, you did." Griffin grins at her. "*I* didn't know if *you'd* come."

"*Meow.*"

He initially froze up in there, when he saw her come in. Something about the collision of coming straight from headquarters and his actual life to meet this woman who seems like she's from his dreams. But this is good. The cat gives them something to do to get rid of the awkward.

He moves in and reaches out to stroke the happy beast Savvy holds close to her, taking the chance to inhale that earthy, herby, floral scent of hers. The cat relaxes and rubs the sides of her head all over his hand.

"I think she likes you," Savvy says with a laugh.

Is it possible Savvy is more beautiful, more vibrant than in Paris? Or is he just hopelessly relieved she showed up? He's missed her laugh. It rings through him like a bell.

"I had a whole romantic plan," Griffin says.

If he's not mistaken, her hold on the cat gets tighter.

"But I can see that we probably need to change it. You're keeping her?"

Savvy nods. "Obviously."

"Do you need to hit a pet store? I know you have the dog. . . ."

"Actually, I don't anymore." Savvy says the words fast.

"Did you ever?" Griffin asks, and lets her see he's amused that she lied to him.

Savvy hesitates, then says, "No, not really."

She ducks her head.

"I understand. So, pet store? Then, would you be comfortable with me helping you get everything set up? . . . I understand if you're not, we could always reschedule."

"Griffin," she says, and he stops babbling. "I'm comfortable. But . . ."

"Oh, right," he says. "You work with an animal rescue. You said it's local. Should we take her there to get checked out?"

"I'm afraid so," she says.

"Why afraid?"

"My mother, ah, helps run it. You can nope out at this point. It's a little early to inflict her and my friends on you. We can reschedule."

He should be worried by this development and the apology on her face and that offer, but he isn't. "We should never have expected any old first—or third—date. You're not getting rid of me that easy."

Savvy sighs. "I guess not. All right, remember, I warned you."

17

✦ ✦ ✦

The Goddess and the Professor

Griffin takes the turn onto the gravel-and-dirt road Savvy points out. The rescue's compound—Savvy's word, not his—isn't so far outside the city limits, but might as well be a world away. One of the great things about Atlanta and the South in general is that you never have to go far to find wild places. The country is always waiting nearby, in the shadow of the city.

The road is flanked by heavy forest. Griffin drives slow and easy along it to minimize the jostling, though the cat sits content and calm in Savvy's lap. He's never seen a cat so chill, no carrier necessary. The tiny creature kneads her skirt periodically, making all the biscuits (in a way in which no one actually makes biscuits).

"You're being so kind to do this," Savvy says.

She's texting with someone as she speaks, and he can practically feel her getting more nervous. Griffin's not that concerned about meeting her friends or even her mom. He tends to score well with parents. And if there's one thing he's picked up on about Savvy, it's that she makes her own decisions. He only needs her to like him.

"I'm actually being selfish," he says, "because I'm doing it to spend more time with you."

"Like I said. Not everyone is down with a date becoming a cat adoption."

Lights appear in the distance up the road, a scattering of

them around a big old rambling Victorian house lit up like Christmas.

"The Farmhouse," Savvy says. "We shouldn't have to stay long."

"It's okay, seriously," Griffin says. "I'm looking forward to it."

"Why?" she asks, skeptical.

"It's something you care about."

"Oh. Right." Savvy sighs as if he has no idea what he's in for. "It's just. My mother is anti-romance. For me."

"She doesn't believe in love?" The word hangs heavy between them. He should have used something gentler.

"No, she does," Savvy says. "She just doesn't think it's a good thing. She sees it as a liability."

Well, that certainly sounds like the opposite of healthy. He's already gathered Savvy's dad isn't in the picture.

"Interesting," Griffin says neutrally.

Savvy points as they near the house. "Park in the drive there."

He does and notes there are a number of other vehicles. Before they're even out of the car, the front screen door of the house bangs open. A few women come out and wait on the porch. There are several dogs roaming around the yard, and a horse tethered outside a nearby barn. Some big fenced-in areas are clearly for animals being rehabbed.

It's all bigger than Griffin expected, but then that makes sense if Savvy has to travel abroad for her public relations work with them. She mentioned earlier that some of the animals they rehab are of the more exotic or special-needs variety.

"Here we go," Savvy says. "Prepared?"

"I'll be fine." Griffin gets out before Savvy can respond and strides around to open the door for her. She climbs out with her cat still gathered against her and murmurs, "Famous last words. Thank you."

Griffin notices that Savvy carefully makes sure he is walking alongside her as they approach the house. A woman wearing a jumpsuit with honest-to-god rhinestones comes down into the yard. "Let me see her," she coos. She ignores Griffin and fusses with the cat Savvy holds.

"Mom," Savvy says. "This is Griffin."

"Hi, Griffin," her mother says, still with eyes only for the little cat. He almost wishes it stayed that way when she does look at him. "Who are you? And why are you with my daughter?"

"Mom, cool it," Savvy says. "Ignore her rudeness," she tells Griffin.

He appreciates the interference, but knows better than to go along with it. "I'm Griffin Carter, ma'am," he says, and lets his best drawl sneak out. "I teach antiquities at the university."

Savvy's mother sniffs. "Don't 'ma'am' me. I can see right through your charm."

Okayyyy. Savvy gifts him with a sympathetic smile. "Mom's name is Claudia."

Her mother frowns at her.

The other women enter the arena then, meandering off the porch. "I'm Brie," says a petite younger woman in a pink dress. "A professor, hmm?" She gives Savvy a significant eyebrow raise.

The other woman wears a tidy striped suit and looks him up and down. "Are you on a date?"

"Elle, Brie, you leave him alone too," Savvy says.

"Nice to meet all of you." Griffin smiles to sell it. He suddenly senses that while Savvy makes her own decisions, these people are incredibly important to her—it's obvious the reverse is true too. He gives an appreciative glance around them at all the well-kept buildings. It truly is an impressive array. Practically . . . "What a magical place," he says.

The women look at him. "It is?" Savvy asks.

"Why do you say that?" Savvy's mother asks.

The four women look around the property, and, finally, Savvy's mother shrugs. "Unusual choice of words."

Griffin isn't sure how he screwed up there, but he did somehow. Tough crowd.

Savvy intercedes. "Let's go inside so you can take a look at this little one, Mom."

"You haven't named her yet?" Claudia says with far too much disapproval.

"She only just found her," Griffin says to cut through the sharp edge in Savvy's mother's reaction. "But it's a great question—what are you going to name her?"

Savvy considers, holding the cat up so they can stare at each other. "I think . . . Paris," she says, and slides a grin to Griffin.

He didn't expect it and he is unexpectedly touched. "We'll always have Paris," he says, light.

Savvy beams at him and he blinks.

"This is fascinating," Brie says, and claps her hands together under her chin.

"Is it?" Savvy's mother returns.

Another woman enters the fray then, coming out from the front door to join them. "I'm Auntie Simone," she says. "Can I see Paris? Y'all get Griffin settled inside, please?"

Savvy hands the cat over to Auntie Simone. She nods toward the door. "This way," she says. And then, lower, as Griffin follows, "I told you so."

"What? I like them." He plays innocent.

"Uh-huh." She raises her brows.

"I like that they obviously care for you."

"Ooh," Brie says from eavesdropping close behind them, "he's smooth."

"Never trust a smooth talker," Claudia says.

Savvy shoots her a death glare. They cross the threshold

into the house, and Griffin isn't sure what he expected inside the gabled and turreted hulking Victorian, but nothing this . . . comfortable. The furniture is mismatched in a way that seems intentional, or at least, exactly how it should be. Small glass bottles are stoppered and situated in antique cases, which remind him of his grandma's house. A broom stands in the corner and the floors are all wood, dotted with occasional carpets.

"Also . . . magical?" Savvy's mother says as she sails past him.

"Cozy," Griffin says, not taking the bait.

"Hmmph." Savvy's mother follows her auntie Simone, and Savvy is gnawing on her lip as she watches them leave the room.

"Go," Griffin says.

"Huh?" Savvy says. She shakes her head. "No way. I'll stay with you."

"Go with Paris," Griffin says. "Brie and . . ."

"Elle," supplies the suited friend.

"Elle will keep me company. I'll be fine."

Brie grins at him like a shark and he's not so sure anymore, but he's faced down revenants and wizards before. He can face down two skeptical friends.

"Yes, go on, Sav," Brie says. "We'll be gentle."

Griffin takes in the swirling tattoo sleeves on her bare arms as she comes over and loops one through his. She steers him farther into the living room and to a worn green velvet sofa. Elle breezes past and sets up in a chair next to a fireplace with crackling flames. Is that a . . . Yes, she has a small frog on her knee, and is stroking its head.

"Be good to him," Savvy says. "I mean it." She hurries out in the direction her mother and Auntie Simone went with her cat.

"Nice pet," Griffin says to Elle.

"Her name is Peggy," Elle says as if it's totally normal to have a frog on your knee. At an animal rescue, Griffin supposes it is.

A fluffy white dog trots into the room then and prances all the way to Griffin to give him a thorough and somewhat intrusive sniff exam. "That's Captain Bear," Brie says. Then, instead of calling the dog off: "Good boy." She smiles at Griffin. "Now, about this date. Savvy didn't mention it and that's extremely unusual."

"I can't imagine why she'd keep secrets. You all seem so low-key about things."

Brie coughs a laugh. "Oh, well, he's funny. Did you catch that, Elle?"

"I did." Elle continues to stroke the frog's head.

"Now," Brie says, "have you ever had your palm read?" She reaches over and waves her hand for him to put his out.

"No, thanks," Griffin says.

Brie waves her hand again, keeping it extended.

Savvy pokes her head in from the hallway and takes in the scene. "Brie, stop that."

Brie sighs but puts her hand down. "She used to be fun. Before she met you."

"You don't know when we met, though," Griffin says. Why did he say that? Huge mistake.

"That's true," Elle says. "When did you meet?"

Captain Bear has, as least, finally discovered all the information his nose can provide and settles down at Brie's feet. A loud bird caw sounds outside the door, and Brie and Elle ignore it. "Do you rescue birds here too?" Griffin asks.

"Occasionally," Brie says.

Claudia returns then, carrying a steaming teacup on a saucer. The good china, if he's not mistaken.

"What a terrible hostess I'm being," she says, and it reads as fake. "Sorry about that. I brought you some tea." She hands it to Griffin, and he takes the saucer carefully despite the exchange of glances between Elle and Brie.

"Now," Claudia says, "Savvy tells me you're a very nice boy. Drink up."

Griffin picks up the tea and inhales. Some kind of green, if he's not mistaken, but with some extra herbs in it. He'd rather not, but he'll have to choke it down. They're all watching him.

Savvy swans into the room with Auntie Simone behind her, carrying Paris the cat. "No!" Savvy says, and lunges forward to intercept the teacup on the way to his mouth. "Don't drink that!"

Griffin blinks. "What is it, poison?"

Savvy sniffs it. "No. But it would taste like it."

She pours it into the pot of a nearby plant, then turns to Simone and holds out her hands. Auntie Simone has a wry smile as she passes over Paris, who returns gratefully to Savvy's arms.

"We can go now," Savvy says.

"So soon?" her mother asks, all innocence. "But I have so many questions for this man."

Griffin doesn't need to be told twice. He gets up and is surprised when Paris makes a small "meow" and reaches a paw toward him. Savvy grins. "She wants to come to you."

Griffin accepts the cat and her purr thrums through him as he cradles her carefully. When he looks up, Brie and Elle have softened.

Claudia shakes her head. "I guess you are a nice man."

She sounds so disappointed.

"It was a pleasure meeting you all," Griffin lies.

A small pain to go through to get to know Savvy better. He wishes he could tell them, *I won't be scared off.*

If Savvy wasn't certain Griffin is one of the good ones before, she is now. Her familiar went to him. On her own.

And he's not running for the hills—though he might be, if

he knew her mother tried to hand over the tea equivalent of truth serum. There are trust issues with men and then there are her *mother's* trust issues with them. Claudia wasn't happy about the date, and Savvy's not looking forward to the more in-depth lecture she's sure to get later.

They get back in the car, Griffin passing Paris in to Savvy, where the cat settles into her lap. She remembers the not-so-light interrogation she already got from her mother. "Who is he? Where did you meet him? Why did he use the word 'magical'?"

Thank the goddess for Auntie Simone: "'Magical' is a good word."

"And he's a professor," Savvy said.

"Well," her mother huffed, "he almost gave me a heart attack. I thought our cloaking spells weren't holding."

Savvy rolled her eyes. Auntie Simone stroked the back of leopard Paris and said, "This is a special girl, right here, for my special Savvy." And Savvy got teary again.

"Where to next?" Griffin asks, bringing her back to the present.

"This has not been a fun date for you. I'm sorry."

"It's not over yet, but—" Savvy laughs when his stomach interrupts with a growl. Griffin sheepishly continues, "I could eat. You?"

"My house? Pizza? Settling Paris in?" Savvy smiles as he glances over at her. "I promise there will be no more interfering friends or rude moms or aunties."

"Auntie Simone seems nice. I mean they all seem nice—"

"Griffin, I've met them, it's okay. They're a lot."

He laughs and it's a good sound. A sound Savvy could get used to. Like the purr of her familiar.

She realizes something in that moment. That missing-something feeling? It's gone.

In this car, right now, she might have everything she needs. She doesn't care if this isn't what she's supposed to want. She does.

If she's honest with herself, she always has.

Now

18

✦ ✦ ✦

Griffin

Griffin realizes it's ridiculous to not leave the bedroom until Savvy wakes the next morning. For one thing, he's starving. But the bangs and crashes from downstairs are increasing in volume—while Savvy slumbers peacefully. He's 99 percent positive the racket Brie and Elle are making is designed to bring him running. He's not falling for it.

So instead he sits in the corner of the guest room in a pink-painted wooden chair, uncomfortable as it is. He's learned a few things in the past twenty-four hours that would have made his first meeting with Savvy's friends and her mother make a helluva lot more sense. And that explain her mother being against their relationship and their marriage. Some of them are the same things that keep him from racing out into Brie's and Elle's sights.

Paris lies on Savvy's chest in the form he's used to, her pointy kitty chin just beneath Savvy's. Her green irises practically glowed before the sun came up to diffuse it. He suspects—and hopes—that she's helping to restore Savvy's equilibrium. He straightens when Paris stretches and then gently steps off to one side of the bed.

A moment later Savvy's eyes flutter open, and then she bolts upright. "We're losing too much time," she says, and leaps out of the bed.

Griffin stands and puts what's meant to be a calming hand on her arm. "It's okay. Take it easy. How are you feeling?"

"Me? I'm fine." She stares at his hand as if she's not sure whether to lean into it or push it away.

Which brings up something Griffin needs to understand. "Last night, when you said we're not back together so quickly—did you mean it?"

Savvy blinks at him with gorgeous green eyes. "Of course I meant it. You saw how they reacted. . . . I know there's this thing between us . . . but how could we? We have to get through all this, but it's pretty clear that our lives are not compatible."

Griffin thinks of their perfect, frenzied fucking in the back seat of Diego's car—which, by the way, he is never getting back—and can't agree. She was holding back before. Maybe he was too. The result of them letting go and just *being* themselves with each other counts as definitive proof they are suited. The rest are details, and those are his specialty.

"We are, though." He takes a step forward, ready to prove it.

Savvy isn't unaffected. He knows exactly what she's remembering. The same heat that he is, effortless and immediate between them. Her pupils go huge and her lips part. She wants him too, but she shakes her head. "There's no time. We'll talk later. Now we have to—"

The door to the bedroom crashes open and Griffin turns his head, gaping, as Brie struts in with the capybara trundling alongside her. Elle follows with a tea tray. Her little frog is perched on her shoulder.

"Meow," says Paris, apparently by way of greeting.

"This is insanity," Griffin says.

"See?" Savvy says. "This is my normal."

Griffin swallows. *He* was her normal. He doesn't say it. The hell of it is, she could be right. The logical part of him knows that. The rest of him wants to close the bedroom door and stay in here all day convincing her they belong together.

"We brought caffeine," Elle offers.

Savvy gratefully moves around him to pluck a cup off the tray. "Truly you are goddesses among all beings." She drinks deep.

"We could've been murdered, by the way," Brie says, raising her eyebrows to Griffin in challenge. "Those noises could have been your *hunters*."

"We're a little stealthier than that."

Brie mimics mouthing the words back at him. He has no counter that won't sink them immediately to elementary school tactics. Fine.

"Sticks and stones," he says.

"In this world, words can hurt you," Savvy says.

Right.

Brie smiles. "Correct, and you know . . ."

"No, Brie," Savvy says, setting down the cup to lift a finger for emphasis. That she says it eases his worry somewhat: She still cares. They *will* talk. Later.

If they survive.

"So, do you have thoughts on what we do next?" Griffin asks her. He has plenty of his own, but he knows Savvy well enough to hear her out first.

She picks up a piece of toast, hesitates, then passes it to Griffin. She takes another and bites into it, chewing.

"What are your thoughts?" she asks around the mouthful.

This is, in Griffin's expert opinion, a trap.

"You first," he says.

"No, go ahead," she says. "You've been awake longer than me. You must have some plans." She rolls her neck around in a slow circle and he wants to banish Elle and Brie from the room and kiss the skin there. "What are they?"

Griffin follows the words, barely.

"Now this is fun," Brie says, and sits down on the bed. With her left hand she strokes Captain Bear's head, with her right Paris's.

"Fine," Griffin says, and sinks back into his chair. The three women loom around him like the Fates, but here he goes anyway. "My plan is we do whatever Savvy says."

"Damn it," Brie says.

Elle nods. "He passed."

Savvy has the tiniest hint of a smile. "For now." She sits back on the bed and takes another drink of coffee. "We need to visit the Farmhouse."

"Okay, logical," Brie says.

"But since I'm persona non grata, we'll have to sneak in. Otherwise, Circe will know."

"If we're doing it on the down low, why do you need to go at all? We can instead, if it's for supplies or brooms." Brie continues petting the familiars.

"I need to get into the Spellbindery," Savvy says.

The other two gasp.

"Why?" Elle asks, and Brie nods along.

"I think . . ." Savvy waits for a second. Griffin can see her weighing whether to put her theory out there.

"Go on. We're all friends here," Griffin says.

"We are?" Brie sounds skeptical. "I mean, *we* are." She indicates herself, Savvy, and Elle.

"I don't even know what the Spellbindery *is*." Griffin tries not to sound irritated. "Let her explain."

Brie waggles her head sarcastically, but doesn't protest aloud.

"Okay," Savvy says, not quite looking at him, "bear with me. We were talking last night about how far apart our versions of history are, what led up to the accords. You mentioned that it's too bad we can't go back and see the past. But what if we could see? What happened back then?"

Whatever Griffin expected her to say, that wasn't it. "How?"

"We have a record," she says. "It shouldn't be that hard to access it."

"Oh really," Brie says. "Except it's forbidden."

"Assuming it's the right thing to do, I believe it will let me show him," Savvy says. "And I think it is."

"I do love a good conspiracy theory," Elle says with care, "but are you sure it's worth the risk?"

"No, I'm not sure," Savvy says. "But it feels like an important thing to know—the truth. That might explain why the Butcher and Mother Circe are acting the way they are."

"It might give us a way to reason with them, instead of this escalating until it blows up the accords," Griffin says. "An insight into how to get them to call off the bounty."

"Exactly what I'm hoping," Savvy says.

"But taking him?" Brie asks with a head jerk toward Griffin.

"I need him to see it. I wouldn't believe me otherwise—how can I expect him to?" She turns to Griffin. "That is, if you're willing to come. You have your own people to worry about. And you'll be behind enemy lines."

"I already said I was on board." Griffin is not leaving her side again until and unless he has to. "My people will be fine for a while longer. I'm not afraid."

"You should be," Brie mutters.

He ignores her.

"So, the plan," Savvy says. She turns to her friends. "Are you two okay with this? It's all right if you're not."

"Hell yes, we're in," Brie says. "We're the distraction, aren't we? Please tell me we are."

Savvy meets Griffin's eyes. He wishes they'd stay on him, but they shift back to her friends. "You are."

Her friends are delighted by this. Griffin wonders how risky it is, sneaking into the belly of the cauldron. Sensing his discomfort, Paris hops down and rubs against his leg.

Damned if it doesn't make him feel better.

Savvy and her friends stand in the front yard with their brooms in hand. The early-morning sunlight blazes down on the rainbow of fall trees that line the quiet street.

Griffin hears another telltale buzz from his phone. He's been ignoring the notifications from his brothers and Diego flooding his text messages. His dad has called a couple of times too. He should return those, but he knows none of them will approve of what he's doing and he doesn't want to put them at more risk than they already are. He meant what he said. They're in less danger without him, and perfectly capable of handling themselves.

So he turns the phone all the way off and tucks it away in his pocket.

He flashes back to yesterday morning, and how he expected to be a married man by now. He's not eager to find out if the Butcher's been lying this whole time, but he owes Savvy the chance to show him. He'd rather act based on fact than legend, even if the two are different. Even if the truth is difficult to accept.

Savvy has finally changed out of her tattered wedding dress, into black on black—jeans, a loose top, boots. All she needs is the pointy hat to be the modern witch personified. And yet he finds the picture pretty, because she's in it. He is in so much trouble. But then again, he knew that the day they met.

"You coming?" Savvy asks.

"On that?" Griffin asks, though the answer is obvious. She definitely means the thick-handled broom she's hovering side-saddle on.

"You'll be a little late to the party otherwise." Savvy studies him. "You don't have to do this."

"Yes, I do. We're better off together—" And when he sees that she's about to argue: "—for now."

That suffices.

"How many hunters can say they've traveled by broom?" Savvy asks, and reaches a hand behind her to pat the wood.

"I'm going to guess zero."

"What are you," Brie says, "scared?"

That's enough of that. Griffin strides forward and after a second's awkward pause scooches on behind Savvy. That makes things better, her nearness, that herbal scent of hers.

"Hold on," she says, and flies them straight up at hell-ride speed.

He snakes his arm around her torso. He can both hear and feel how hard she's laughing.

"Having fun?" he asks.

"Yes!" she calls back. "You?"

They're above the clouds, and Brie and Elle join them.

"Yes," he says right into her ear, and hopes it gives her the same chills he has.

Griffin suspects the physics of flying through space actually bends several of the rules of time *and* space, not to mention the obvious lack of windburn and not tumbling off what's in essence a narrow stick traveling at high speed. It shouldn't work, but it does. Magic.

The flight doesn't take long, and then they're descending into woods on the outskirts of the Farmhouse property. Griffin lingers instead of releasing Savvy right away. She doesn't seem to mind. Elle and Brie are still on the way.

"You might want to . . ." she says at last, tilting her head to one side. She puts her feet down and so does he, and then her broom shrinks down as he watches, and she tucks it away in her back pocket.

If Big Rob got a look at that, he would be so envious he'd undoubtedly try to create a shrink ray.

Elle and Brie descend then, the croaking frog the only familiar in evidence. They land lightly and their brooms downsize just as quickly as Savvy's. "So," Brie stage-whispers, "what's next?"

"We'll want Peggy in full," Savvy says.

"Of course." Elle maneuvers into a slightly larger space between the trees and sets down Peggy the frog.

Griffin raises skeptical eyebrows but waits. And manages to keep from gasping aloud when the frog demonstrates the reverse of what the broom did, growing larger and paler until Peggy is a milky-white horse with a spotted gray nose.

Their cat is a leopard. A capybara masquerades as a fluffy white dog. The frog is a horse. Why not?

"Now," Savvy says, "if you breach the boundary first, we should be able to sneak in under the disturbance of the spell."

"I am so uncomfortable with him knowing this stuff," Brie says.

"I promise I'll cast a protection solely to keep him out after we're done."

"You will?" Griffin says at the same time Brie says, "Okay then."

"Compromise makes the world go 'round," Savvy says.

Brie raises an eyebrow and Griffin figures they might be having the same thought. Savvy isn't much of a compromiser. More of a getting-her-way-er.

"What now?" Elle prompts.

"You two go in by the main road making as much noise as possible. We'll follow."

Brie makes a face. "You're sure you're fine to be alone with him and his . . ."

Savvy places a hand on her hip. "Do not say it."

"Fine," Brie says, but she gives a direct look at Griffin's crotch and he can't help shaking his head and laughing.

"I promise not to distract her," he says. "With my magic penis."

"Hey," Savvy says. "This is no time for jokes."

"At least, I'll try not to too much, anyway," Griffin adds.

"Good enough," Brie says.

Savvy sighs. "I think I liked it better when you were openly fighting. Let's go."

Elle swings up onto Peggy's bare back and then reaches out a hand for Brie, who takes it and leaps up and over to sit behind her.

"Make sure they hear you coming," Savvy says.

Brie grins. "Oh, we will."

Elle whistles and Peggy canters forward into the trees, headed toward the dirt-and-gravel road that leads first to the barn where Griffin and Savvy were supposed to tie the knot and then the Farmhouse.

19

✦ ✦ ✦

Savvy

The woods are quiet and familiar around her, the sun above throwing shadows of the tree cover like a blanket draped over her shoulders. Savvy can't be lulled by that. She would never have thought it possible to feel so far from a place she loves as much as home—the Farmhouse—while being so close to it. But here she is, about to sneak as far inside as possible, to the beating heart of C.R.O.N.E., bringing a hunter with her. The Spellbindery is the most sacred space to her witchkin, the nerve center of their history.

But this is the fastest way to see—and to make Griffin see. One of the first things any field witch learns is that information is the key to success. Understanding a situation is the first step to resolving it. The position she and Griffin are in is still bewildering in so many ways.

There's something underlying it that eludes her. Not for much longer, though. Is it a risk to violate the rules? Brie and Elle probably assume she's only minorly transgressing, but her plan goes further than that.

"Should we follow?" Griffin asks.

Savvy doesn't answer, just silently moves deeper into the forest. She's aware that Griffin is behind her, but she has to give it to him. He doesn't make a sound. Not a broken branch, not a crunch on fallen leaves.

The first non-woods sounds come about ten minutes later, as they near the barn. The gallop of hooves and Brie hollering like she's the witchy answer to Paul Revere. "We're coming! Here we are!"

Savvy creeps close enough to the edge of the woods for a look, and Griffin joins her. The entire community must be there, meeting, given the number of vehicles and brooms propped against the outer wall of the barn, no doubt voting on what to do about Mother Circe's orders and Savvy. Her mother won't sell her out so quickly, but there are others who won't be okay ignoring or even delaying the head crone's orders.

This explains why Claudia hasn't tracked her down yet. She's managing things here.

Brie's hollering gets louder as she and Elle thunder toward the barn on Pegasus—and ride straight into the midst of it through the open doors, shocking a broomsquire who's come out to see what's up. There's an uproar from inside at their entrance.

"We need to hurry," Savvy says.

Because if she's right, and everyone is at the coven gathering, then the house will be unattended.

She removes her broom, which grows in her palm, and gestures for Griffin to join her astride it. Then she guides them low and slow—but faster than they could ever go on foot—through the trees. This was a game they used to play, forest tag on their brooms. Avoiding the trunks, steering through them, is second nature to her. They used to do it with only moonlight as guide.

Savvy stops when the Farmhouse comes into view. A lit torch stands beside the porch, and a similar flare appears in the turret window, visible even on such a bright, blue-sky day. "No one's here," Savvy says. "Thank the goddess."

"How do you know?" Griffin asks.

"I just do." The lights, for one—that's the combination that signals a community meeting. Anyone who happened to be out and came home to find it would head straight to the barn. The only ones exempt would be the instructors for the little witchkin, but their buildings are farther back on the property, to protect them from becoming embroiled in daily crises.

Savvy does a quick working to conceal the two of them, though a skilled witch would certainly be able to dispel it if they tried. "Let's go," she says, and stashes her pocket broom.

She realizes she's reached down and taken Griffin's hand automatically. The heat of it in hers shouldn't feel right, but it does. They lope across the yard holding hands. A *squawk squawk* greets them, and she looks up to see Cretin's silhouette perch on the roof of the porch.

"Shhh," she says.

The raven tilts her head, as inscrutable as her mother can be.

"Please?" she adds.

The raven stays quiet, so that's as good as they're going to get.

"You were talking to the bird?" Griffin asks low. "Whose is it?"

"Guess," she says, and presses the door open, giving it a second in case someone *has* been left behind. No one calls out or meets them, which is a good sign.

"Claudia's," Griffin says.

Savvy glances over her shoulder and nods. "Yes, but how did you—"

"Your mother would have either a raven or a peacock as a familiar, nothing in between."

Savvy snorts. "Only the male peafowl have the bright feather display and she insists on a female familiar."

Griffin nods as if he's earned a point, and maybe he has.

"This way," Savvy says. But then notices Griffin isn't following. He's gawking at the living room and the opening to the kitchen. "What?"

"This is not how it looked when I was here before."

"Oh." *Right.* Savvy remembers the panic he created when he used the word "magical" after her mother and Auntie Simone had cloaked all the magical objects on his first visit, the night they found Paris. "This is what it really looks like. Voilà."

The downstairs still has sitting furniture and the like, but it also has large paintings of famed heroic witches and operatives—including a portrait of Mother Circe herself in her prime. There are crusty grimoires on the bookshelves and an apothecary's dream stand of spell ingredients that line the wall just outside the kitchen. And an alligator that was an early familiar of Mother Circe's stuffed and hanging from the ceiling.

"Okay," Griffin says. "Does our house also look different in reality?"

"No," Savvy says. "There were just lots of hidden things. You had some too, right?"

Griffin shifts uncomfortably. "The basement might have a secret room."

"A secret room?" Savvy shakes her head. She never bothered him down there. "What a pair we are."

"Don't make that sound like a bad thing," Griffin says. The heat and intensity as he looks at her almost distracts her from why they're here. Almost.

"The meeting will end eventually," Savvy says. "Brie and Elle can only do so much. We have to hurry."

"Lead on, goddess."

The way he says his nickname for her makes her want to stop and climb on top of him. *We're not doing that right now. We're fighting for our futures. Our futures which will most likely be separate.*

Savvy starts up the stairs. Here's where she has to hope the Farmhouse still trusts her. The inner sanctum, the Spellbindery, isn't in one precise location. It moves. The Farmhouse is a cousin to Llanada Villa, later known as the Winchester Mystery House. Sarah Lockwood Pardee was a witch who did the initial design for C.R.O.N.E.'s property here before she even became a Winchester. If people really knew the truth about what the place out West hides, they'd find it much more than an odd tourist attraction.

What Sarah Winchester mainly did was teach the boards of the house how to shift and hide and be unmappable. While the Farmhouse behaves with the common rooms, the Spellbindery is itself suffused with magic. It can be found only by those it wants to find it.

Part of the final testing of every young witch here is to locate it without assistance and be admitted. Once there, you find that your name has been added to the Registry of Witchkin, a giant book that produces new pages as it needs them. Savvy was seventeen when she located the room, a year earlier than most do.

Should she have brought Griffin here? What are the odds the Spellbindery will let her find it with him in tow? She was optimistic earlier, possibly too much so. . . .

Just as she turns to ask him to wait downstairs, there's a tug at her that comes from no one in particular. It's the spirit of the house.

"Do you feel that?" Griffin asks.

She nods.

"We're meant to go up," he says.

Her shock is as much a presence as the sensation that is definitely pulling them on. They climb upward on the curving wooden stairs. The spiral gets tighter the higher the staircase goes. She hopes it's not some hardwired trick that the builder laid, but she doesn't think it is. The energy behind the tug doesn't strike her as hostile. She had thought it might *allow* Griffin here, not encourage him.

But, if anything, it's . . . inviting. Almost like the room wants them to find it.

Why would it welcome a hunter? Why any of this? The question about everything that's happened since yesterday.

They reach the top of the spiral staircase, and a landing opens out onto a variety of rooms. Only one door is open. To the top turret.

"We keep going up," Savvy says.

There's a distant *squawk* from Cretin outside, but she can't worry about that now. There's a thin light shining down from above on this last narrow set of wooden steps. When she found the room, all those years ago, it was tucked away in the belly of the house. She feels a little unease at how far this location puts them from the entrance.

There's nothing to do but keep climbing. And so they do.

The stairs creak underfoot. Savvy counts them. Thirteen.

Sarah Winchester was fond of thirteens.

The round room comes into view when she reaches the last one. The Spellbindery.

No matter where it is, the roof is a dome traced with mythic symbols; the paths of ley lines and the stars are drawn in graceful arcs. The walls are dotted with long, wide windows. Here is no different. There's the sound of a fountain, though none in view. The Registry of Witchkin stands open on one pedestal, and Savvy has the weirdest impulse to show Griffin her name in it.

There's no time for being sentimental.

"Wow," he says as she moves and he steps inside.

There's a small covered desk in the corner that holds the documentation related to operations; every successful mission, and the few failed ones, is detailed from assignment to closure. Rows of secret journals documenting the history of C.R.O.N.E., going back to when it was just a loose coven, are shelved beside a bubbling cauldron. Elle is one of the operatives who keep today's records up to date. Some of the books are hollow, containing important objects instead of written records.

In fact, one journal protects the most significant artifact in the entire room: the signing quill—from a raven in Cretin's line, this one another of Mother Circe's familiars—used to formalize the accords that meant hunters and witchkin were to live distanced, mostly safe lives out of view of the public eye. Up till now, at least.

Accessing the books is frowned upon, but allowed. Accessing the quill is the forbidden part. As is bringing an outsider here.

First things first. She heads to the large iron cauldron, the pool of water within sleek and silver as a mirror.

"Remember when you said it's too bad we can't go back in time? See what happened?"

"I do, but I wasn't advocating for time travel." He pauses, a furrow between his brows. "You can't time travel, can you?"

"We can't alter anything that is necessary to the ultimate stability of nature, and time is one of those things. But we can bear witness to our history." Savvy indicates the shelves full of thick leather volumes with rough-hewn pages. "Those are journals."

"Too bad we don't have time to read them."

"Fortunately, there are other ways to see the past. Only some of them are in writing." The quill must hold some hint of what occurred between the Butcher and his men and Circe and her coven. Exactly what she and Griffin need to witness.

She runs her fingers along the leather spines and finds the tome in question, removes it from the shelf. There doesn't seem to be any need to do a spell, not when the house is participating. "You led us here, so let us see," Savvy says, then lays the book flat and waits for it to open.

Nothing happens.

Savvy gnaws on her lip, considering. A distant *squawk* reaches her.

She closes her eyes and concentrates and when she opens them she touches the cover and it gives beneath her fingers, gliding open. And there it is, tucked inside the hollow volume.

The quill, a dark, gleaming feather with a sharp point at one end.

Griffin is riveted as she holds the quill by the feathered end and lowers it toward the gazing pool in the cauldron. She speaks the Latin and—

"Wait, you're not going to dip that, are you?" Griffin interrupts with horror.

"It's okay, I promise." She can't help smiling at his concern for the old object. She submerges it the rest of the way and the pool begins to bubble, and then she removes her hand and closes her eyes and calls for it to show what it has borne witness to.

When she opens her eyes, a scene appears in the air before them, similar to the ones that appear when she communicates with other witches through her amulet, but more detailed. To Savvy's surprise, there are only four figures present. Two are Mother Circe and the Butcher, and they look only slightly younger than they did at the wedding. Her with gray hair, him bald. The leaders' teeth gleam, bared at each other.

The others are their seconds, seemingly. A wide-eyed woman in her early twenties wearing a hooded robe, and a man of similar age sporting thick leather.

There is no sign of a battle at all. Only of the treaty itself on a desk. Mother Circe—again, looking nearly as old as she did at the wedding, not middle-aged as she did when Savvy first met her as a teenager—holds out her hands and the young woman jerks. Mother Circe speaks, and gestures to the young man. He also begins moving in a strange way. The two walk toward each other in fits and starts as Mother Circe chants and—conducts them. Yes, she's controlling their movements. The Butcher stands by and watches as she directs them to each other and their hands close around each other's throats.

"What?" Savvy hears Griffin voice the same question she has.

Circe throws her head back to release a cackle as the two fall, collapsing to the ground so there's no doubt they are dead. Then Circe removes the quill from the pocket of her skirt and squats to stab the palms of their downed allies. She advances toward the table, the document waiting there.

The Butcher stands at her side and waits as she signs—with the blood of the two Circe has forced to kill each other—and then extends his hand for the quill. She presses it into his palm. They exchange a secret smile, and the signs of age melt away from them. . . . Twenty years, thirty, gone in the blink of eye. Their skin firm and forms young, their limbs moving with greater ease. Circe looks as she did when Savvy first encountered her.

What does it mean?

Footsteps land heavily on the stairs, pulling Savvy out of her focus on the vision. They've lingered too long.

Savvy plunges her hand into the water and pulls out the quill, dry as bone. "But why? I don't understand."

To use magic to control another witch is forbidden, and for good reason. Savvy can't imagine a greater evil.

She *witnessed* Mother Circe use her power to force both a witch *and* a hunter to kill each other. And then she and the Butcher signed the accords with the blood of the slain. They grew younger after the ritual and signing. What more context could she need for that? The thought walks up her spine like a set of cold fingers.

There must be some explanation. There must. Or everything I've been taught is a lie.

Savvy puts the quill into her pocket and pushes Griffin behind her, against the wall of shelves, despite his protest. "Savvy, I—"

"Shh, quiet now," she says. She's not ready to hear him acknowledge what she just showed him. She can't defend Circe's role in what they've seen.

She hopes it'll be Brie or Elle, coming with a warning. But

they'd be louder. She expects her mother, given Cretin's cries, and she's right. Claudia comes through the door.

"Savannah, you shouldn't be here." Her tone is long-suffering. "The others are on their way here. Your friends tried to stop me, but I knew you must be here when they showed up. You can leave, Savvy, and I'll handle him. Come back later. This will blow over."

Savvy understands in an instant. Her mother is offering to make Griffin disappear or turn him over to Mother Circe and possibly the Butcher too.

"No," Savvy says. "No one touches him. I'm going to figure out why this is happening and then I'm going to stop it. I saw. I watched. . . . The quill . . ."

"I can defend myself," Griffin says.

"Not here," Savvy says. That would only make things even worse.

"I'm sorry," Claudia says. "I truly am. But there's no other way."

Savvy still has the wand, but she won't use it on her family, on her sisters. And she also knows the house welcomed them—both of them. Suddenly, she even thinks she knows why the room brought them all the way here, to the top of the house. To make their escape easier.

"Do you trust me?" she asks Griffin.

He hesitates, but: "With my life."

"Good." Because the one thing she's certain of now: they *are* in the fight of their lives. She's been lied to. They all have. But she doesn't know for what game, what larger stakes, yet.

Savvy holds out her hand and Griffin takes it.

"Don't," Claudia says. "You're going to make this harder on all of us."

"I didn't start it," Savvy says, "but I'm sorry about that. I don't—"

Feet pound up the stairs and Auntie Simone rushes into the room, but Savvy is already pulling Griffin over toward a window. "You mind opening that—with your foot?" she asks.

"You sure?"

She nods. Griffin kicks through the glass, shattering the quiet.

Savvy's broom is in her hand. "Don't come after us," she says.

"I'll make no promises." Claudia has her hand on her hip.

Auntie Simone puts a quelling hand on her mother's arm, gripping it. "Hurry," she says. "The others will have to act if they see you here."

Savvy realizes Auntie Simone is letting them go. Brie and Elle are the last to join and Savvy gives them the slightest shake of her head. *Don't follow now.*

Brie frowns, but she and Elle stay put.

And then Savvy is on her broom and Griffin is behind her, and they're leaving the Spellbindery, steering into the air and out. She waves a hand and the broken glass shards fly up and knit back into window behind them. They flee into the brilliant blue sky.

The realization hits like a blow. C.R.O.N.E. has lied to her and cast her out. In that moment, Savvy isn't sure what home is anymore, and if she has one.

20

Griffin

As they depart, Griffin is baffled by the repercussions of what Savvy conjured up out of the quill. It doesn't settle anything. But it must tarnish Savvy's view of Mother Circe as the hero of the day—when she expected it to do the opposite, and prove Griffin's version of history wrong.

The Butcher's actions don't paint him as a hero either. In fact, it sure looked like both Circe and the Butcher profited by growing younger through the accords. But . . . how?

What they saw . . . Mother Circe basically used her magic to murder one of her own and one of the Butcher's. The parallels between what they've been asking of Savvy and Griffin are obvious . . . but they haven't been forced to do anything.

That he knows of.

Then there's the fact that Savvy's mother and Auntie Simone struck him as not having any good options for moving forward either. Claudia was willing to dispatch him, and Auntie Simone wouldn't have been so quick to let them escape together if she had other ideas how to resolve this. He's relieved Savvy forbade her mother from acting against him. Still, it all *spells* more trouble, no pun intended.

He devoted his whole life to H.U.N.T.E.R. and it stings to discover he's being used, even if he doesn't know for what.

Still, no one from the Farmhouse seems to be chasing them. That's something. They're well clear of the property in minutes. A reprieve that's bound to be short-lived, given that their own people aren't the only ones they have to worry about hunting them down.

None of it makes sense. Griffin much prefers logic to mystery.

The parting words of Auntie Simone only served to remind him that both of them are out in the cold, except for their closest friends and family.

Which is why he took the journal beside the book Savvy accessed off the shelf and tucked it under his waistband. It has pages, he confirmed with his thumb, and he hopes it contains the kind of knowledge *he* can access. He needs to tell her.

"Savvy," he says over the wind, "we have to talk. Can we stop?"

"I need to think first," she says over her shoulder. He can hear the strain in her voice. "I'm not ready to talk about it yet. Where can we go to regroup?"

Griffin protects people. It's second nature. Savvy is hurting and he needs to be able to give her some insight that will comfort her. Books have always been the way Griffin discovers what he needs to keep his people and his world safe.

But he doesn't know that anything in the book he took will do that. Right now, that vision is an all-too-real reminder that despite the Butcher and Mother Circe cooperating then, their two camps couldn't be further apart now.

So he decides to keep the book to himself, until he knows what it holds. Instead he searches the possibilities of a safe landing place on his side and realizes he does have an answer.

"I have an idea," Griffin says. "I don't think they'll have gone back there."

"Where?"

"Diego's cabin."

Savvy's broom hitches then steadies. "That place is real?"

Griffin needs the release of the laugh, short as it is. "Who knew?"

"All right, where am I going?" Savvy asks.

Griffin guides her as she flies, the few fluffy white clouds around them a surreal kind of scenery.

He tries to ignore his wonder at the fact that he is flying. When he was a kid, he used to make his brothers watch the Superman movies. They were always the Batman fans in the family, more into the gadgets and the cars. But give him Superman any day. Solving problems by outsmarting the bad guys as much as muscle. Truth, justice, loyalty. Love.

So, he's not hand in hand with Lois Lane over Metropolis. Instead he's being flown *by* Savvy. Savvy, who must be reeling that the origins of her coven aren't as squeaky clean as she believed. But the cognitive dissonance between the reality of *her*—and if he's being honest, Brie, Elle, Auntie Simone, even Claudia—against what he's always been told about witches is potent. The house back there, and its sacred room, welcomed him. Tangibly. He felt an invitation. And it let him and Savvy see a huge secret, and a seeming liability.

But *why* would the house invite him if humans—especially hunters involved in thwarting bad supernatural elements—are the enemies of witches? He's beginning to seriously consider that Savvy's correct about their missions being closer than he's been taught . . . and also that both of them have learned many different lies.

Take that vision of Mother Circe and the Butcher, after what was supposed to be the largest battle in their history, with heavy casualties on both sides. Mother Circe was far beyond injured or cowed, as he was taught. And the Butcher, at least from what they saw, let her take out one of his men. And they both looked old before, not after.

They looked like they did at the wedding.

"Just down here," he says, and points at the cabin. "The one with the bottle tree."

Savvy lands them near it. She walks over and dreamily touches one of the blue glass pieces hung on a branch. She looks over her shoulder, not quite meeting his eyes. "This tree has a trace of magic in it."

"What?" Griffin doesn't doubt her, but . . . "Diego said it was his idea. He made it with his mom."

"It offers some protection," she says. "I never got the vibe off Diego, but his mom must've had at least a little natural witch in her." At Griffin's gape, she says, "We don't all join covens and become practicing witches. Some families leave and it's fine. We lose track of them unless someone finds their way back."

"Every time I think I have a handle on the reality we inhabit, it shifts," Griffin says carefully.

Savvy walks closer to him. "I don't know what we saw back there."

"Yes, you do."

"Fine, I do, but I don't understand what it means yet."

He sets his fingers on her shoulder. "Whatever it does, I'm not sorry we met."

Savvy moves away and he almost reaches out to her. Almost. He hopes Savvy knows he noticed she didn't respond in kind. She's retreating. And he isn't certain that he shouldn't do the same.

"I hope Diego has some food, because I can't think when I'm hungry, as you know," she says, and gives him a weak smile. "I'd rather save any conjuring energy because . . ." She shrugs.

"Because who knows what you'll need it for next? I get it. He bought groceries yesterday." Griffin wants to smack his forehead. "Shit. There's a security system. Big Rob put it in. I don't know how I forgot."

Savvy raises her brows. "I can take care of it."

"You are so smug!" Griffin protests. "Big Rob is a technological genius."

"And I am a different kind of genius." She grins and the bravado strikes Griffin as both true—in spirit—and a false front. "Wanna bet me I can't get us in there?" she asks.

For now, Griffin lets her have the pretense that everything is only a moderate disaster, not a full-on catastrophe. He sighs. "No. You would never offer a bet if you didn't know you'd win."

She raises her pointer finger and taps him on the shoulder. "Correct."

She turns to face the house and holds her hands out, palms up. She closes her eyes and chants under her breath, and he hears a small pop and looks up to see a puff of smoke coming from a detail above the door that just looked like a decoration. "How long will it take them to get here if they notice the cameras aren't working?" Savvy asks, opening her eyes.

"At least an hour."

"All right, then we have an hour. I'll set a boundary warning that'll let us know if someone's getting close."

"I'll—uh—make us some sandwiches." Griffin grumbles it. He wants to argue that they should let his people in. They might have ideas or intel. He's also positive Savvy will run if he suggests it.

He doesn't like the fact that she's doing all this work to keep them safe. Even though he knows that's a dumb macho thing to think. He can't help it. He can be a little dumb and macho, so what? He's a warrior, for fuck's sake.

"Truly the most important action of the moment," Savvy says as if reading his thoughts. "It'll help keep me from getting drained again."

Fine, maybe sometimes warriors make sandwiches.

Savvy turns the knob and the door opens for her. Griffin doesn't bother to ask if it was locked.

"I'm going to use the bathroom, splash some water on my face." He nods toward the hallway and Savvy peels off in that direction.

214   GWENDA BOND

Griffin heads straight for the kitchen. He removes the book he took from the so-called Spellbindery and stashes it in one of the cabinets. He'll buy time to look at it as soon as he can. And then he'll tell Savvy . . . something. Hopefully something useful.

He rummages around Diego's pantry, glad his friend actually values good food and not the junk his brothers would've bought. Sourdough, roasted turkey, avocado, and—oh, there's cooked bacon in the fridge too. He adds a couple of slices then puts the plates on the table. Savvy swans in and practically turns into a heart-eyes emoji at the sight.

Yeah, definitely worth it. Sometimes warriors make sandwiches.

She takes a seat and picks up hers. Griffin sits down across from her and digs into his own. A moment almost like the normal they had at their home before. Except there should be no more secrets. But there are. Griffin's got one. Savvy probably does too. Are they incapable of being honest with each other?

There's a distance between them and it's filled by that question.

"Thank you, professor," Savvy says. She takes a bite, chews, and swallows. Then she pauses. "*Are* you a professor, or is that just your cover?"

"I'm as much a professor as you are a goddess," Griffin says. "So yes. But mostly I'm an operative."

"Same." Savvy nods. "I only pretend to know about PR."

"And the animals at the Farmhouse," Griffin says, putting it together. "They're familiars. You said you had a dog in London, but then said later it was made-up?"

"In reality, Leggy the lemur." Savvy takes another bite. They're talking like acquaintances. He hates it. "I brought her back here for training and so she could find her witch."

"And Paris?"

"I'd almost given up on finding a familiar when she showed up. A total surprise. I hope she's not too mad when we don't come back to Brie's to get her right away." Savvy has already eaten half her sandwich. She glances around them. "Diego's place is nice. Not what I expected."

"Same." Griffin feels like she's gotten enough sustenance in for him to broach what he's been thinking. "What we saw . . . it doesn't match either of their stories. Therefore, we still don't know the truth. And time travel isn't an option."

Savvy tilts her head in consideration. God, she's gorgeous.

"Hmmm," she says. Then, "No. No way."

"No way what?"

"No way to the bonkers idea I just had."

"You might as well say it. I at least want to hear it."

Savvy settles an elbow on the table. "I need to track the source of all this. I want to know what Mother Circe is doing."

"Well, yeah, me too."

"I mean to track her down."

There's so much they can't explain. "Are you sure it's a good idea?"

"No, which is why it would have to be through unofficial channels. What we saw—she would've been in her seventies around then, and that was over three hundred years ago. He looked about the same?"

Griffin nods.

"She took the name Circe when she founded the coven, no one knows who she was before. . . . But they were old again at the wedding. Both of them. It can't be a coincidence. And us . . ."

"A hunter and a witch," Griffin says. "I had the same thought."

"They want us to kill each other, don't they?" Savvy shakes her head. "Mother Circe is a yaga. Finding her using an indirect approach will take some work."

Griffin picks up the reference right away. "You mean yaga as in Baba Yaga?"

"Sort of. It's more of an honorary term. Most yagas aren't members of C.R.O.N.E., they're just witches who prefer to be alone when they get older. Like the rest of them, Circe prefers to live in isolation. A simple location spell won't turn up where she is, no matter how close. And if I ask my mother . . . I can't. Not yet. It's too dangerous to involve them."

Savvy studies the table and Griffin is suddenly finding this all far less academic. She's chewing her lip in the way she does when she's nervous or worried.

"What is it?" he asks gently. "We're in this together, aren't we?"

Savvy doesn't answer at first. "We don't have much of a choice."

Lukewarm. "So, tell me the crazy part of what you're thinking."

Savvy drums her fingers. This idea is making her more nervous. Interesting. "The only way I know to find her is through Melissa. She isn't part of the coven, but she was sent to Mother Circe briefly before she left. Circe banished her. Yagas are territorial. She'll probably be using the same place now."

Griffin blinks. "Melissa the Gorgon? As in your ex? The one who's been trying to kill us?"

"We were teenagers," Savvy says. "It lasted two weeks."

"She doesn't seem over you," Griffin says. He adds, "Which is unsurprising. You are not the kind of woman someone gets over."

"Sweet talker," she says. She grows serious. "You may have to, Griffin. Get over me."

"You keep saying." He breezes past that. "Melissa seems pretty devoted to taking you out. . . . And she was pretty scary back there."

"But she didn't actually hurt anyone except the people there to harm us—that must mean something?"

Griffin is still skeptical. "I tangled with her in Paris, you know."

Savvy gapes. "Melissa was mixed up in the catacombs business?"

"Her and two other guys." Griffin looks up at the ceiling. "I may have told her to never practice necromancy again or we would have to hunt and stop her. Which she obviously did in front of us."

"Are you telling me that your job requires you to try to capture her or something? We don't have time for that."

"I'm just sharing, in case it becomes relevant." Griffin pauses. "So you think she would do this? Help you?"

Savvy sighs. "Probably. But I'll have to do something truly terrible to convince her."

Griffin balks at that. "Well, then, no, we'll find another way."

"By which I mean apologize to her."

"Oh." Griffin thought she meant the kind of terrible that involved more sacrifices or maybe agreeing to go out with her again. "Is that so bad?"

"Wait and see," Savvy says, grim. "But I'll do it. I'm gambling she has more reason to hate Mother Circe than she does me."

"How do we find her?" Griffin asks.

"I'm on it." Savvy sweeps up the last crumbs on her plate with a finger.

"Right." Griffin gets up. "I'm going to see what weapons Diego has hidden out here. I'm not going into this empty-handed."

"My hero," Savvy says, and though there's a note of irony, Griffin's stupid macho streak purrs like Paris the cat at the words.

Griffin doesn't indulge the spike of guilt at not answering texts at the same time he's riffling through Diego's gear. There was nothing in the bedroom, nothing socked away in the closet. But there's an attic and that's where he hits the jackpot. Diego has a small arsenal of H.U.N.T.E.R. gear stashed up here, as if he's long thought of this place as their apocalypse stronghold.

Like they wouldn't be scattered to the four winds fighting it, should it ever occur.

Anyway, this is only a personal apocalypse. A relationship apocalypse. To have any chance of working things out long-term, finding a way to be together, they have to figure out not only what is happening, but *why* it's happening, and some way to stop it.

That's a lot of hurdles.

He focuses on the problem he can solve. Which is not daring Melissa the Gorgon to come out and play without some major firepower. In a locked trunk that uses their universal code, there's a tranquilizer gun with self-steering bullets, a handful of robot bugs that can be handy as both spies and as tiny attack vessels (think steering one into someone's eye—as Griffin once did to a cyclops terrorizing a small town in Colorado), a Taser with some special mods. Oh, and a grenade that forms a protective plasma barrier that uses some previously gathered magic to hold its shape.

Griffin also liberates an extra black utility vest and gray camo pants that are both a little big on him and packs the pockets and pouches with the handiest of the supplies.

When he comes back downstairs, Savvy is outside facing the lake—there's much less activity today, as they close in on Sunday evening. Most families have gone back to the city to prepare for the week, their fun over.

He slides the door open and goes out to join her. He walks softly so as not to startle her, and because it's second nature, but then it occurs to him that he's approached so that whatever he does to signal his arrival probably *will* startle her.

So he moves slowly to stand beside her. He finds her eyes are closed, a peaceful expression on her beautiful face, her hair ruffled by the breeze off the water.

"Like what you see?" she teases without changing her stance or opening her eyes.

Of course he couldn't sneak up on her. He doesn't know why he assumed he could. "What do you think?" he asks, voice husky.

She turns her head and looks at him. The invitation is clear and he takes it, stepping in to her and claiming her mouth, just as she claims his back. The kiss is scorching, and he tries to fill it with all the promises he wants to make. She groans, strokes a hand against his cheek, rubbing at the stubble there, and around his neck, and then she pulls back and leaves their foreheads touching.

"It is very hard to imagine never doing that again," she says.

Griffin won't even entertain the thought. "Then don't."

"I think I have to," she says, and looks at the ground.

He follows her eyes and sees the journal he brought from the Farmhouse at her feet.

"You should stay here and read that," she says. "Then go home. We're in separate corners. That's where we belong."

"Savvy," Griffin says, "I should have told you I took it—I would have. I wanted to know that it was useful first. We *are* in this together."

"Your friends are almost here. I better go," Savvy says with a trace of regret, and reaches into her pocket. She removes her broom and it grows in her hand.

"Savvy, wait, let's talk this through."

"I'm done talking," Savvy says. "Don't come after me. Please."

Griffin watches as she flies away to the soundtrack of screeching cars pulling up out front. But he can't turn his back on his obligations, either. He needs to discover what the Butcher's part of this is. He'd give anything to follow her.

She doesn't want him to.

So he picks up the book and goes back inside. Time to meet his people.

Six Months Ago

21

✦✦✦

The Goddess and the Professor

Savvy takes in the inside of the sports bar in front of her and Griffin. Obviously, even for people who like sports bars, there's a range that goes from something like gastropub to pub grub to grubby grub. The joint they're entering—the sign identifies it as O'Hooligan's—is somewhere in the third category.

"Diego picked this place, didn't he?" Savvy's feet stick to the floor, victim of an epoch's worth of spills.

"How did you guess?" Griffin asks.

"A hunch."

Speaking of which, Diego and Griffin's brothers and his parents are piled into a table in the corner with the clearest view of the medium-sized TV mounted on the back wall.

"Isn't this great?" Diego asks as they get closer. He stands up and flings his arms out, nearly decking Griffin's bearded brother Jacob, who ducks. "We practically have the entire place to ourselves."

This is true. The Carters, Diego, and Savvy appear to be the only ones here to watch the game. Savvy tried to talk Brie and Elle into coming out with her, but they declined once she revealed where they were going. Brie accused her of making up the place. "'O'Hooligan's' sounds like a Mad Libs for businesses I don't want to go to."

Personally, Savvy likes basketball, but in that she's more or less alone in her friend group. She's more inclined to follow the

WNBA than college undergraduate men's games, but beggars and daters can't be choosers. Apparently, it's a tradition for Griffin's family to get together to watch anytime the Bulldogs make it past the first round of the SEC tourney because Griffin's parents met during the tourney in college, despite the fact that neither of them attended either the games or the University of Georgia.

Two seats are left at the end of the table near Griffin's parents, Roman and Jackie. Savvy takes the one closest to Jackie, who gives her a big welcoming grin. She has an effortless sense of easy stability about her, and is currently sporting a Bulldogs hoodie and still managing to look pulled-together with a sleek gray bob.

At times like this, it's hard to believe that only three months have passed since she and Griffin started officially dating. His family and friends have been a lot less dramatic about it than hers. Her mother is a broken record on how much of a mistake she thinks Savvy's being involved with him is.

Griffin's mother pushes an empty beige coffee mug over to Savvy, pulls her purse up off the floor, and pours a healthy portion from the white wine bottle she has stashed in it into the mug.

"Diego never asks if they only have beer," Jackie says by way of explanation.

"I don't mind beer, but . . ." Savvy takes a grateful sip of crisp sauvignon blanc. "This is more my speed, thank you."

"Hey," Diego protests, "beer is what you're supposed to drink during games—well, or liquor, if your team is losing."

Griffin's dad shakes his head. Savvy unofficially thinks of him as James Bond, Sr., because he's the most polished, handsome older gentleman she's ever met. She's chosen well, since she suspects this is exactly how Griffin will age.

Hold up. How long has that thought been buried in her brain?

She knows things feel serious between them, but she isn't convinced they should. . . . *Why not? You are surrounded by his family and they're treating you like one of them.*

Yeah, and he doesn't even know who I really am. He never can.

"What's wrong?" Griffin asks, holding the beer Diego has supplied him with and leaning in to her ear.

"Nothing," she says, and wishes he were less perceptive about her moods. "Now," she says to the table, "I want to hear the story. I've heard the quick version, but . . . I want to hear it from the sources."

"The game's on," Diego says, and when Jackie shoots him a look, sits down and puts his chin on his hands, rapt. "But yes, please tell the story again."

Everyone at the table focuses on Griffin's parents, despite how many times they must have heard this, and it's beyond sweet. Griffin slides a hand onto Savvy's thigh under the table and she puts hers into it; there's no way she'll be able to focus and listen otherwise. The light touch is enough to make her pulse speed up.

"Do you want to start this time?" Griffin's mom asks.

"Oh, no," his dad says. "You're much better at it than me."

His mom nods. "True." She settles her hands around her wine-filled coffee mug. "It was a March, not unlike this one. Unseasonably cool. I had an ancient Toyota that barely ran."

"Spoiler alert," Diego puts in.

"Shhh," Jackie gently shushes him.

"All my friends were going to a Bulldogs bonfire because they had tickets from one of their boyfriends. I gave them a ride over to Athens, but I wanted to go see a Camper Van Beethoven reunion show instead. I bravely decided to go on my own. There was a big rumor that some members of R.E.M. would be sitting in."

"A true rumor," Roman puts in. "Peter Buck was there."

"And Michael Stipe stepped in for a duet on 'Eye of Fatima.'" Jackie smiles at him. "There was this guy there who was also alone. And very cute. We ended up bouncing around next to each other, singing all the lyrics word for word like huge dorks."

"I think you mean like the extremely cool people we were and still are," Roman puts in.

Savvy laughs and Griffin squeezes her hand.

Jacob nudges Quinn. "Would you say our parents are cool?"

"Cooler than you," Griffin teases.

"Hard to argue," Quinn says.

Jackie leans forward. "Anyway, I left right after, because brave as I was, I wasn't brave enough to introduce myself to strange cute boys."

"She left before I could catch her."

"And yet somehow you managed," Savvy says.

"This is the good part," Roman says with a grin. "May I?"

Griffin's mom nods and takes a sip from her mug.

"I stayed after to buy merch and meet the band, which is of course what all extremely cool people do," Roman says.

"Obviously," Jackie says.

"And so I'd be sobered up when driving back. I had . . . an early-morning assignment due. I'm just about to get onto the interstate exit back to the city when I see this sad little car pulled over by the median. I can just make out the shape of a woman's head inside, where she's alone in the driver's seat."

"My friends were staying over, but I had to get back," Jackie explains. "I'd gotten out of the car to check out the tire and it—it felt like there was something creepy watching me. I got back in and locked the doors. It was well after midnight by this time. I was scared to death."

Savvy keeps a smile pinned to her face, but what she's really thinking is: *Always listen to that intuition. There probably was some-*

thing out there. Instincts are great warning signals for things that go bump and hang out next to interstates at night.

"So when I pulled over behind her and knocked on her window, she screamed." Roman is dry. "It was very romantic."

"Then I saw who it was. I have never jumped out of a car and started talking to a stranger so fast in my life. . . . He even went and checked out the woods and scared away a stray cat."

"An enormous tomcat," he says, and something about it bugs Savvy, but she mentally waves it off.

"There was no hope for my car, so he used his Triple A to get it towed to town. And instead of calling my friends—which he asked me if I wanted to—I let him give me a ride home." She nudges him with a shoulder. "And a good-night kiss."

"We were married just a year later," Roman says.

"Fast," Savvy says.

"Just the amount of time we needed," his dad says.

"Well, I'm never getting married," Diego declares, not that anyone asked him.

Savvy usually would chime in and say the same. But, tonight, she doesn't. She glances at Griffin and their eyes meet and they smile at each other and . . . she realizes she's in deep.

She's completely in love with him.

And she can't bring herself to see it as a disaster.

She almost blurts it out, but somehow manages not to. She *loves* Griffin.

Griffin is never bothered by hearing the story about how his parents met—except the part where it diverges from reality without his mom knowing.

The "tomcat" in the woods was actually a lesser chupacabra that had been attacking women in the area. His dad came back with more experienced operatives and put it down the next day.

"It's a great story," Savvy says, breaking eye contact with him. "Thanks for sharing it."

"You know who else has a great story?" Diego asks. "Jacob. He's moving in with you and Quinn, Griff."

"What?" This is the first Griffin's heard of it. "What happened?"

"Someone bought my building—jacking up the rent. They want to renovate, so they're basically making it cost too much to stay." Jacob sighs. "It'll just be for a little while."

"The couch is yours," Griffin says.

Yes, Griffin and Quinn share an apartment, a nice one, and now apparently it's going to be all the brothers together. Which is going to make things dicier in terms of Savvy being around. Quinn's almost slipped up several times. Jacob is meticulous, but . . .

"You could move to my place," Savvy says.

Jacob says, "What?"

"Not you," Savvy says. "Griffin. You're over all the time anyway. Paris would love it. I have the space. . . ." She trails off. "Forget I said anything. Too soon for moving in, right? Too soon."

He can tell she's as surprised by the offer as he is. "Maybe not," he says. He turns to Jacob and Quinn. "Would you want to take over my lease together?"

He can see that Jacob wants to jump on it, but is hesitating to avoid forcing Griffin into a position where he has to say yes to Savvy. But . . . Griffin realizes he wants to. He's 100 percent all-in with this woman. Head over heels for her.

"Just to be clear," he says to her, "we're talking about moving in together? For good?"

Savvy hesitates then nods. "Yes, we are."

His mother has a hand to her heart and is exchanging ridiculously beaming smiles with his dad.

"The only things is, I have a lot of books and junk and—" Griffin is suddenly panicking, thinking of all the ways he can't move in with Savvy no matter how much he wants to. Where will he store his weapons?

"You can have the basement for an office," she says. "But if you're not ready—"

"It's not that."

Roman catches his eye. "I'll help you move in—we can tinker with the downstairs a bit, if that's okay, Savvy? I did some contracting work in college. And our buddy Rob can fix up anything."

Savvy shrugs. "That's fine with me. If you're moving in, I want you to be comfortable."

Renovations are permanent. Griffin can't keep himself from leaning in to kiss the side of her mouth. "This is big. I'm excited."

"Me too," Savvy says, sounding faintly surprised, as their eyes hold again. She inclines her head and her lips meet his for a slightly longer kiss.

"Aw, man," Diego says, "another round for the table. I see where this is going. I'm going to lose my wingman for sure."

Savvy chooses this moment to select a crinkly french fry from an abandoned appetizer basket on the table and fling it at Diego.

Everyone cracks up, even Diego, and Griffin thinks, *This is it. This is my family.*

She can't ever know the truth about his job, but it can work. Look at his mom and dad. It can work.

No matter how impossible it seems, it has to.

Now

22

✦ ✦ ✦

Savvy

Savvy shields herself from sight as she flies back into the city toward Melissa's address, which she found on, yes, the internet. The old ways aren't always the most convenient. She meant what she said about saving her power as much as possible.

Besides, it turns out Melissa the Gorgon has a wildly popular Insta account followed by people who think she's just very committed to her arty hair snakes, unaware they have real poison fangs. Whether they're the result of a glamour or some sort of absorption spell for animal familiars, now that Savvy can't say. At least she knows where she's going. Melissa tagged the building she lives in once in a photo, a former girls' school converted into posh lofts.

She even has her own hashtag, #modernmedusa. Griffin would probably lose it at that.

Griffin. Savvy was only scanning for more magic after the unexpected discovery at the bottle tree. There the book was, obviously hastily stashed. He's still lying to her. They've both been lied to about a lot of things.

She can't keep lying to herself.

The way he reacted at the barn when the truth about her was revealed keeps returning to Savvy in the odd moment. His disgust and betrayal. She tries to square it with things he's said and done since that prove he doesn't view her as evil. That might seem like a low bar, but for a hunter and a witch, it's confusingly difficult, to say the least. She doesn't view *him* as evil either, and that's troubling too, given what she knows— correction: thought she knew—about hunters.

And then there's the physical part of it all. The fact is, the sex has always been great between them. But now . . . even that kiss . . . the attraction is combustible. She *can't* imagine never kissing him again, never seeing him again, never crawling under the covers together in their bed to go to sleep with Paris curled up at their feet.

But she also can't imagine how they can possibly be together. She isn't even sure she'll make it through this. And that's doing what will be perceived by Melissa as begging for her help (because that's exactly what it is) and then trying to get the drop on Mother Circe.

She's troubled by the lack of action from Claudia and Auntie Simone. The Spellbindery will have alerted them. She shouldn't have removed the quill and Griffin shouldn't have taken the book. That vision made it clear that this is turning out to be about more than just whether she and Griffin individually, let alone together, can survive.

People only keep secrets this size for reasons they can't or won't share. Mother Circe is definitely not who she claims to be, *and* she's up to something. Savvy will figure out what it is or die trying. She doesn't see any other choice.

Obviously she'd rather live—even if the solo life she always envisioned for herself working for C.R.O.N.E. no longer seems like an option either. Whatever else Mother Circe is, she's a murderer. The proof is still in Savvy's possession.

Brie tries to call using Savvy's locket, a glow at her throat, and Savvy ignores it. It's better if she does this alone. Everyone else will be safer this way.

The old schoolhouse in Grant Park with its magnificent redone façade comes into view below. She checked it out on her phone earlier, and Melissa must do well for herself via Instagram influencing and freelance necromancy. The Roosevelt is a nice place, with spacious, high-ceilinged apartments. Not exactly the kind of Gothic abode she expected.

Hopefully that means she doesn't actually need the money from Savvy's bounty.

Savvy lands in front of the grand brick edifice's main entrance, tall wooden doors with windows, a graceful arch detail above. Her plan is simple: find Melissa's apartment and knock on the door. Melissa might not lose her temper so destructively that way. People don't like wrecking their own things, and Savvy is afraid if she lures her out here, Melissa might raze the whole building without stopping to think.

There's a sushi delivery guy coming out as Savvy nears the door, and she makes it so he doesn't see her as she catches it and slips inside. A bank of mailboxes is visible along the back of the entryway. Jackpot.

Savvy walks over and starts scanning the names. She didn't realize Melissa lived this close by, but there's no reason for C.R.O.N.E. to know or do anything about it unless she's breaking or directly challenging their rules. She's flown under the radar, so to speak.

Finally, top row, last one, there she is. Apartment number 313. Melissa Sanger and, written in script below, "aka @ModernMedusa." Of the 240,000 IG followers.

She appreciated Griffin not judging her for having a necromancer ex-girlfriend . . . even if it was in high school. And pre-necromancy. The fact that she's bi came up in the sanitized personal histories they gave each other. He didn't make a big deal of it then. He is a good guy, hunter or not.

But he's not for me. I'm not for him. We were a pair of fools lying to each other and to ourselves.

She heads over to the elevator bank and presses the up button.

She flashes back to their first time meeting each other and then later at the Savoy. When the car starts going up, she gives a tragic little hop.

The elevator stops and Savvy gets off. She can't be sure what kind of protections Melissa has, and if she's already been alerted to her approach. Nothing to do for it now but hurry. Savvy can't do a shielding spell if she wants to talk to Melissa. She has to be open.

Three thirteen isn't far up the hall.

She knocks, once, twice.

"Fucking thank you," Melissa says as she opens the door. "What's the point of sushi without the fucking extra wasabi?" She blinks in momentary confusion, then raises her hands. Black shadows—she *is* weaker than before, they're wispy—begin to form.

"Wait. I'm not here to fight," Savvy says.

"Too bad," Melissa says, and her hair snakes hiss and snap. One strikes at Savvy.

"Wait!" Savvy dodges and holds up her hands in the universal gesture for peacemaking. "Please? Can I come in and talk? I'm serious."

Melissa frowns—no, scowls. "Why?"

"I need to apologize for some things."

Melissa crosses her arms. "You must want something else too. And I'd still really like to murder you."

Savvy is encouraged by the lack of physical escalation. "Yes, and acknowledged. . . . But I'm willing to grovel."

There's a tense moment. Savvy braces for an attack.

"Fine." Melissa nods. "I'll hear you out."

They stand there awkwardly. "Well, you coming or what?" Melissa finally says. She turns on her bare foot and goes back inside.

There's a lot about the last two days Savvy could never have predicted or anticipated. A lot that she'd have scoffed at the very suggestion of. Her entering Melissa the Gorgon's apartment? Voluntarily? Definitely one of those things.

Melissa is in the same black dress as before, sans boots, and she now seems unconcerned that Savvy's here. It's her turf, after all. She leads Savvy into a large open living room that could have come straight out of an interior design magazine. Muted rugs and a comfy couch. There's a ring light and green backdrop in one corner.

Also, Melissa apparently recharges by consuming mass amounts of sushi. Which, respect.

She has a huge spread on a low table and she sinks down to a floor cushion. She plucks up a piece of tuna sashimi and feeds it to one of her head snakes, which gobbles it greedily.

Oh. She's eating for . . . several, then.

"Well," Melissa says, and pops some nigiri into her own mouth. And, around the bite, "Are you groveling or what? Better make it good."

Savvy proceeds farther into the room and sits on the edge of the couch.

"Sure, make yourself at home," Melissa says. "Let's hear it."

Savvy takes a breath. "I should have been more sensitive about how I ended things. . . . We were kids, but I knew it was wrong to do it in front of everyone. I'm sorry. Truly. That was messed up."

Melissa and her head snakes go completely still. Which Savvy has never seen before—the snakes are *always* moving.

Savvy figures this means Melissa wants more groveling. Whatever it takes. "It was shitty. I was shitty. I'm sorry if I . . . broke your heart. But I do need your help. I need to find Mother Circe—without her knowing. You're the only one I know who's ever visited her who isn't part of the coven. Please—"

"Stop!" Melissa says, and the snakes snap as one. She points chopsticks at Savvy. "You think you breaking up with me is my problem with you?"

Uh. "I assumed?"

"Well, you assumed wrong. But then, Savannah Wilde, you always did have your broom so far in the clouds you couldn't see what those of us stuck on Earth were doing."

Uh-oh.

"What about the 'my sweet' stuff?"

Melissa sighs. "Have you really never encountered sarcasm before?"

Savvy gapes.

Melissa feeds one of her snakes another bite of sashimi. "Savvy, would you like to know what broke my heart? Would you like to know what *I* want out of this, in order to show you the way to Circe?"

Savvy wants to say no. She would rather leave. She has no idea where Melissa's going with all this. But she needs to find Circe. Melissa basically just admitted she knows how to do that.

"Let me have it," Savvy says. "Don't hold back."

"Oh," Melissa says with a dry laugh, "I won't. It wasn't breaking up with me that was the bad part. We were kids. Fine." She rolls her eyes. "It was the fact that you told everyone I hurt my familiars. I loved them. My magic—it wasn't like yours, like any of yours. It did dark things without me meaning it. I . . . That's when I realized I am a natural necromancer, not a witch at all. That was the beginning of me losing everything."

Savvy can barely breathe. It was rare for a witch to have multiple familiars, but an exception had been made. She remembers discovering Melissa in one of the barns with her three snakes, dead. Melissa had freaked out at Savvy's arrival. She'd asked Savvy to wait, let her explain. Savvy didn't listen. She had run, screaming, to tell everyone. "But—"

"Yes, you found me with them. But when I left, I took them

with me, all the way through the dark woods to Mother Circe. She taught me how to wake them, how to bond them to me to keep them alive in this fashion. We're the same now. Me and my familiars." The snakes appear to be watching Savvy, as solemn as snakes can be. Looking closer, Savvy sees the hints of gray on the edges of their scales. "We're bonded as close as we can be. We're one being."

"You must be— No, Melissa, no." Savvy must misunderstand. Her hand floats to her heart.

"Trading part of my life to keep them animate? Yes." Melissa nods over at the corner. "I expend as little actual power as possible, usually. I'm only active when I have to be—I make most of my money performing as a modern witch for strangers on camera. Mother Circe taught me how to conserve. For them. And then she kicked me out. I was on my own."

"I had no idea." Savvy feels sick. "Why would she do that?"

"There's only room in the coven for one dark-magic worker, in her eyes," Melissa says. "You must have finally figured out the truth about her. Congratulations."

"She uses dark magic?" Part of Savvy's doubt and confusion eases, even as horror spikes inside her. The ritual, the sacrifice.

"Duh," Melissa says, and takes another bite.

"I didn't know—but it makes sense." Based on what she and Griffin saw in the vision . . . Taking away people's will and then signing a contract in their blood is the height of dark working. What doesn't gel is how Mother Circe's been able to hide it from the coven for all these years. . . . *And* why would they let her kick out a teenager, all those years ago? Savvy assumed Melissa's infractions were the worst possible or that it had been her choice to go. She can't imagine making her way on her own at sixteen, confused, barely understanding her powers. "Melissa, I . . . I am so sorry."

Melissa's eyes have a sheen to them. "Now, that one, I think that was real. Sorry I tried to kill you and the hunter. Twice."

"Griffin said you were in Paris, reanimating the catacombs, last year too—why?"

"I was hired by someone who wanted to be confidential. Along with two other necromancers. . . . The timeline was specific. They paid promptly even though we failed at the job."

"You never found out who it was?" Savvy asks.

"No. You know?"

"No." *Maybe*. But she can't figure out what the Butcher and Circe would've gotten out of it.

"Oh well." Melissa dons a grin, which strikes Savvy as a false front. She recognizes it because she's been known to do the same thing. "I should thank you—the shot I took at you earlier? It should've wiped me out, but somehow it didn't."

"What?" Savvy is confused. "Why?"

"Circe told me years ago that the positive energy of a community could shore me up. Today was proof it works. We must still have some kind of link. Yes, you shut me down, but I'm not empty. I tried to bond with other necromancers, but . . ." She shakes her head. "Didn't work, not for long."

Savvy nods, reeling. "It didn't, because you're not like them. Not really." This is another entire facet of her world, previously hidden, that she's discovering. Her mother and Auntie Simone can't know the truth about Circe.

Melissa gathers her hands in her lap. "You can make all this up to me."

"How?" Savvy asks. "I'll do anything—" She qualifies, "Except let you take us in for a bounty."

"How kind, now that you know what I risked earlier, and what it would probably do to me if I attempted it again. I don't need the money." Melissa holds up a finger and says, "What I want is back in."

Savvy understands in theory—if the good energy can help her, coming back is logical. But how could Melissa ever bear to live under Mother Circe's rule again after being put out in the cold at sixteen?

"I get it," Savvy says. "But there's a problem. About what you're asking."

"Of course there is," Melissa says.

"I'm on the outs right now, as you know, so I can't promise you the coven or C.R.O.N.E. will accept you back," Savvy says. She hurries on as Melissa looks at her with what now seems like despair. "I don't even know if I'll be a part of it again when all this is done. But I swear to you that I will do everything I can to make it right." Savvy considers what Melissa said about her solaring earlier to dispel the necromantic magic and its impact on her. There are healing spells that are much gentler. "Can I help you now?"

Savvy extends her palm, summoning light to it. The snakes—like Melissa apparently—are confused, somewhere in between ready to attack and standing down.

"Can I try?" Savvy asks. "Based on what you said, I think it'll shorten your recovery time. And it definitely won't hurt."

Melissa hesitates, then nods.

Savvy turns her palm over, and the milky light spills over the snakes and Melissa. When it's done, there's a long silence.

And that's when Melissa the Gorgon, aka @ModernMedusa, aka Savvy's teenage fling, aka a woman who plays the part of a fearsome witch for Instagram likes, and *could* be a fearsome necromancer in real life but isn't, all to keep her familiars "sort of" alive, bursts into tears.

"Let me get my boots on," Melissa manages, and clambers to her feet. "We'll leave right away. The old one will never see us coming."

Good. If Savvy has her way, she won't see them at all.

23

+ + +

Griffin

The biggest shock to Griffin isn't the arrival of his family and Diego in two separate vehicles, the cavalry arriving. It isn't that Savvy found the book he removed and has taken off on her own—and that she seems to think that's for the best. It's not even that he can't dismiss the idea that maybe she's right.

No, the biggest surprise is his mother's presence. Jackie's climbing out of the passenger side of his dad's SUV when he reaches it.

"Mom?" She shouldn't be here. *Fuck*. He'd all but forgotten that he also blew his dad's cover. He kicks the pavement. Another thing that's technically his fault. Without the wedding, that would never have happened. "How are you?" he asks her.

"How are *you*?" she counters, and walks over to pull him into a fierce hug.

He didn't realize how much he needed it. He hugs his mom back, the two of them rocking together in the sunshine, and meets his father's eyes over her head. The street is otherwise quiet, a small kindness.

"Where's Savvy?" Jackie asks, pulling back a bit. "Is she safe?"

"We're . . . she's not here. She just left."

Jackie frowns. "You let her go?"

"I don't have much standing to stop her." Jackie might as well have laser vision into his heart, and she trains it on him now. So he deflects. "How are you dealing with all this?" He indicates his dad and his brothers.

Jake, Quinn, and Diego are going in and out of the cabin, transferring some things into the SUVs. The plan must not be to stay here.

"All what, sweetie?" Jackie asks.

Griffin never gets frustrated with his mom, but he does now. He turns to his dad, flummoxed, with his hands up.

"She knew," Roman says.

"Oh, all *that*," Jackie says. "Your father's job! I've known since before we got married. Your father isn't nearly as slick as he thinks, and neither are you boys. But it felt like you needed to maintain the illusion."

"The existence of H.U.N.T.E.R. is secret—we have to maintain our covers." Without that, they wouldn't be in this mess. He can't believe it. To his dad, he asks, "Did you know she was on to you?"

Roman looks chagrined. "Not so much."

Jackie smiles. "I figured it out, and Savvy would've too, eventually. Now, I didn't know she was a witch. But it makes sense."

Griffin tilts his head to the left, then to the right. He's not seeing any angle where it does. "How so?"

"She's very impressive," Jackie says as if it's obvious.

He can't argue. But . . . "Yeah, well, her being a witch is only one of our problems."

They don't seem to be able to trust each other.

His mother projects an aura of motherly disappointment. "Why is it a problem at all? It seems like a solution to me— you're obviously perfect for each other."

"They're our enemies."

"She's not your enemy. Your brother told me she saved all your lives."

Griffin doesn't know how to counter that. "Ah, Dad, help? Can you explain it?"

"Not really," he says. "The Butcher is refusing to be sensible and call off the hit on you. Mother Circe is doing the same thing. But we're not going to let anything happen to you. So we're taking you home to regroup."

"Do you have a way to get ahold of Savvy?" Jackie asks.

Sure, he has her number. She has a phone and so does he. But she's not going to answer if he calls. "She's out gathering intel."

"Good," his father says. "On?"

"Circe. We . . . found out some things."

"Good. We need it. But . . . is she being careful?" Roman asks.

Griffin decides not to reveal Savvy's plan to convince a necromancer to help her out. Or that she's not intending to report back to him. His nerves about her being on her own kick up and he reminds himself that she's the one who left him here.

Diego trots out holding up the book that came between them. "This was on the kitchen table—what is it?"

Griffin's grateful for the subject change. "A journal I took from the Farmhouse, aka witch headquarters. It's a long story, but we watched the signing of the accords." He explains the ways it didn't match what either of them had anticipated. "They signed it in the blood of their dead followers."

"You're sure this was real?" Roman asks, his shock plain. "The Butcher and Circe in this together?"

Diego is wordless, a unique reaction for him.

"Savvy certainly believed it." Griffin nods. "And I have no reason to doubt it. What else do you know about the accords? From our history?"

Roman thinks. "There *were* casualties, but they were signed anyway."

"Is there a detailed record of who died? So we can confirm the vision was real?"

Roman frowns. "I'm not sure. We can check with Rob."

"He's still with us?"

He nods. "He's still with us."

"I'm calling him." Griffin digs out his phone and selects Big Rob from his contacts.

His friend answers on the first ring. "Griffin, that you?"

"It is." He braces his hand on the hood.

There's ambient noise. "Good to hear from you—I'm on my way to your folks' house."

"Do you still have archive access?" Griffin mentally crosses his fingers.

"Couldn't keep me out even if I didn't." The grin is audible. "What do you need to know?"

"The casualty report at the accords signing in 1693."

"I don't have to look that up, I went through a minor fascination with the accords as a kid. There were two casualties that day—an operative on our side, promising man, and a witch. It was losing those two that led directly to the signing. The Butcher made Mother Circe see that they had to end the bloodshed."

"Interesting," Griffin says. Because that's not what happened. At all. But who died does match up. "Are there any descriptions of the Butcher from that time?"

"Hale and hearty, the warrior everyone followed without question, that kind of thing," Rob says. "Of course, he wrote the early histories."

"Got it," Griffin says. "See you soon—I'll explain more then. And, Rob, thanks."

"We're family," Rob says, just before he hangs up.

"Helpful?" Roman prods.

"Yes, and the journal might clarify it more."

"Okay then," Roman says, and takes charge. "You, back seat, read while we go home. Jake, Quinn, you follow us and shout if you see any trouble coming. Diego, you get in with us."

Diego nods and pointedly speaks to Griffin. "Yeah, I need a ride, since my car is . . . who knows where."

"It's at Brie's," Griffin says. "And I'm keeping it."

Diego gives him a look like he's gone insane. "Fine, because I'm not going near that witch to get it back."

Jackie clears her throat. "Is that how we talk about women?"

"She *is* a witch!" Diego protests.

"Mm-hmm." Jackie shakes her head with disappointment. "So is the woman I still want to be my daughter-in-law. Frankly, I'm jealous. I think I'd make a great witch."

"You would, honey," Roman says.

Griffin considers revealing what Savvy said about Diego's mother and the traces of magic, but decides not to just yet. He also doesn't point out that his dad recently negotiated with the Butcher and came up with the verdict that Griffin would have to take out said prospective daughter-in-law. He's obviously not doing that, but she feels further away with every second.

The world has gone mad. Griffin grabs the book that might help make sense of it and gets in the SUV.

As they travel back to the city, Griffin's head is spinning. The journal plunges him back into the daily record-keeping of a young witch historian named Diana in the 1690s.

The information is written in looping, slanted penmanship with flourishes on letters like "S," and fairly formal diction, on age-yellowed pages of woven paper bound into a leather casing. Griffin's antiquities training comes in handy for deciphering the phonetic spellings and period slang the writing is peppered with.

There are lists of new spells and their ingredients that are being covered in informal lessons among the coven members. A report of a village that had been razed, by some accounts by hunters, and others by random marauders. Another report that Mother Circe will be visiting her home coven in the woods soon, and how they are preparing to welcome their leader after her travels abroad. Griffin figures the contacts she made back then must have allowed her to build C.R.O.N.E. into a world-wide organization, with chapters around the globe . . . just as the Butcher's did for him.

The throughline isn't completely the opposite of what Griffin *or* Savvy learned growing up and in training. Villages *were* being destroyed, and the writings make it clear that some of that was due to ever-escalating conflicts between early groups of witches and hunters. The hunters plainly feared and despised the witches, and vice versa. Each side clearly blamed the other for the deaths and destruction. But on the witches' part, things changed when they started to be openly targeted by villagers too.

Salem happens.

The hunters now follow a leader, a former Butcher, who hath presented himself an expert on witchcraft for the triales taking place in Mass. He tells the people of Salem Village the signes indicating workings. These are inkorrect, but women have been tried and hanged through the courtes. One was a natural witch and the Mother swears she wille be avenged. More women are expected to follow. The Butcher is said to take a foul delight in the persecution, whispering in the ears of the lawmen snakelike. He sees an opportunitie to destroy more witchkin.

That first reference to the Butcher being in charge of the hunters occurs in late 1692. The young historian notes repeatedly that Mother Circe places the blame for the continued hysteria squarely upon his shoulders. The entries become less frequent and harsher in tone.

As Griffin reads, he feels as if he's a witness to what happens in Salem as it escalates far beyond anyone's control, a mania that begins infecting other towns. Most of the witches in Diana's particular coven seem to be deep in hiding in the woods, hoping their spells will keep them safe. The women being persecuted in Salem—for the most part—seem not to be witches at all. There are some efforts on the coven's part to help them escape, save them, but the success or failure isn't documented.

And none of that prevents Diana and the witches of her coven from taking umbrage at the effort to wipe out others for practicing witchcraft, charges valid or not. Plans are developed, with Mother Circe intending to make a large move with her coven in May of 1693 to ensure their safety. The exact location isn't noted, but Griffin is guessing somewhere near Salem from the context. He wonders when this particular coven moved to Atlanta, when it officially became C.R.O.N.E., and then expanded into other chapters with their own covens. He has so many things to ask Savvy, but his biggest takeaway from the book so far is that during the Salem trials period, witches were just trying to live, to stay alive, not acting as aggressors.

Until that spring.

The young historian keeping the diary has been hand-selected by Mother Circe to attend her during a battle to directly challenge the Butcher and his hunters. Her strategy is to weaken the hunters' defenses, showing them they cannot stand against the witches, and then get the Butcher to sign the accords. She has gifted Diana with a quill made from a feather molted by her own raven. The quality of the writing becomes steadier due to it.

The entries during the battle are short. Diana worries that Mother Circe is too frail to survive, though her magic is strong. But *then* she chronicles Circe being granted a meeting with the Butcher that she returns from in high spirits. A cease-fire is called. Diana's last entry says that the signing of accords to bring public peace is scheduled for that afternoon. Diana is excited, because she and an envoy from the Butcher's side will be the only witnesses. Mother Circe has cautioned her to bring no defensive spells or weapons. The other side isn't to have weapons either.

To document such an occasion is her dream.

Griffin's hands are shaking when he finishes reading. Because he knows what happened. Diana and the Butcher's man were made to kill each other. But the question remains . . . why? The accords weren't just about secrecy from the rest of the world, obviously. The Butcher and Circe both got younger after the killings and received greater status as a result of the signing. The question is: Why break the accords now, 330 years later? Why use Griffin and Savvy to do it? And why in this roundabout way?

Griffin closes the book, and soon they're back in the city, driving into his parents' giant garage at their house in the suburbs, the automatic door shutting on his parents' SUV and his brothers'. Big Rob's car is already here, and he opens the door from the house to meet them. Roman gets out and Griffin hears Big Rob say, "We have freelancers outside. Down the street."

They begin discussing what to do about the mercenaries.

Griffin smooths his hands over the journal's leather cover and considers what his next move should be. Both sides covered up what really happened that day with lies. Griffin's afraid the actual history might be repeating itself, which means someone *is* due to die. Sooner rather than later.

He can't let it be Savvy.

24

Paris

Captain Bear and I are in agreement. Humans, much as we love them, are not so bright. Peggy, as usual, disagrees, because she says Elle is brilliant.

Prove it is my feeling, but I mostly keep it to myself.

The two of them have tried to talk me down, but if *their* humans hadn't come back without my Savvy or my Griffin then I wouldn't have to take matters into my own capable, magnificent paws. I know full well, better than anyone, the trouble those two can get into without supervision.

I've been listening to Brie and Elle fret over where they've gone. I have my suspicions that this situation is nearly out of control. I don't trust Mother Circe or this Butcher man. I only trust my Savvy and my Griffin. The bond between Savvy and me doesn't tell me where she is, but it *does* tell me she is in trouble.

I'm clearly the only one who can manage this situation and save her. So.

I preen into my true leopard form and start my negotiations with a loud *"YOWL!"*

"What is it?" Brie asks me, Elle hovering behind her. "Do you know, Cap?"

Captain waves his little arms around, trying to communicate my distress. Peggy croaks.

Now that I've got Brie's and Elle's attention, I make my case.

I pad my beautiful body to the door and back to them a couple of times and then I run at the door and jump up to hit it with one sleek shoulder.

"I think she wants to go out?" Elle says.

Like I said. Brilliant? Please.

I repeat my run and jump, my muscles poetry in motion. "*YOWL!*"

Brie hurries over and opens the front door, chanting to conceal us from her neighbor. I proceed directly to the pink car in the driveway. You can't give humans even the slightest way to misunderstand or they will. I lift my paw in an elegant gesture and touch the handle.

"She wants us to go somewhere, I think?" Brie comes to my side and frowns. "Where?"

Stronger emotion shoots through my bond with Savvy. Fear. Hers. *"YOWL!"*

"Uh, how can she direct us where to go?" Elle asks.

My frustration knows no bounds. But then I have an idea. I nudge Elle's hip until she takes her phone out of her pocket.

I nod my gorgeous face at it. "YOWL!"

Hurry, human.

Elle asks, "Savvy? You want me to call her?"

"She's not answering," Brie says. "I tried, Paris."

I shake my head.

Elle and Brie exchange a look. "No," Brie says. "No, no, not him."

"YOWL!" I insist.

Elle swallows, then asks, "Griffin?"

I bob my nose up and down, staring at them so there's no doubt.

Elle finally shrugs and dodges Brie to call him. I hear his voice answer: "Elle?"

"Where are you?" Elle asks. "I think . . . Paris wants to see you."

I purr and turn to look at Peggy. Fine, maybe her human *is* the smartest. But mine, both of mine, are *home*.

And I'm not letting anyone take my home away from me.

25

✦ ✦ ✦

Savvy

Savvy's roughly tracking where she and Melissa are headed. Georgia's wild places are sometimes remote, sometimes not. In this case, they head outside Atlanta proper, in a different direction than the Farmhouse. She and Melissa soar over hills and mountains with twisty roads, tiny communities, and breathtaking tree-covered landscapes. As in literally *breath stealing* when Melissa careens down into the forest, barely controlling her broom.

Turns out necromancers don't fly that often. Savvy steers smoothly behind her unlikely accomplice, winding through fairly spaced-out trees. Melissa slows, and they stop in a circular copse with oddly shaped stones standing around it. The blackened bones of a fire are left in the center, a faint scent of ash in the air.

"She's had a conjure fire here, calling someone to her," Melissa says, and then half tumbles off her broom and manages to plant it in the ground in a semi-graceful recovery. "I'm just a little out of practice," she says, patting one of her snakes with a nervous hand.

She's speaking softly, and Savvy follows her lead on that.

"I didn't say a word," Savvy says, and dismounts from her broom, allowing it to shrink down. "We should shield ourselves."

Melissa nods agreement and crosses the clearing. She reaches down to pluck a handful of some lacy violet ground cover along the tree line. Savvy navigates to the opposite edge of the rough-hewn circle and gathers a pinch of kudzu and red-veined leaves of sorrel.

Savvy and Melissa pick out a few more plants and tuck them into the leftovers of the fire. Savvy chants in Latin under her breath, weaving a spell to conceal them. Melissa mumbles in what sounds like plain English, an occasional profanity thrown in like spice.

The two of them stand back, satisfied, or at least Savvy is. A vaguely floral scent now mixes in with the smoke.

Melissa's snakes hiss. It's the only moment of warning before a thunderous crash sounds in the near distance. Then another. Like a huge dinosaur is coming their way. To be fair, Savvy has seen things that strange.

She expected to have to search out Mother Circe's hut, but she must be on her way to them. An icy suspicion forms.

"Did you summon her?" Savvy asks Melissa, and suddenly she deserves the world's largest dunce cap. Has she learned nothing? That she trusted a necromancer so easily is shameful.

"I just animated her leftover magic enough to draw her back. She sticks close to this area. If you did your spell right, she shouldn't see us."

Melissa makes it sound like no big deal. It is quite possibly a huge deal, a huge *crashing* deal.

"You sure about that?" Savvy counters.

"Mostly sure." Melissa's snakes writhe through the air as if they're dancing. "And no."

Savvy could ask if this is an intentional betrayal, but there's no point. She can't know if she's still being a fool, believing anything Melissa the Gorgon has said. Though, she'll have to hope Melissa's need is real. That might keep her from fully tossing Savvy under the coming witch bus.

Another *crash*. And another.

Savvy's instincts scream she should run, but she tests the

cloaking spell and it holds. So she stays put, waiting as the crashes come closer and closer. Louder and louder. She came here to find Mother Circe and get a glimpse of her current activities and that's what she'll do. She won't wish Griffin were here beside her.

She won't.

She's still lying to herself, then, after everything.

The loudest *CRASH* yet comes, bone-rattling. The trees just outside the circle where they stand flatten under the step of a giant chicken foot with curved claws. Then they rise again in its wake, unbothered, just as they've stood for hundreds of years.

Another enormous chicken foot stomps into the dirt and then stays put. Savvy stares up at the witch's hut above them, a small wooden house with a chimney that releases smoke into the air. If it sat on the ground instead of on top of chicken legs, and if it didn't have scraggly, hesitantly moving wings below the windows on the sides, it might look like any old hut in the woods. But, no, this house walks or, as now, stands on legs as tall as the trees.

She's heard stories that the yagas all eventually end up inhabiting either large-scale shoes or a chicken-legged hut like this, à la the original Baba Yaga herself, the Russian witch. Some design choices just make sense. A classic never goes out of style.

Savvy has a moment to consider if this is how hysteria presents, musing on the immutability of housing fashions among isolationist witchkin.

She waits for a long minute to see if Mother Circe senses their presence and descends to confront them.

And one moment more. The birds seem hesitant to sing. The leaves of the tree canopies rustle together, but quietly.

Nothing happens.

"I guess we're going up," she says. It's partly a test to determine if Melissa is her ally or not.

"Guess so," Melissa grumbles.

Perhaps Savvy is too quick to rule out the benefit of the doubt where other people are concerned.

"You don't have to," Savvy says. "You've fulfilled your end by helping me find her."

Melissa tilts her head this way and that and then sinks to the ground beside the dead fire. "Okay, I'll wait here then."

Or perhaps Savvy shouldn't have expected her to completely change personalities lightning fast, even if she is a friend instead of an enemy. *Figures.*

So you're on your own. That's fine. It's where you always planned to be.

She studies the hut again, and decides to go for an aerial approach rather than risking a climb. Too bad Paris isn't here to scamper up a tree and spy for her.

Savvy climbs onto her broom and rises exceedingly slowly, inch by inch, bit by bit, just in case Circe's got unseen spying capacity or wards set up that she might trip. Despite Melissa's contention that she's too cocky to shield from magic users . . . No cloaking spell is unbreakable, after all.

And she's already learned that she doesn't understand how Circe's magic works. *"You must have finally figured out the truth about her."* But Savvy hadn't. She still hasn't.

Once she's at the level of the residential part of the hut, above the legs but just below the windows, she studies the sides and drifts next to a window more shadowed than the others. The better to see inside. Her broom holds her just so as she leans over to barely peer in through glass that ought to shatter with those bony-legged, ground-shaking strides but doesn't.

She almost loses her focus and plummets to the ground— something she hasn't done since she was a beginning flier at age seven.

The Butcher and Circe sit at a wooden table, a teapot between them, steaming cups in their aged hands. Saucers placed in front of them. They're both dressed as if it's a date. Him in a suit, her in a dress. How quaint.

They're chatting. Laughing.

Like old friends.

The confirmation settles into Savvy. They're in on this together. What is their endgame?

Something else about the scene, the two of them together at the table, tickles at her memory. But she can't place it. . . .

So she studies the parts of the space visible to her for anything else she can learn. The two of them are seemingly alone. Mother Circe's abode is lavishly decorated, and her spell supplies are extravagant, with plenty of colored-glass bottles and ancient books and a rack of wands.

Nothing here would give her away to a coven member as anything but a respectable leader. Anger builds inside Savvy. She believed in this witch. In her version of history. And she's angry on Griffin's behalf too. The Butcher built her people up as monsters, maybe because he's sitting beside one.

Savvy hesitates. There's one thing she doesn't see here that she anticipated: Mother Circe's familiar. A raven like her mom's Cretin. In fact, Circe's familiar is an ancestor of Cretin's called Craven, and Claudia's familiar was a gift from Circe. Auntie Simone could have had one too, but declined, satisfied with her ostrich.

The raven could be on patrol outside. A familiar *shouldn't* be able to penetrate the spell that hides her and Melissa, but she isn't willing to bank on it.

Wait. There she is. The large black bird lands on the opposite windowsill (whew) and squawks. Mother Circe points and raises the window with a gesture, not getting up. The bird flies over to her and perches on a hanging rest behind her chair.

Savvy gasps at the person who enters through the window on a familiar broom. A face she knows as well as her own.

Her mother is here. Claudia's eyes widen, but she nods to Circe, then to the Butcher. Pleasantly.

Savvy realizes the table is set for three.

Circe gestures again and the third chair at the table scrapes out. Her mother sits in it, and waits as the teakettle rises into the air and pours liquid into her cup. She smiles at the two elders, again so pleasant it makes Savvy's teeth ache. Since when does her mother smile like that?

And, for the life of her, Savvy can't fathom why she'd be here at this point. She's reportedly already made her entreaties on Savvy's behalf, on ears that refused to budge. Savvy remembers the message conveyed through Cretin to Brie about Savvy taking out the hunter. . . .

Savvy's heart has been broken, hastily put back together, hardened, softened, cracked, crumbled, hurt, and filled. All in the last twenty-four hours.

This is the world she always wanted to be a part of. One of the people pulling the secret strings behind reality, keeping it intact, no matter what it takes. Savvy is a spy.

For the first time ever, she wishes she weren't. If she were anything else, she wouldn't have to wonder if her mother is betraying her right now. She wouldn't have to lie to herself about missing Griffin like an ache.

Yes, Savvy has always thought she'd end up alone, was taught *by her mother* to put it all on the line for the mission and nothing more. She's been taught so many things that have turned out to be wrong.

Her mother always said no one else would love her enough to risk everything for her. But she knows, in this moment, that she'd risk anything for Griffin.

That's when Claudia looks straight at the window where

Savvy hovers. There's no doubt in Savvy's mind Claudia sees her.

Savvy hopes that she gets the chance to tell Griffin how she feels. She's afraid that she won't.

26

✦ ✦ ✦

Griffin

Griffin paces around the mini headquarters in his dad's no-longer-secret room downstairs in the house where he grew up. There are a couple of computer consoles, a library of important texts, and cabinets filled with wonder gadgets.

He thought he understood the broad parameters of how familiars work before this. But then, he didn't know that his cat could become a leopard in a blink, or a capybara could turn into a dog. Or that Peggy is actually a horse who's sometimes in frog's clothing.

Nor did he realize that said leopard, aka his sweet lap cat Paris, could vocally lobby people to do her bidding in a way more complicated than *pats* or *food, please*. Ever since he heard her yowl in the background of the call from Elle and then gave Savvy's friends his parents' address, he can't sit still. Because the thing he is certain about is that familiars are bonded with their witches. If Paris is freaking out, there's a reason and it has something to do with Savvy.

Who isn't answering his calls. Or her friends', apparently. And who, Brie grudgingly reported, is invisible to locator spells at present.

Big Rob is currently seated at one of the consoles and has already found Melissa the Gorgon, aka @ModernMedusa (she's internet famous—who knew?), tracked down her address, and hacked into the security system of her (very posh) building.

Savvy wasn't seen going in—figures—but Rob caught some brief glitches in footage outside a window that the blueprints and rental records told him should belong to Melissa. A large enough disturbance that it would account for two people leaving by air.

Diego and Quinn have gone to check it out in person, making sure the freelancers spotted them leaving—so they wouldn't follow, but stay put for now where Griffin is. If they attack the house, Big Rob and his dad have set up a nice surprise from the roof, where Jacob is concealed and ready to take them out.

Griffin is a bundle of barely contained nerves waiting for the arrival of the witches and his cat. They're the best lead he has on finding Savvy.

His phone buzzes and he unlocks it.

No one's here, but the windows are open. And there's a bunch of leftover sushi—ok to consume?

Griffin bites back a growl of frustration and ignores the question. Only Diego would want to risk food poisoning at a time like this.

Get back here. I might need you.

The door to this room—like Griffin's at his and Savvy's house—is concealed by a seemingly ordinary bookshelf. They've left it open. Footsteps sound on the stairs, and then an enormous Paris streaks into the room, circling Griffin in obvious distress. He rubs her giant cheeks. "It's okay, we're going to find her."

Brie and Elle are not far behind her, trailed by Jacob. "Anything?" Brie asks.

"We think she left with Melissa the Gorgon, but they were hidden from the cameras."

"Why did you let her go confab with a necromancer again?" Brie's hand is on her hip.

"For the last time, you know Savvy as well as I do—I didn't let her do anything. She was insistent this was the best way for her to find Mother Circe." *But I should have stopped her from going alone. I made a huge mistake. And I'm afraid she's paying for it.*

Paris steps in between Griffin and Brie and says, *"Yowl."*

Which Griffin interprets as: *We do not have time for this.*

"Paris, can you find her?" Griffin asks.

Paris bobs her head up and down in an unmistakable yes.

"I hate to be the voice of reason," Big Rob says, "but how is that going to work without causing the greater Atlanta area to lose their entire minds? You can't traipse around town with a loose leopard."

Paris levels a stare at Big Rob and then transforms into a small cat in front of him. He gapes. "Oh. Okay. Did we know . . ."

Griffin shakes his head. "We did not, not until yesterday. Familiars also use glamours."

"Huh," Big Rob says. He scoots out from the console and stands to offer his hand to Elle and Brie. "I'm Rob."

Brie crosses her arms, but Elle shakes. "Elle, and this is Brie. Why weren't you in the wedding party?"

"On duty."

Griffin has his own theory about how Paris can lead him to Savvy. So, first things first. . . . "Looks like they left through a window. I'm going to need to be able to fly with Paris to look for her."

"Ahahaha, no," Brie says. "How would you?"

They don't have time for this. "Brie, I know you're not my biggest fan—"

"Putting it mildly. If my girl is hurt then I blame—"

Jackie chooses that moment to enter, shutting everyone up. The secret room is getting crowded. She has a tray of cheese and crackers. "Snacks," she says. "Any word from Savvy?" She pauses. "Because I would hate to think you're down here bickering while she needs you. All of you."

Direct hit. Wow. Even Brie has a chastened moment.

His mother's presence makes Griffin ask a new question. "Has anyone talked to Claudia?"

He's asking Brie and Elle, obviously. "Not since the big interruption earlier," Brie admits. "She is not going to be happy." She grins. "*You* should definitely call her."

Great. Claudia tolerates Griffin at best. She has never been a fan of him as right for her daughter. Not that he has the impression she'd find any man right for her daughter; according to Savvy, her father is only known to her as "the mistake." If anything, Claudia will be more convinced than ever that Griffin is one too.

But desperate times, desperate measures. She might have an idea where Circe is so he can narrow down where to start looking. His mother gives him an encouraging nod.

He turns his back on Brie, takes out his phone, and dials her. Nothing.

"You want to try?" he asks Brie.

Brie nods and pulls a locket—similar to the one Savvy wears—from beneath the neck of her pink T-shirt and grips it, concentrating.

They wait.

"She's not answering," Brie says.

"Try Auntie Simone," Elle puts in.

"Good idea," Brie says.

The locket glows brighter and then Auntie Simone's face hovers in the air in front of Brie.

"Whoa," Big Rob says, "that is cool."

"What is it?" Auntie Simone takes in Griffin and Brie. "Where is Savvy?"

"She went to find Mother Circe," Griffin said. "Do you know where she is?"

"Alone?" Auntie Simone frowns and shakes her head. "Claudia went to meet with Circe."

"Why?" Brie butts in.

"I didn't agree with her," Auntie Simone says. "She thinks she can make a deal."

Griffin's mind races. Surely Claudia wouldn't let anything happen to Savvy, but . . .

"Can you tell where Claudia is?" he asks.

The witches all look at one another. "She'll know if I do a locator spell," Simone says. "It's . . . not something witches do to each other except in extreme circumstances."

Paris chooses that moment to *YOWL* again.

"The circumstances *are* extreme," Griffin says. "Please? I have to find Savvy. Paris is upset—something's wrong."

Brie nods. "Do it. Savvy has some sort of ward up. I can't find her—and we think she's with Melissa the Gorgon."

Auntie Simone's eyes go wide at that. "All right. Give me a few minutes."

Her visage disappears, and Griffin starts to pace, as much as he can in the crowded room. "How long will this take?"

He's afraid it will be longer than Savvy has. Everyone else must be picking up on his vibes *or* they are as worried as he is. Neither is a comfort.

The tense wait finally comes to an end when Brie's locket glows and she holds it up. Auntie Simone appears in front of them again. "I can give you about a square mile to search—she was moving. It's woods."

Brie's phone pings and she takes it out. "I've got the pin."

Big Rob whistles. "You can do geographical coordinates? That is so rad."

Griffin waves to Brie. "Send it to me—I'm going to get Savvy."

"We're coming with you," Brie says, and motions to Elle.

"No," Griffin says. "You stay here. The more people out there, the more ways it can go sideways."

Elle seems to be considering his point.

"But—" Brie starts.

Griffin makes her meet his eyes. "I promise you I'll bring Savvy back." Paris stalks over and paws Griffin's leg. "And I'll take Paris."

Brie hesitates. "Okay, but if you *don't* bring her back, you're done for."

He couldn't agree more. He has to do this.

Griffin turns to his dad. "You still have a four-wheeler around here?"

Griffin gets in the loaded-up pickup truck in his parents' garage. He has a rough area of where to start, a hapless-regular-hunter disguise, and Paris to assist. This is an extraction. He meant what he said. If he went in with too many people, nothing good would come of it.

Paris nudges his elbow with her head, once, twice as they get ready to leave the garage. *Here we go.*

As he pulls out in the truck, two freelancers leave their posts up the street, stalking his way. The man in the black cloak and the Slasher with his messed-up face. Griffin lifts a hand to wave to them, and the distraction is all Jacob needs to hit the Slasher with his nullifying ray. He goes down, the black-cloaked man looking alarmed as Roman stalks across the yard toward them.

"No one's following us to your mama," Griffin says, and guns the motor.

He drives fast, gritting his teeth, worried, for a thirty-minute haul outside the city and off the interstate onto county roads to the area Auntie Simone told him about. Forest surrounds them on both sides of rolling hills.

Best-case scenario, Savvy is relatively easy for him and Paris to find and bring home. Worst, he makes his last stand here. But it'll be worth it, because it's for her.

He shouldn't have tried to protect her from the book. She didn't need that—she needed the truth. More, he should never have let her push him away. Not when he believes the only shot they have at getting through this is together. It's the only way he *wants* to. What good is the future, if it can't be the two of them?

He has the beginnings of an idea about how that might be possible and he wants to share it with Savvy. Let them convince each other; then the rest of their world might follow.

He gets out and Paris jumps to follow. He shuts the door and walks back to release the gate on the back of the truck. Quickly, he lowers a ramp and then hops up and climbs on the ATV waiting in the bed. Brie, of course, made a fuss about how these things are bad for nature. It's the best option he has right now. A mountain bike is too slow.

The other reason he didn't want anyone else to come is that he doesn't fully trust Claudia. Hard to feel guilty when the feeling is so mutual. But Paris's encouraging reactions once they neared this spot reassure him that he's not on a wild witch chase.

The ATV roars to life, handles vibrating under his palms. Paris waits at the bottom of the ramp.

"Ready," he says. "Set, go."

Paris takes off into the forest and Griffin guns the motor, giving chase. He maneuvers through the trees and down the steep sloping hill, keeping Paris in sight. The leopard is booking it—although Paris is holding back on Griffin's account. She could go forty miles per hour, if she were running flat out. A fact courtesy of Big Rob.

He thinks he hears something, even over the growl of the motor, so he slows and cuts the engine for a second. Paris also stops short.

There it is. A tremendously loud *crash* in the distance somewhere ahead. Followed by another. Simone told him he'd know Mother Circe's place when he found it.

"What the hell is that?"

Paris looks at him as the sound repeats, then turns and heads toward it. The big cat pauses to checks that Griffin is behind her.

Fine, guess we're going toward that sound.

"Lead on," he says, and marvels that talking to a shapeshifting black leopard now seems normal. It's an encouraging sign. He's adjusting. He just needs Savvy to. He restarts the ATV and gives it gas.

They both speed up as they continue. The crashes get closer and closer, plainly audible over the loud rumble of his vehicle.

He wonders at what point the thing doing the crashing is going to hear *him*.

He's trying to decide when to cut the engine and proceed on foot when Paris pulls up short and makes the loud sawing sound that's her roar. That settles that. He chokes the ATV and leaps off it, jogging to the big cat's side.

She is in a long, low, defensive crouch, continuing with her sawing call. A warning. *My territory.*

Griffin searches ahead through the trees and—

There's a familiar silhouette. For a moment, his hopes soar. Snakes weave through the air around Melissa the Gorgon's head, some sort of living nightmare halo.

"Where's Savvy?" he demands.

One of the snakes strikes at the air. "Could you be any louder? Why not just bring a parade with you?" Melissa glances at Paris. "No offense. *You're* fine."

Griffin needs to know Savvy is okay. He has to. He stalks

forward, Paris shadowing him. "Go, find her," he tells Paris, and she doesn't need to hear it twice. She vaults ahead, around Melissa, and deeper into the trees.

"Where is she?" Griffin asks again. "Why isn't she with you? Did you do something to her?"

"God, why should I answer anything?" She huffs. "You won't believe me."

Griffin inhales deeply, lets it out. Otherwise, he's going to lose his shit. "You should answer because if Savvy's not all right, I'm responsible. But I'll need someone to take it out on."

Melissa sniffs. "Oh, big bad hunter. I'm shaking." She holds out her hands, palms up, calling shadows to them. "Try me."

This is a distraction. Much as it might feel nice to indulge in some fighting, burn off some of the anxious fear inside him, it's meaningless unless it gets him to Savvy. "I don't have time to waste. Where is she?"

Melissa rolls her eyes and nods her head back. "I mean, duh, her cat went that way. I thought you were supposed to be smart."

Enough of this. Griffin sets off, striding right past her. To his amazement, she follows him. "She didn't call for you. She's got this. She'll be fine."

The undercurrent of doubt in Melissa's tone kicks his worry into overdrive. He wants to shout for Savvy, but he assumes she's in stealth mode. She won't be happy if he alerts someone else to her presence.

"You really are desperate for her, aren't you?" Melissa says it like this is news.

Griffin doesn't dignify it with an answer.

She laughs. "I never would've believed it. A hunter and a witch. Jesus, you should have a reality show."

She would say that, given her online presence. "We like to keep a lower profile, @ModernMedusa. We're not performers."

Her snakes wag around her in an offended halo. "It's a living. You know, Savvy's a lot less judgmental than you." She snarls. "I can't believe I just said that."

Griffin speeds up, puts some distance between him and Melissa. He's scanning ahead when Paris's sawing call reaches him. Is Savvy in trouble?

And that's it, the end of his rope. He runs.

27

✦ ✦ ✦

Savvy

Savvy can't believe it. It's not possible. The fact that she's entertaining the idea that her own mother would betray her says everything about her training. But not about her *heart*. Her heart would break yet again.

Her mother stares at her through the window. Savvy searches and finds the protections she and Melissa cast dispelling.

Savvy drops back to the ground and searches for Melissa. She's gone.

"Melissa?" she calls softly. Nothing.

Knew I shouldn't have trusted her. But that's not true. She thought the two of them were making progress toward an odd friendship.

Savvy is learning a lot of things about herself, none of them pleasant.

She looks up and Cretin is now perched on the windowsill where she hovered moments before, staring down at her. Instead of inside with his mistress. Only her mother will get the benefit of Cretin's senses, but she can't swear that's not a big deal.

Nothing to do but get out of here, stat.

She climbs onto her broom. She'll fly low until she's clear of the hut and then head above the trees.

She makes it a dozen yards before she spots a dark shape heading straight at her, low, and braces for an attack. Until recognition flows between them. Paris.

Her heart pounds in her chest. What does it mean? Why is Paris here?

She lands and waits. Paris reaches her and stands up to place her huge paws on Savvy's shoulders. Savvy's eyes sting. So she isn't entirely alone.

"How?" she whispers.

Paris puts her paws down and crooks her head for Savvy to follow. They travel fast through the trees, Paris on a mission. Eventually, they're greeted by breaking branches that indicate someone else coming toward them.

Griffin appears like a mirage. A tall drink of water in a desert. Her hunter in the middle of the forest, clearly hunting for *her*. Less than a quarter mile away from Mother Circe's chicken-legged hut, here's her love.

She should be offended he assumed she'd need his help. Her heart doesn't care. It only cares that maybe she hasn't lost her last chance after all.

"Looking for someone?" Savvy asks breathlessly.

Griffin's relief is written on his dirt-streaked face. "Paris thought you might need backup."

"Good girl," Savvy says, and gives her familiar a scratch behind one soft ear.

Griffin walks all the way to Savvy, eyes pinned on her as if she's the only thing he's ever wanted to see in his life. It's beyond sexy and, ridiculous as it is, here, now, with everything that's going on, she presses her thighs together.

"Until this is over, we stick together," he says.

She's cautious. She knows what she has to lose. *Everything, and my heart.* "If it makes sense," she says.

"It's the only thing that makes sense." Griffin comes even closer. "Some things are negotiable. This isn't. You'll understand why soon enough, but just promise me."

"I'll do my best." He has no clue what she's confirmed, that the Butcher and Circe are working together. Still. That maybe her mother is in league with them.

Melissa stomps out of the woods then, awkwardly carrying her broom. "You're alive," she says to Savvy. "Good."

When Savvy raises a brow at her, she says, "Dead people can't keep their promises."

"She's not wrong," Griffin says. He lifts his hand to stroke it up and down Savvy's arm as if confirming she's real and unhurt.

"We better get out of here," Savvy says. "Mother Circe didn't see me, but—"

"But your mother did." Claudia *tsks* as she descends from above them. Cretin sits on the end of her broom. "What were you thinking coming here? She wants you dead."

Savvy's mouth opens and closes while she tries to settle on an answer.

"Claudia," Griffin says, "why are *you* here? Why didn't you answer when we called you?"

Claudia shrugs. "Like I'd leave something this important to chance. You got Simone to find me anyway, I take it."

"Yes." Griffin speaks to Savvy. "So that I could find *you*." Then, to Claudia: "I'm not here by chance, I'm a highly trained operative and I had Paris with me."

"Bless your heart," Claudia says.

Griffin and Savvy exchange a look. "Ouch," Savvy murmurs. "Seriously, Mom, what are you doing out here?"

Claudia hops off her broom until she's right beside Savvy and Griffin. She waves her hand to indicate how close they're standing. Savvy hadn't realized. She doesn't move.

"What were you doing?" Savvy asks her again. "I want an answer."

"Showing up for my daughter. And it's a good thing I did. Were you going to do something stupid like make yourself known to her?"

Savvy stands her ground. "Did you know *he'd* be there? Did you know about the two of them?"

"He who?" Griffin asks.

"The Butcher," Savvy and Claudia say in unison.

Claudia sighs. "Oh, honey, we can't get into it on this mountainside. She's far too close." She looks at Melissa. "You're back."

So she *did* know Melissa was sent away. Savvy files that away.

Claudia's next words are to all of them: "Let's get out of here."

"We're going to my parents'," Griffin says, and his tone makes it clear this isn't up for discussion or Claudia's approval. "Is it okay to leave my vehicles out here? I don't want to be the breadcrumbs that lead the bad witch back to us."

"I don't think Circe cares about going four-wheeling," Melissa says. "Should be fine."

Savvy boggles. Griffin came on an honest-to-god rescue mission for her. It makes her feel . . . toasty warm. Like she's wrapped in his arms. Like maybe she's not alone after all.

She suspects her mother is still holding information back. *Not for long.*

"Fine." Savvy makes a face and flirts with Griffin. "I suppose that means you're flying with me."

His hair is messy, and she knows he's been running his fingers through it. *Worried for me.*

"I like flying with you," he says.

"You do?" Savvy is surprised. "It doesn't freak you out? Because *eeeevil* witches fly?"

Griffin makes a big show of looking around, high, low, behind Savvy and up into the air. Then right at her. "I don't see any."

"You always were smooth," she says.

"Now that's a lie, and we both know it."

Savvy has almost forgotten about their company until Melissa snorts. "God, get a room," she says.

"Give me a ride?" Griffin asks.

Savvy's insides, outsides, everysides melt at the words. *Yes.* "Get on."

She mounts her broom and he climbs on behind her. "For the record," he says into her ear, "I didn't just mean this flight."

Her irritatingly soft heart races and she has to keep herself from saying, *Yes, please,* out loud.

Paris shrinks down and delicately takes her usual spot in front. Savvy angles them upward into the sky, following her mother, dodging Melissa and her erratic broomhandling.

Wonders will apparently never cease.

Savvy wishes she'd stopped to ask why they're headed to Griffin's parents' house. Won't Jackie be reeling from all the revelations from the wedding, still? And she's noticed Brie isn't calling her anymore.

So she shouldn't be surprised at the horde that greets them, rushing out the front door onto the lawn—which has a patch of black, smoking ground in the center—to surround them with relieved smiles and good cheer. But she is.

Tears threaten again, and she breathes them away. She shrinks down her broom and stashes it, and Griffin slides his hand into hers. She leaves it there. She needs steadying. Sensing it, Paris rubs her small cat body against her legs.

In front of Savvy: Brie and Elle; Griffin's entire family, including his mom; Big Rob; Diego; *and* Auntie Simone.

Diego jumps forward, holding out one of those hunter Tasers. "I'll take out the necromancer!"

Oh no.

Griffin speaks before she can. "That won't be necessary. Melissa is a . . ."

"Friend," Savvy supplies. She nods to her, and Melissa nods back, with no snarky comment.

Brie reaches forward and plucks the Taser from an outraged Diego's hand. "I'll just hold on to this."

"She can't do that, can she?" Diego asks seemingly anyone.

Jackie pats his shoulder. After which she steps forward, opens her arms, and says, "Savvy, come here."

Savvy hesitates only briefly before diving forward to accept the hug. Jackie strokes her hair as if she's a little girl. "I'm so glad you're all right," she says to Savvy.

"She's *my* daughter," Claudia says. "Of course she's all right."

Savvy can't help laughing. Only *her* mom would feel competitive over a hug. "Love you, Mom," she tosses back over her shoulder. Though she still has lots of questions for her.

"I hope she'll be my daughter too," Jackie says.

Savvy wants to ask, *You do? Isn't that still impossible? I want it to be possible.*

She pulls back and turns to Griffin. "I know we all have a lot to discuss, but Griffin, can we talk first?"

The crowd that would usually protest—anything, literally anything—stays quiet for once.

Griffin nods and steps forward, takes her hand, and leads her inside. They don't speak as they head upstairs. Griffin's parents' house is a suburban castle, tastefully decorated but with whimsical touches from his mother's taste in art and eye for color. Photos of Griffin and his brothers and the grinning Carters dot the walls in the upper hallway.

Savvy's had the full tour, and so she knows where they're going: Griffin's childhood bedroom. Third door on the left. She begins to marshal her arguments. She wants to clear up any misunderstandings, especially the ones of her own making. He came for her, and that has to mean something—that he cares for her enough to want to see this through.

But she isn't used to putting herself out there. Griffin is the only person she *wants* to know all of her, and that has worked out *so* well thus far.

The bedroom is a study in teen Griffin. Academic trophies. Instead of rock-band posters on the walls, old maps of foreign countries and surrounding counties. Telling, in retrospect. Shelves lined with books on esoteric subjects he laughingly dismissed to her as his Dungeons & Dragons–phase fodder.

They stand silently inside the door for a second, not facing each other, but looking at the room as if it's a fascinating chasm and they are on its brink.

Savvy pivots so she's facing Griffin. She should be looking at him for this. Not to mention, his face is such a nice view.

"I—" he starts in an argumentative tone.

"Wait." She puts her fingers on his lips. They soften, something like the whisper of a kiss against her fingertips. "I need to say something."

She removes her hand.

"Okay, but . . ."

She gives him a commanding look that says, *I'm talking now.* He nods for her to continue.

"I haven't always been honest, not just with you, but with myself. There was part of me, when this blew up . . . I know you're aware I never planned to get married. I always figured I'd be fine on my own. I had everything I needed. I was raised to believe that. My mom passed her old hurt on to me. And I just took it."

She can tell he wants to argue. It must be killing him to stay quiet, but he does. It's not easy for her to be so open and talk emotions—risk emotions—and yet, she has to.

"In the woods, I realized something . . . devastating. That I almost decided to let you go, to go back to believing that, even though I always secretly wanted love. Before we met, I always made myself believe that it was enough to have a job I loved, and that was important to me. I believed in that first. I made a mistake. I want to live my life so it's about who I can give all of my heart to. Who I would do anything for. And it's not just the job." She swallows. Here it is. "I realized I want the truth *for us*. I'm willing to fight for us. Even though I still don't understand how it can work out, with everything against us and . . ."

"Savvy, when I thought I might have lost you . . . I couldn't deal with it. I messed up, with the book, not telling you. I was an idiot who thought I needed to protect you from something I didn't. But you have to know . . . I'd fight the whole goddamn world for you."

Her heart flutters in her chest, butterflies in her belly. "You would?"

Griffin's mouth quirks up on one side. "Well, after this."

He reaches out and pulls her flush against him and they crash into each other, mouths colliding, hearts too. Promises in each kiss. Savvy pulls back, despite not wanting to.

"Griffin, we don't have time."

"We have time." He bends and sweeps her up into his arms. She has never felt hotter or safer than at this moment.

"Well, if you say so." She grins. "I love you, professor."

"And I love you, goddess."

"Show me."

He deposits her on the bed and she scoots back to make room for him. She slides her hand between them to find his cock hard and ready through the fabric of his pants. For her. Only for her.

He unbuttons her jeans and helps her shuck them down and off.

She has a thought. "Did you lock the door?"

"No one in this house is stupid enough to disturb us right now."

"Your turn." She helps him get his pants off, and after some fumbling with the far too many snaps and Velcros on his vest, that too. Skin is necessary. So necessary.

He makes a feast of her with his eyes and then lowers to take one nipple in his mouth, his hand cupping the fullness of her other breast. He sucks hard and she moans. He slides his hand down and cradles her pussy, sliding one finger inside, then another. "Meant for me."

"I need you inside me. Now."

He makes a noise that has to be agreement, but something occurs to her fevered brain. "I promised you a ride."

"I might die, but I'll deny you nothing." He flips onto his back and she straddles him, and at another moment she might tease him. She might go slow. She might try to kill him and make sure he dies happy.

This is not that moment. She needs him. He needs her.

She positions herself, holding his cock, and then sinks down and down until he's filling her up. His hands cup her ass.

The awed expression on his face and the sensation as he thrusts up into her is almost too much. They rock together in a symphony. There's nothing except this, them. He fucks up into her and she meets every move of his hips with a roll of her own. The stars show up behind her eyes quickly, she's so close.

He flips her beneath him and grinds into her, two fingers between them on her clit. "That's it, come for me. Come for me."

She holds nothing back, a scream that she doesn't care if anyone hears, the stars for both of them, the thunder of her heartbeat in her ears. Griffin roars and thrusts into her one last time, right there with her. They breathe, just breathe, recovering.

He props himself up on his forearms and gazes at her. She

leans up to kiss him. This man she loves. She drags in a breath, releases it.

"We better go to work," she says.

"About that," he says, still panting. "I have an idea."

Two Months Ago

28

✦ ✦ ✦

The Goddess and the Professor

Griffin was early, so he's already well settled into their usual corner table at their favorite taco place. Strands of hot pepper–shaped lights line the tops of the walls, and there are already two margaritas—rocks, salt—on the table. One for him, one for Savvy. He's even ordered already, because Savvy texted him to, since *she's* running ten minutes late.

You know what I want, she wrote.

He hopes he does. And he considers ordering a shot of tequila, in case he's wrong. Sipping this margarita is doing nothing for his rare case of nerves. He's confident in his decision, so it's not that. He knows Savvy will love the vintage ring he's picked out to pop the question, small diamonds around an elegant emerald in an antique gold setting. Lovely and understated. Nothing in the jewelry department could compete with the woman who's going to wear it, so why try? He knows all that, but . . .

He *also* knows she's been honest about the fact that, before they met, she didn't see herself as a long-term-relationship person. She'd never envisioned any version of the proverbial white picket fence. Or the big wedding. "Hashtag crone life, hashtag spinsterville," she'd joked early on, with a serious undercurrent.

But then she invited him to move in with her, and their lives have blended better than he could have imagined. This might seem fast from the outside, less than a year in, but he feels in his bones that they are right together. He doesn't want to wait to make it forever, and he thinks—hopes, prays—Savvy will agree.

Griffin has always figured he'd have a family of his own, but the outlines were fuzzy. He could never quite picture who would be standing beside him. At least not in the same detail with which he could picture his future with H.U.N.T.E.R.

When he thinks of the future now, it's Savvy first, before anything else. Which frightens him, especially since he'll have to continue to hide a large part of his life. It doesn't seem possible to have a solid relationship that lasts forever built on such a fundamental lie, but . . . there's his parents. If this is the only way he and Savvy can be together, he'll make it work.

He'll pray his guilt doesn't eat away at their happiness. Because Savvy deserves happiness. She deserves his whole self, and that he can't give it to her is a thing he'll just have to live with. . . . Somehow.

She rushes through the door then in jeans and a T-shirt, still the most glorious sight of his day, and he straightens. She greets their waiter, coincidentally headed to the table with their order. She dumps her purse in the empty chair next to Griffin, leans down to give him a quick kiss, then settles into the chair across from him.

"Sorry," she says. "I had to go out to the Farmhouse, and my mom took the opportunity to neg our relationship yet again."

The waiter slides three racks with three varieties of taco between them, along with the appropriate salsas, and plates for each of them.

"But you can't argue that I have perfect timing." Savvy selects a taco right away, smiling.

He can't. It's true. In fact, he decides then and there, she's perfect, period. He reaches into his jacket pocket and pulls out the box.

Savvy wasn't sure she'd make it to dinner. Not after being called out to the Farmhouse to help find a fox familiar-in-training that got lost in the woods. It turns out that Paris has a nose for tracking.

Then her mom took yet another chance to tell her that she shouldn't be wasting her time on a relationship that can never work, despite the fact that Savvy is happy in it. She loves Griffin, more every day. So she shakes off her mother's downer take and grabs a taco.

She's fairly certain she got the worst of the leaves out of her hair and dirt off her jeans. She's already taken the first bite of her carnitas taco—heaven must be wrapped in a corn tortilla—when she notices how Griffin's looking at her.

Damn. "Do I have something on my face?" she asks, and swallows. "Sorry, I'm starving. I had to help out at the rescue. One of the, um, animals in rehab ran into the forest. All hands on deck."

"Your mother asks an awful lot of you," Griffin says. "How is that PR?"

She shrugs. "Other duties as required."

"There's just a little . . ." He reaches over and plucks a leaf from the side of her head.

"Oops," she says, and he smiles at her. But it's not a taco-night, easy smile.

He seems . . . not quite her normal Griffin. She hates lying to him. Maybe he's picked up on that. Probably not, though. She's an exceptional liar. You have to be in order to be a good C.R.O.N.E. agent. Usually, she's proud of all those assets. With Griffin, she regrets that one, while recognizing it's the only reason they can be together.

He clears his throat.

She sets down the taco. "Okay, you're scaring me. What's up?"

He shakes his head, his strong, masculine jaw tight. "Nothing to be scared about. I hope."

He hopes? "Griffin, out with it."

"Okay, if you insist. . . ." He brings his right hand from un-der the table, holding a small box in it. "I had a whole romantic speech, but you . . . you're *you* and I'm both nervous and also can't wait to share this with you. I wish I could share everything with you. I know we've been together less than a year, but . . ." He opens the small case with his other hand. There's a ring in it, sitting pretty in the velvet.

She blinks at it wide-eyed, then at him.

"Savannah Wilde, will you marry me?"

She runs through all the reasons this is a terrible idea. There are a lot of them. How could it not be a disaster? Then, she pauses. . . .

It's Griffin. Griffin across their favorite table at their favorite weeknight dinner place. The person who made the missing-something feeling go away. And he's offering to make it forever.

This is what she wants, *who* she wants. It's what she's always wanted, but never dared to dream would happen.

"You're proposing to me at taco night?" Savvy asks. Before he can answer, she says, "Yes!" And then louder, to the entire restaurant, she calls out, "She said yes!"

"I think that's my line." Griffin cracks up and so does she as they both get up for a kiss. He spins her around in his arms. The people around them cheer.

"You know what? Let's do it as soon as possible," Savvy says. "This will *have* to shut my mom up."

"The sooner, the better," Griffin says, and Savvy leans into another kiss.

Hot damn.

She said *yes* to him. This will be an adventure.

Now

29

✦ ✦ ✦

Griffin

Griffin tugs his shirt back over his head, then tosses Savvy her jeans. She catches them easily. He'd give anything to extend this interlude, but they can't—they've stolen as much time as possible.

But that's all right, because they're fighting for each other. To be together.

And, if he has his way, to fix the barriers set up to keep them apart. He's already outlined the broad strokes of his theory about the past.

"So the signing ceremony was also a secret compact?" Savvy asks, and shimmies into her pants.

"That's what I think after reading Diana's take."

"Diana?"

"It was her journal. She was barely into adulthood. She and the hunter we saw die weren't supposed to bring weapons or defend themselves. It was obviously meant to be a sacrifice from the start."

Savvy finishes dressing. "The Butcher and Circe seemed chummy today. Which figures, if they've *always* been working together."

"Or at least for the last three hundred and thirty years. You still have the quill, right?"

"Of course."

A knock sounds at the door.

Savvy raises her brows at him. "We really must have been gone for a while."

"Or I gave them too much credit." He lingers for a last moment alone with her. One more kiss, a gentle meeting of their lips. Savvy is still his. That means they have to get through this.

"Ready?" he asks her.

She nods.

Another knock sounds, and Griffin opens the door to his bedroom. Diego stands in the hall, eyes averted. "I told them we shouldn't hurry you, but Savvy's mother is getting antsy and that woman is *a lot*. . . ."

"Diego," Griffin warns.

"Oh, come on," Savvy puts in. "We both know it's true."

Diego looks up, given tacit permission, and gives Savvy a thumbs-up. "I knew you'd get back together."

Griffin snorts. "You did, huh? What was all that earlier then?"

"Ah, I was just being supportive," he says. "Speaking of, Big Rob says we have more company out there, even after Jacob and Roman took care of the first two. At least they're not coming en masse. Different recovery times—you have the necromancer to thank for that. Words I never thought I'd say," he grumbles. "Anyway, there's also food."

"Did you say food?" Savvy perks up and sails past Griffin into the hallway. "And we're plotting our next moves? Two of my favorite things." She pauses to kiss Diego on the cheek. "Thanks for the support."

Diego puts his hand on the spot and Griffin resists the urge to punch him. Or to explain exactly how his support manifested itself.

Paris meets them at the bottom of the stairs.

They find everyone—even Big Rob, whom Griffin would expect to be glued to a computer in the basement—in the kitchen. Familiars perch on or sit behind their witches, in various states of glamour or none. Auntie Simone is holding a black-and-white-feathered chicken in her lap. The table itself houses an eclectic spread that is probably the result of every menu in his parents' takeout-night drawer.

"Tacos?" Savvy asks hopefully.

Brie lifts both hands into the air and then points in front of her. "Over here."

Savvy grabs a plate and loads it up with food, sinks into a chair Brie's been saving for her. Griffin will do the same in a moment. You don't skip meals before a big mission. And this is going to be the biggest of his life.

Claudia is sitting at the island instead of the table, her huge raven and Melissa the Gorgon alongside her. The raven is side-eyeing the hair snakes. "I don't suppose anyone has a plan," Claudia says.

Auntie Simone shushes her. "Claudia, just wait."

"I have a question, Mom," Savvy says. "One you haven't answered. Did you know about the Butcher and Circe?"

Her mother frowns. "What do you mean? I asked for a meeting between them in the hope of peacemaking. They refused to budge and I went on my way to find you."

Hmmm . . . Griffin jumps in. "And—leaving aside me and Savvy—how would you feel if you found out they were conspirators? That they have been since the beginning—all the way back to Salem?"

Claudia rises. She cuts an intimidating figure, sparkling jumpsuit and all. "Well, I could never leave aside my daughter, but no matter what the circumstances, if I found out something like that I'd be . . ." She tilts her face, considering, impeccably glam makeup in place. "Apoplectic."

"I was hoping you'd say that." Griffin goes to stand behind the chair Savvy's in. "That's exactly what we believe. The accords might have been legitimate, but it was also a blood sacrifice—Circe forced a witch and a hunter to kill each other, while they both watched. Near as we can figure, we're meant to be some sort of repeat of that. I don't know why they didn't come for us directly, but . . . I don't plan to pay back that favor." Griffin pauses. "No one here is on the hook to do anything more. Savvy and I have a strategy to get us out of this, and we'd love help from any of you willing. But we understand if your vows to your respective organizations are too strong to break."

The room is quiet enough to hear a grenade pin drop.

Everyone starts talking at once.

"Of course—"

"Your brothers are—"

"Tell us what to do."

Roman motions for silence. "Of course everyone here is in, yes?" He waits as the nods go around the table. "What do you have in mind?"

Griffin lifts a hand. "Let's call it forced retirement. For both of them. Then, if it works, we do things differently going forward." No one protests. He wasn't positive that would be the case. A good omen. "First things first, we get the both of them where we have a home-court advantage."

"The Farmhouse is best, if possible," Savvy says. Savvy asks Claudia, "Will the coven follow us or her?"

"Us," Auntie Simone cuts in, without hesitation. "What do you think we were discussing at the meeting? We may lose a few, but no one is going to butt in. They know you'd do the same for them."

Claudia nods.

Savvy's hand floats up to her heart. She's surprised and touched, he can tell. He needs to work on making it clear to her how amazing she is, and how much love she commands.

"Okay, we have some calls to make, then," Griffin says. "I'll take the Butcher, and Savvy, you've got Mother Circe."

"I think we need to do something first, and you're not going to like it," Savvy says with a wince.

Griffin knew this had gone too smoothly. "What is it?"

Savvy was incorrect. Griffin doesn't just not like this. He outright *loathes* it. When they've come so close to this moment in the recent past, it feels way too close for comfort. But he can't argue with Savvy's logic.

They're on the front lawn, unshielded, their friends either waiting on the sidewalk, in cars nearby, or inside—likely— peeking out the windows. The early-evening skies fit the melancholy scene.

The mercenaries up the street will be watching too, and hopefully report their movements. Quinn and Jacob left out the back door and are going to get the drop on them as soon as they make their calls and start to move on Griffin or Savvy.

"Farewell, Griffin," Savvy says, and reaches her hands out to him as if they're parting for one last time.

"I *hate* that it has to be this way," Griffin says, which is the complete truth.

"We just can't be together," Savvy says.

And, even knowing it's playacting, the words hurt, ugly to his ears.

"If only things were different . . ." Griffin says. The closest he can get to agreement. Because soon, very soon, they will be.

Savvy slides her cheek against his, stubbly because he hasn't shaved in two days. She gives him a searing kiss, licking her tongue into his mouth, and while he meets it with his own, that is entirely unfair. He wants to carry her up to his childhood bedroom and make love to her again.

Which she must know.

"See you soon," he murmurs into her ear. "And you'll pay for that later."

"Promises, promises," she whispers.

She pushes dramatically away and stalks across the yard toward her coven and their familiars. They're all on brooms, ready to depart. Paris is waiting patiently. Savvy hesitates and gives him one last, longing look back, then takes out her pocket broom, grows it, and climbs on. Paris hops in front of her and Griffin silently tries to send the cat a message: *Watch over her until I get there.*

The heartfelt fake parting for show is done.

His dad opens the front door. "Everything okay, son?" he asks.

Griffin watches until they fly out of sight. "It will be."

Savvy and her crew are going ahead to the Farmhouse. Griffin isn't happy about the separation, but he understands it's brief and will help bolster their chances of luring the Butcher and Circe to the same spot independent of each other. They might be less eager to cooperate if they think Griffin and Savvy—and their allies—are working together. They're assuming that the Butcher's and Circe's centuries of self-preservation instincts are still intact.

The command center downstairs will be Griffin's backdrop.

Once he's back inside, Griffin moves quickly. "Let's hurry," he says.

There are too many variables at play for Griffin's liking. But they need to outmaneuver the Butcher and Circe and so it's all or nothing.

"How you feeling?" Roman asks as the two of them head down into the basement.

"Like I should be by her side, even now."

"You will be, just a little while longer. Griff . . . I'm so proud of you."

Griffin pauses. "You are?"

"I am. You're making this something we can do with a clean

conscience—I know I'm ready to atone for taking orders from that bastard." He sighs. "Imagine if your mother hadn't known. Or if she left me, because of his lying ass."

"I'd rather not," Griffin says.

"Yes, well, thank you, son."

Griffin has to swallow against emotion. His dad is his first and biggest hero.

"Go time," his father says, and pats him on the back.

Griffin nods, and they enter the mini headquarters. Big Rob and Diego are waiting—Big Rob because he's in charge of the call, Diego because he isn't good at following orders. Quinn and Jacob will meet them back upstairs in the garage once their freelancer sweep up is done.

Griffin takes the console seat. He has the journal in front of him, carefully out of sight. Roman wanted a look at it before, while they were loading up on gear and weaponry. "Call him," Griffin says.

Big Rob brings up the video call, and everyone else stays carefully out of sight.

The Butcher is in a home library when he answers, weapons hanging on the wall behind him. Griffin wouldn't have figured him for a reader. Or, for that matter, someone who uses his own weapons. What's on the walls and shelves around him are probably those hollow books interior designers use and replica armaments.

"You," the Butcher says. "Have you killed the witch?"

A muscle in Griffin's jaw is so tight it jumps, but he manages to keep his tone even. "No," he says. "But you'll call off the hunt on me, permanently."

The Butcher scoffs. "Why would I do that? You can't even be a good soldier. A shame. Your father's a good man, always toes the line."

Griffin can imagine that Roman's head is about to explode now too. Taking this man down is going to be an extremely satisfying endeavor.

He holds up the journal. "Well, I've seen evidence of your collusion with Mother Circe. At their Farmhouse. I've parted ways with Savannah, but I don't think many of our operatives would be thrilled to learn about your working *with* our enemy all these years."

"You upstart, you think with your prick—"

Griffin leans back. "You know what? Forget what I said. I'll just head there and reveal it all anyway. Then you'll be the one dealing with assassins."

There's an outraged roar as Griffin makes a slashing sign across his neck and Big Rob cuts the feed.

"You think he'll go for it?" he asks his father.

"I think he's already yelling for his private security to get ready for an expedition."

"Then let's hit it," Griffin says, and gets up. "We need to make it there first."

✦ ✦ ✦

30

Savvy

L anding at the Farmhouse is surreal. With the upheaval of the past day and a half, it seems strangely calm. Like any ordinary day when Savvy shows up to visit—if anything, quieter. A few familiars toddle around outside, mostly dogs and cats, though she spots a possum and raccoon pair that are going to be nigh impossible to separate.

The other witchkin must be going about their business. Of course, they had no warning of Savvy's return. The only formal heads-up from her mom went to the minders of the children, to keep them safely over on the school grounds and away from the Farmhouse. They're going to continue to do this on the fly, so to speak.

Saying goodbye to Griffin, even as pretend, took more effort than it should have.

That's why we're doing this. So you don't have to for real.

Savvy spins around to take the peace in. Time to disturb it.

Her mother, Auntie Simone, Elle, Brie, and Melissa cluster around her. "Let's call her," she says.

"Out here?" her mother asks.

"As good a place as any. I want it clear where I am. This'll save us the time of locating the Spellbindery again."

"The house may have divided loyalties," Auntie Simone says.

Savvy doesn't think so, after how cooperative it was for her and Griffin. But Auntie Simone knows its bones and heart better than she does. Her familiar Orange has grown back to

ostrich form, taller than any of them—meaner too—her shadow
falling partially over her mistress.

"Can I be with you? For the call?" Melissa asks. It must be
deeply odd for her to be back here, for the first time in more
than a decade.

"No," Savvy says, and adds, before Melissa can be hurt,
"None of you should be. I want her to think she's only coming
to face off against me."

"Sweetie, are you set on all this?" Claudia asks. "I didn't
want to bring it up in front of *them,* but . . . there's no going
back from this. For any of us."

"Why would we want to?" Brie asks. "It's been lies all the
way down."

"What Brie said." Savvy frowns. "We're in this with *them.*"

"Okay, I just wanted to make sure." Claudia sniffs. "Someone has to voice every side."

"My decision is made." Savvy exchanges a glance with Brie
and Elle, who nod agreement. "Remember, stay over there,"
she says, and steps out of the group to face them with the Farmhouse behind her.

She takes her locket in her hand and finds the thread of energy connecting her to the rest of the coven. She tugs on it and
then envisions darkness, and it swirls into motion in the air in
front of her as she pictures the witch she's calling. And, finally,
out of the darkness, a vision resolves. Mother Circe, backlit dimly.

The crone wears the same dress she had on earlier, high-
necked and black, as if she's dressed for a funeral. For all Savvy
knows, she's still sitting at her table drinking tea with the man
who's supposed to be her enemy. Her mouth curls in distaste at
the sight of Savvy.

"I told your mother, no mercy," Circe says, which is some
opening. "You refuse to kill the hunter, you are as good as dead
to me. And yet, your insolence is boundless."

Savvy holds her spine straight. She won't shrink from this woman. "I know you intended us both as your sacrifices—the hunter and me. I know all about your real origin story."

"What are you talking about, child?"

"I'm not a child, I'm a witch—and I'm going to be known as the witch who brought your rule of our coven to a close. I know about Salem, about your partnership with the Butcher. The only thing I can't figure out is . . . why try to get us to kill each other now?" Savvy jerks her head behind her, indicating the Farmhouse. "After this little talk, I'll be calling everyone here to reveal the truth. Today. They deserve to know. Then we'll see who's as good as dead."

Mother Circe's mouth opens, and Savvy squeezes her hand around her locket and starts to drop the thread connecting them. Before she can, Mother Circe shifts so Savvy can see more of where she is.

It isn't her yaga hut after all. No, there's a line of shelves behind her. A round section of wall that Savvy recognizes.

She's in the Spellbindery.

"Now, now," Mother Circe says. "You must know I cannot let you do that."

Mother Circe lifts her hands, and the air flickers above her palms. Within seconds, fireballs hover over her hands.

"No, no," Savvy says, thinking fast. How did she know to come here? What Savvy intended?

It could've been someone from the other side—or . . . She looks at her friends in turn, then at Auntie Simone with her quiet patience, then at Melissa with her recent history of trying to kill Savvy. They're all as shocked as Savvy.

There's only one person who isn't. Savvy's body goes cold, her knees weaken, and then she looks at her mother. "Why?"

"Everything you've worked so hard for—everything *we* have," Claudia says defensively. "I couldn't let you risk destroying it all,

not when I know how strong she is. The both of them. She'll let
you go, I have a promise. . . . You would have given up everything
for him. They can never love us as much as we do them. Your
duty is to your sisters."

Savvy is shaking. "She would never let me go. And I don't
want to live without Griffin. I have to stop her. All you've done
is make it harder."

Savvy finds the core of her inner strength.

Auntie Simone pivots to Claudia. "What were you thinking?"

"Circe will destroy the evidence and then things will be all
right," Claudia insists. She is so stubborn. "I can't let Savvy be
hurt."

Savvy's not bothering to tell her that she and Griffin have the
evidence. The quill and the book are still in their possession—
good thing they didn't reveal that to Claudia before either. She
must have assumed they were planning to bluff.

An upper window blows out, glass shattering, smoke roiling
from the Farmhouse. There's no time to wait for Griffin and his
people to arrive. They have to act now or Circe will destroy the
Farmhouse and the legacy hidden within it. Something that,
despite everything, Savvy *does* believe is worth preserving and
protecting. They can only move forward if that history is acknowledged, by both sides.

She pictures the Registry of Witchkin burning, and she can't
let it happen.

Melissa puts a hand on Savvy's wrist and says to her, Brie,
and Elle, "I'm still linked to you all. Remember."

Savvy doesn't get the significance of that now, but nods:
Noted.

Auntie Simone and Orange are blocking her mother's access
to Savvy, even as Claudia keeps protesting. "Savannah, listen to
me. I did it for you. You can't trust them."

Cretin caws from high above, a warning call.

Savvy is certain her mother means what she says. That she did what she thought was right.

But she didn't bother to ask what Savvy wanted. And the irony is that it's her *mother* she couldn't trust. Griffin might have taken that book, but he wouldn't betray her like this.

She went against an important rule of being an operative: *Trust your instincts.* Claudia was way too comfy-cozy with Circe and the Butcher. She's not evil, she's mistrustful—and that, another irony, is what likely made her so easy for Circe to manipulate. If this wasn't personal before, it is now.

"I know you thought it was the right call, but it wasn't. Keep her contained," Savvy says to Auntie Simone, who nods. Then Savvy looks at her friends. "Four against one. At least we have decent odds."

She, Brie, Elle, and Melissa form a line facing the house, their familiars at their sides. Well, except Peggy, whom Elle cups in her hand.

"You stay here, Captain. Help Auntie keep her out," Brie says to Captain Bear in capybara form, and kisses him on the top of his head. He growls and lumbers in their direction.

Paris makes that eerie sawing call of hers, harsh and chilling. "Find her," Savvy says, and strides forward to open the porch door.

Paris doesn't need to be told twice. She streaks into the house, and Savvy and the rest follow.

Savvy weaves a spell of air, strengthened by Brie, to surround them so they and their familiars will have no trouble breathing, no need to fear the smoke inside.

So much for the all-hands-on-deck united confrontation they had planned. Griffin will be on his way. But they wanted everyone to be in place before Circe or the Butcher arrived. All points are converging in a way that feels out of control.

One thing at a time.

Paris leads them up the second set of stairs. The Spellbindery isn't where it was before; it's on the far side of the second floor. The heat announces it as they approach.

"Stand back," Savvy cautions, and summons the wind with greater strength, like she did at the wedding. Brie assists, but Elle's holding back and Savvy thinks she knows why.

The door blows in, flames shooting out at them.

"Allow me." Elle extends her hands, Peggy on her shoulder.

Of course. Peggy's form, even though it's a glamour, makes Elle more readily able to summon water. Elle marches in front of the rest into the room and applies what's essentially a targeted magical sprinkler system to the pockets of fire.

Some things are obviously destroyed, charred and ruined as the flames begin to die down. But Savvy is relieved to see the Registry on its pedestal, unburned, even as the row of journals is the worse for wear. Do healing spells work on books? Something to figure out later.

The biggest what-and-where-the-fuck, however, relates to Circe. She's nowhere to be seen.

The shattered window lets in air that feels practically crisp combining with the warmth in here. The flames nearly doused, Savvy drops the spell protecting them and breathes in the scent of ash.

"We have to find her," Savvy says.

"We may have another problem," Brie says from beside the window, pointing outside.

Savvy joins her.

Two caravans of SUVs are headed their way, trying to force each other off the road, dipping in and out of the fields alongside it while doing so. Weapons blaze with occasional fire from the back of a truck, including one that takes out a big section of road. The SUV driving toward it manages to go off-road at the last second.

Above the vehicles, Circe flies. Her yaga hut makes long, ground-vibrating strides across the landscape on its chicken legs behind the convoy. If it steps on one of the cars, it'll crush it. There's no doubt in Savvy's mind.

Griffin is in one of them.

"This is under control," Elle says, meaning the blaze is out.

"Good, because nothing else is." Savvy takes out her broom, grows it. "Here we go."

✦ ✦ ✦

31

Griffin

oly hell. That's what Griffin thinks when he spots the Farmhouse in the distance, smoke streaming out of an upper floor.

Hang on, Savvy, we're coming.

As if things haven't already gone enough to shit. They hit Atlanta traffic, and even though they didn't stay in it, it slowed them down. What it means is that the Butcher's two SUVs arrived at roughly the same time theirs did, managing to get the jump on them and turn onto the road to the Farmhouse first. Griffin has since passed the vehicles, and almost run them off the road twice.

The old bugger's guards are tough, though, and manage to navigate away through the fields and then back to give chase. Possibly assisted by his accomplice Mother Circe's magic. Luckily, Griffin has Diego to lean out the window and toss a grenade that erupts into spikes that stick in the ground—finally, one vehicle is out, front tires flattened, fishtailing.

Griffin guns the engine. His dad, Big Rob, and his brothers are in the truck behind him now, Quinn in the bed throwing challenges in the way of the other pursuing SUV as fast as he can.

"Oh shit," Diego says.

"What?" Griffin checks the rearview. And does a double take.

"Yes, we're being pursued by a giant chicken-legged house."

Holy hell again.

"Hold on." Because if they don't get out of the way before that thing reaches them, any of them, the outcome won't be pretty.

He grits his teeth and presses the gas pedal harder, throwing up dirt and gravel in their wake. He breathes slightly easier when Savvy launches out of the no-longer-smoking window on her broom, streaking toward them—and toward the old bat he now spots flying in their direction, two ravens swooping around her. He can't tell if they're supporting or attacking her.

At least Savvy isn't alone: Brie, Elle, and even Melissa are in the sky too, and he's grateful for those odds. Though he does wonder where Claudia and Auntie Simone are. Not to mention the rest of the coven, given that it's supposedly in Savvy's corner.

The house gets closer and closer and finally he decides this is good enough, slams the SUV into park just short of where he normally would. He hops out. Paris races from the front door and over to Griffin. Peggy is behind her, bouncing down the wooden steps and then adopting her horse form as soon as she's down and trotting in their direction too.

"Savvy!" Griffin shouts. Paris greets him with a swipe of tongue on his hand. Savvy wheels around in midair and flies back his way.

Diego unloads a bunch of weapons from the back seat and begins setting up a stronghold, using the truck as a shield. Roman's truck arrives, and the four of them pile out of it with a surplus of gear and weapons, and join him, staying low.

The last of the Butcher's vehicles stops too, maybe two dozen feet away, but no one gets out yet. The chicken-legged hut continues its progress with crashing step after step. Circe steers her broom into an open window, and one of the ravens glides in behind her.

Savvy's still coming back, along with her friends, so he searches around him. That's when he spots Auntie Simone and . . . an ostrich and Captain Bear visibly restraining Claudia from moving. Well, Captain Bear is doing the best he can, up on his hind legs.

Savvy lands beside Griffin, her friends joining one by one but facing the threats instead of them. He scans her for injuries. "Are you okay?"

"Unhurt." It's unlike Savvy to be visibly frazzled, but she is. Sweat streaks her face, and her caramel hair is a messy tangle. "The plan has gone, um, pear-shaped. Fire-shaped. It's bad. My mother flipped on us to Circe."

Oh no. That had to hurt, and badly.

"I'll deal with her later," she adds.

So Savvy doesn't want to wallow in it, and, frankly, they don't have time. "Okay. We need to regroup, fast," he says.

Crash. Crash. Crash.

"We have to stop the hut before it gets here—Circe wants to destroy the Farmhouse. She tried burning the Spellbindery, but we stopped her."

Other witches are emerging from the outbuildings, plainly confused by what they're witnessing.

The Butcher's guards exit their vehicle, and Roman and Jacob rise to shoot tranquilizing bullets at them—which they manage to dodge. They get the old man's door open and there he is, gnarled skin, grimacing. They rush him toward Mother Circe's house, which has stopped walking for the moment.

One of the chicken legs flips up its clawed foot and allows the Butcher to climb in, then lifts him up and deposits him through the window.

The plan was to get the Butcher and Circe both here, so that part worked anyway. They were not, however, meant to have a stronghold to hide in and use for attacks. They were supposed to be cowed by the threat of blackmail.

Circe's hut stays put.

Griffin pulls Savvy into him, needing the touch. "Will the Farmhouse let us all in?"

Savvy nods, their faces almost level. "I think so."

"Everyone inside," Griffin calls. "Her too." He nods toward Auntie Simone and points at Claudia.

"Griffin . . ." Savvy doesn't sound so sure.

"She knows what Circe is aware of," Griffin says. "If they've been talking, maybe she can help."

"She doesn't know we still have the evidence. They meant to destroy it. She betrayed us."

Unspoken: *betrayed me.* Yes, there it is. The hurt.

"And now she can make at least a little of it up, if we're lucky." He files away the rest of the information.

Savvy tilts her head. "I thought you didn't believe in luck."

He never did before he met the remarkable woman in front of him. His meant-to-be partner. His soulmate. A word he would never have considered taking seriously, without the reality of *her*. "I believe in us."

"Me too. You are *still* getting better at the sweet talk, by the way." She motions to Auntie Simone. "It's all right. Bring her."

Griffin doesn't argue. The only thing he's improved at is knowing his own heart and what it not only wants, but *needs*, to feel complete.

Their unlikely cohort falls back toward the Farmhouse, moving carefully and keeping their eyes on the threat at the horizon. Once they're inside, with weapons and familiars in tow, Brie paces in front of the couch. "Should we redo the wards? Against her?"

"Will the house go for it?" Savvy asks Auntie Simone.

"No," Claudia butts in. "She's still the head of our coven."

"Not for much longer," Savvy says, but not looking at her mother.

"Worth a shot," Elle says, and Auntie Simone nods agreement.

Elle and Brie go to the shelves and start gathering supplies.

Griffin circles the stash of weaponry his dad, his brothers, Big Rob, and Diego have deposited inside the door. They're all busy gaping at the ceiling alligator and paintings. The entire house smells of the recent fire until Brie and Elle start their work. The scent begins to dispel almost immediately as they chant and scatter substances from bottles, working their way around the downstairs.

"Do we have anything here that can disable that hut?" Griffin asks. "If we can keep them from moving, that will help."

Big Rob advances on the weapons with a thoughtful expression.

There's a knock on the door. Someone's on the porch. They all freeze.

They should have had a person on lookout. Rookie oversight.

Griffin heads over to answer, and Savvy stays at his side. Through the screen door, they can see several men and women in work clothes waiting, holding severe, pointy brooms. He feels Savvy stiffen, and he can guess it's because Claudia may have lied about the community being on her side. He braces to put her behind him and go for the easiest-to-access weapon in his vest, if necessary.

"Yes?" Savvy asks hesitantly.

There's an awkward silence, and then an older woman among them speaks. "What can we do to help? We brought these." She holds two of the pointy, swordlike brooms. The others lift wands and similar brooms.

Griffin puts an arm around Savvy's waist when she sags into him. "You're with us?" she asks.

"I'm not sold on the hunters," the woman says, "but you're

one of ours." She hesitates and then pulls open the door and steps past Savvy into the house. "Melissa?" she asks, squinting into the room.

Melissa the Gorgon's snakes are curling close around her head, almost as if they're trying to comfort her or be less conspicuous. "Mom?"

Savvy is gaping. "I didn't know you were Melissa's mom," she says to the woman. "She should never have been sent away. I didn't understand what I saw back then. I'm so sorry."

Melissa's mother walks over and reaches out her hands and gently grips her daughter's arms. She ignores the snakes and focuses on her daughter's face. "I thought you left of your own accord—who sent you off?"

"Circe."

"You were sixteen. My baby." The woman's face hardens. "We're definitely on your side," she says to Savvy over her shoulder. "Hunters or no hunters."

"The hunters are surprisingly okay," Melissa the Gorgon says, and if Griffin's not mistaken her eyes gleam with unshed tears.

There's a *crash* outside, then another. Griffin turns and strains to see past the people on the porch, even as he ushers the rest of them inside. The hut is coming for them again.

"This may sound crazy," Savvy says.

"This *is* crazy," Diego says behind her.

Brie and Elle have returned from upstairs. "He's not wrong," Brie says.

"What is it?" Griffin prompts Savvy.

"I think you and I should request a meeting. They'll see it as an opportunity."

Griffin balks instinctively. "That's because it would be one. We know they want us gone."

"So let's make them think they're getting what they want."

She tugs him back inside. "We don't have much time. The others can work on a backup strategy in case we fail. Far easier for them to face us than everyone—or so they'll believe."

He doesn't have a better plan, so he nods agreement. He trusts her.

"Mother, will you have Cretin take a message with the request for us?" she asks Claudia. She's not party to what they discussed outside, so there's no risk of her betraying them again—inadvertently *or* on purpose.

Her mother's hesitation is palpable, but she finally nods. "Perhaps meeting with Circe will open your eyes to the truth."

Griffin can't let it pass. "There's only one truth about Circe, Claudia—she and the Butcher want me and your daughter dead."

"Because you're a hunter," Claudia says.

"Mom, shut up," Savvy says. "I know you acted out of pain, but this is my life. You either help us, *both of us,* or . . . I'm not sure you and I can have a relationship anymore."

Her mother hesitates, and Griffin finally detects a hint of something softer in her eyes. Regret.

"All right," Claudia says. "All right."

It's not an apology, but it is a concession. Griffin sees Savvy's shoulders drop a little, relaxing as she turns to Brie. "Can you handle the note requesting the meeting? There's one more thing I need to see Griffin about in private."

"Got you, sis. And hey, Griffin, maybe you and your magic penis aren't so bad." Brie is already heading to the kitchen and rummaging in a drawer. She takes out a fountain pen, a bottle of ink, and some stationery. Seems a bit much, but witches must take their letters seriously.

"Thanks, Brie. I'll never live that down, huh?"

"Here's hoping that's a problem, right?" she tosses back, already writing. Elle snorts.

Griffin finds his dad and brothers are looking at him with raised eyebrows, but of course it's Diego who asks, "You have a magic penis?"

"Of course I do," he says. What else can he say?

Savvy appears to be doing her best to not smile. "Traitor," he murmurs to her.

"I know it's legit," she says, and winks before heading to the stairs.

Savvy leads Griffin up to the Spellbindery and its semi-charred remains. The remnants of the fire offend him to the soul. These are priceless old papers and objects and Circe just torched them? Who knows what's missing? The antiquarian side of him is screaming in horror. The practical side is just glad that Circe likely doesn't realize she didn't destroy what she meant to. The journal is tucked inside his vest pocket.

"What's up?" he asks.

Savvy shifts back and forth on her feet. "So, I have an idea. It might give us a small advantage . . ."

"And I'm going to hate it?"

She wrinkles her nose. "It's just going to be a little weird is all."

He touches her cheek. "What's a little weird, at this point? Hit me."

32

✦ ✦ ✦

Savvy

Savvy and Griffin pause at the top of the stairs for one last check-in.

Savvy is used to wearing glamours, but she's *not* used to looking at herself from outside. Or to altering her own appearance to match a man's—in this case that of Griffin Carter, her one true love.

"You look a little stiff," she tells him.

Griffin, as her, answers, "This is more than a little weird."

Fair. "Just think of it as being the ultimate double agents."

"Funny," he says.

They're not revealing this trick to anyone—Savvy doesn't think her mother would double-cross them again, but no reason to risk it. And so there's nothing to do but get going. Savvy heads down the stairs first, only belatedly realizing Griffin would have let her take the lead.

No one knows what's up when they come downstairs, obviously. They've mutually agreed to get outside as fast as possible. Savvy's calculus is that this might buy them an element of surprise when they need it most—or at least make their individual reactions harder to predict.

"So, ah," Griffin as Savvy says, "did they take the bait?"

Brie nods. "Cretin brought this back."

Brie extends a small rolled-up scroll of paper and Savvy accidentally reaches out for it, despite the fact that Brie is offering it to the person she thinks is her but is really Griffin.

This is making her head hurt. Griffin slides her a glance from eyes that look like hers and takes it. He opens it where both of them can read.

"'Come if you dare. Bring no seconds.'" Griffin reads the small handwritten script aloud.

"I don't like that 'no seconds' rule," Roman says.

"None of us do," Brie agrees.

"You'll all be here for backup. Think of yourselves as seconds-in-waiting," Savvy says.

She notices Brie squinting at her, as if measuring something.

Roman hesitates, but then . . . "All right. That means we need a signal. A way you can let us know if you need us."

Savvy and Griffin exchange a look. She searches for a good option, one that Griffin would propose re: her magic, when Paris saves them. If she isn't mistaken, the leopard looks amused, her eyes slitted like, *I see what you're doing.*

"Paris will know," Savvy as Griffin blurts. "She'll be the signaler."

Paris bobs her head up and down, satisfied, then sinks to the floor.

Big Rob comes forward and presses one of those fancy Tasers into Savvy's hand. "Um, thanks," she says. "Dude."

Griffin as her slides her a glance about the vocabulary. "Dude" is definitely not a Griffin word. When Big Rob continues to stand here, she pockets the Taser thing and then extends Griffin's hand to clap his friend on the shoulder. That seems to satisfy both of them.

Savvy takes in everyone in the room one last time. Gratitude for them surges within her. Melissa and her mother are talking on the couch, her mother giving a testing touch to one of the snakes, a stroking pet. Melissa stands. "Don't forget what I said before."

Right. About us still being linked. Should've followed up on that.

"Here we go," Griffin as Savvy says, nodding to Melissa.

They drop their hands into each other's and Savvy opens the front door. They step out onto the porch.

"Well, that was harder than I thought it would be," Savvy murmurs as it shuts.

They head down the stairs to the yard. The chicken-legged hut towers over them a dozen yards away. Heavy clouds hang in the darkened sky, a promise of rain in the wind. The rest of the property is quiet—word must have spread and most people are hunkering down, waiting to see what will happen. It's a good thing the kids aren't around.

"Not so easy to imitate me, is it?" Griffin as Savvy asks.

"I should've gone more sexy professor with it," Savvy as Griffin says.

"No more talk like that. We have a meeting—and I am not getting turned on by you while I look like you."

Savvy gives him a devilish grin. "I didn't even think about that."

"Well, don't."

"I'm kidding. I wouldn't."

"Mm-hmm."

She's mostly telling the truth. But the very concept of Griffin makes her go a little soft and warm inside.

They walk slowly closer to the hut and Savvy belatedly wishes they'd pressed for more neutral territory than the old witch's house. But at least they have backup nearby. And the surprise of who's who to play with.

She can admit part of the desire for the face-to-face is that she still doesn't understand why all this happened. Why paint targets on the two of them now? Some fundamental explanation for it eludes her.

Then there's the personal part. The threats to her and Griffin, but also causing her mother to betray her. Claudia is an adult who made her choices, so her actions are her own fault—

but Circe must have manipulated her too. Her relationship with her mother will have to suffer, even if it will be more honest with Savvy's priorities finally clear.

Then there's the larger-scale justice for what the Butcher and Mother Circe did together. But also making Griffin's idea of forging a new way forward a reality. Their two previously opposed sides joining forces to do things differently. That's the dream underlying everything.

This has to work. It's their future together they are fighting for, but that's not the only thing.

They stop in the shadow of the hut, the bony legs stretching tall above them.

"Griffin Carter, I love you."

"Savvy Wilde, I love you."

Mother Circe's raven appears in the window above them, staring down. One of the chicken feet flips over, making a basket they can both fit inside, just the way it did for the Butcher. They move toward it, but Savvy stops and puts her hand on Griffin's (well, her) arm.

"Yeah?" Her own face wears the question.

"Will you, uh, marry me? If we get through this?" she blurts.

"I was going to ask you that," Griffin says.

"I win. Sorry not sorry. Is that a yes?" Savvy as Griffin asks.

"Yes," Griffin as Savvy says.

She can't help laughing. "She said yes!" she calls softly, just for the two of them.

Griffin as her cracks up too.

A loud raven squawk ruptures the moment of levity. *Right. Big-showdown time.*

Savvy holds out Griffin's hand to assist with climbing in, just as Griffin would do if they weren't switched. Then she climbs in after him.

It's a little like being in the world's strangest Ferris-wheel car, the bony claws sticking up around them and the soft, dirty foot pads making it actually feel safe, if smelly. The foot jerks into motion and they clutch each other, but the ride up to the window is smooth. Savvy tentatively holds on to a claw to stand.

The raven stays perched on the sill and Savvy wants to tell her that they aren't intimidated. She grew up with Cretin as a babysitter.

"Move, Craven," Mother Circe's voice says.

The raven launches out of the window, nearly knocking Savvy off the chicken foot. She pats the claw. "Good chicken," she says, because this must have been a familiar originally. A familiar who she hopes enjoys being a house. But who probably doesn't, not with a mistress like Circe. It makes Savvy wonder, honestly. How many loyal animals has she left behind over the years?

"Enter," Mother Circe commands them.

Savvy's impulse is to disobey, but this is why they came. She shepherds Griffin as her to the front—though she knows he'll hate leaving her out here, even for a moment—and he climbs into the window. She follows quickly, so he won't be distracted.

The chicken foot descends, stomping back down. Savvy has a pocket broom, so it's not as if it cuts off an avenue of escape. A small relief.

The table from earlier has been enlarged and reset. The Butcher sits in a high-backed chair on one side, hands folded in front of him. Mother Circe is standing, but now takes another high-backed chair beside him. Two empty, regular-sized chairs wait for them.

Please, try harder to intimidate us.

Savvy winks at Griffin, a signal they planned before. He lifts his hand and then Savvy subtly directs her attention to the chairs, turning them both into de facto thrones as well.

To her surprise, Mother Circe cackles, but it's an amused one. Not a battle cry.

"I underestimated you, girl," she says.

Another piece of her rationale behind the glamours is that Savvy figures Circe and the Butcher needling the wrong one of them and the other responding will actually result in a greater ability to stay focused and not take the bait.

Griffin as her smiles, a baring of teeth. "You have no idea."

Being so close to these two, knowing what they do now, is fascinating. Savvy walks forward and gestures for Griffin to sit first. He hesitates, then does. Savvy pulls her chair out and takes it.

A delayed revelation hits her. She fully expected the interior of Mother Circe's house to be larger than it appears from outside. That should be an uncomplicated working for someone of her age and power.

But the interior doesn't match her projections. They are in one large, simple room—nicely appointed with supplies, yes, but her bed's in the corner that wasn't visible to Savvy earlier. It's a lot like a studio apartment would be, which is to say: small. This larger table takes up much of the rest of the space. Mother Circe doesn't strike Savvy as someone with tiny-house energy.

Interesting.

She could have other residences, of course. Almost certainly does. But Savvy has heard she's been a yaga for years now. Which means she probably takes this hut into whatever wilderness she wants to stay in.

That feels almost like hiding.

Savvy narrows her eyes as she settles into one of the mini thrones she conjured. She examines Mother Circe. The same thing that hit her at the wedding strikes her again. She has aged greatly. After a few hundred years? Why didn't she pick up the significance of that before?

"It seems we are at cross-purposes. The only way to save your family is to sacrifice yourself," Circe says. "You asked for this meeting, girl. So speak."

"By family . . . you mean my mother?" Griffin as Savvy answers. "I'm not too keen on her at the moment."

Savvy would have put it slightly differently . . . which is why they're doing it this way.

Circe hisses, her different-hued eyes narrowing. "She was simply trying to protect you. She didn't realize it was a lost cause."

The Butcher has yet to say anything, which Savvy finds intriguing. She focuses on him, knowing he'll see her interest as Griffin's. "And what about you, Butcher of Salem? Must have been easy to manage the exploits you made your name on with her in your corner, I suppose. Do you have any juice of your own?"

His face, with its gnarled skin, seems larger because of his missing eyebrows and bald head. He leans forward. "You should watch your tongue, boy. Your family is also at risk."

"You know," Savvy as Griffin says, under his scrutiny, "you two do seem like quite a pair. Did she seduce you or the other way around?"

"What do you think?" Circe asks. "Neither of us wanted to die."

The Butcher looks at Circe. "I've always said, if I die, you will go with me. It's still true."

"What does that mean?" Savvy asks.

"Yes," Griffin puts in. "What does it mean?"

Mother Circe has her old hands on the table, in what Savvy assumes is a show of power. They're as effective as any weapons. Or are they?

Savvy sends out an exploratory spell, subtle, meant to detect power. Mother Circe feels . . . weak. And there's something else. An undercurrent of something familiar. She's felt it before.

Savvy frowns. The Butcher is emanating power too, but not much.

She reaches over and puts a hand on Griffin's.

"Let us stop with the theater," Circe says. "You said you know what we did then . . . it clearly didn't last forever. We need your sacrifices to be noble and true. We chose you both because you are among our strongest soldiers. Now that you know, you should cooperate. Then we can manage to go on, remain leaders, strong as ever. Have we not protected the world? In our way?"

Savvy's struggling to grasp at the truth. "Why not just kill us, like you did back then?"

Mother Circe averts her eyes. The Butcher laughs, an ugly, hoarse sound.

"She tried," he says.

"You proved too strong to force, but you were supposed to recognize the truth about each other far sooner," Circe says.

"It seemed easier to let you do it yourselves, then," he says.

"But you keep resisting," Circe says. "We brought you together for a specific purpose."

Griffin responds first. "What do you mean—*you* brought us together?"

Savvy isn't used to hearing her own voice, but she recognizes that note in it. Doubt. And it worries her. Especially when her own hand fists and slams down on the table.

"Tell us," Griffin as her says.

Mother Circe smiles. "Oh, I see," she says. "It's a glamour. Delightful."

Savvy trembles as the truth finally comes into focus. The MI6 agents who followed them around London—forcing her and Griffin's first meeting. The reason she couldn't glamour herself by the Thames that day. It wasn't the mask. It was Circe's doing, Circe's and the Butcher's.

They were there, glamoured as the agents.

Mother Circe lifts her hands again and claps. Savvy's glamours dissolve, which is a thin show of power, but now they are back to being themselves. Savvy wishes she could relax into being back in her own skin, but she can't.

Not when Griffin points across the table. "Explain what you meant."

33

✦ ✦ ✦

Griffin

Griffin is doing his best to keep his rage in check. It's not going well.

Savvy takes a heavy breath beside him. Then she says, "Yes, I think you'd better explain."

Mother Circe is more animated than Griffin has seen her yet. She grins, like she knows she's playing a trump card. He can't bring himself to look at the Butcher, the man he was taught to respect, who is a pathetic liar.

"It's obvious, isn't it?" Circe says. "We introduced you. We had high hopes for you."

Griffin scans back over the day they met. Given what he now knows about glamours . . . "You weren't there."

"They were," Savvy says.

"Oh, sweet boy, yes, we were. First time I traveled abroad in ages. Remember those persnickety MI6 agents? I meant to force you, for you to take care of it then and there. Ultimately, we decided to set you on a collision course. And that's where you disappointed." Mother Circe sits back and waves a hand to the Butcher.

"You were meant to go to war, not to bed," he says gruffly.

"Or," Circe says, "at least to bed and *then* war. I was both surprised and disappointed that we had to send you both to Paris," she says to Savvy. "And then you still didn't figure out the truth about each other and do what we required. But you can make it up. Do your duty. We set the course. We must continue to do so. You can't deny that the coven has done great work in the world. So have the Butcher's men."

"Not because of you," Savvy says. "Either of you."

Griffin is trying to wrap his head around this. Meeting Savvy wasn't fate at all, but these two old power-hungry monsters cooking up a plot to renew *their* vows. He and Savvy weren't meant for love, but hate.

Not that Griffin has ever believed in fate. Or luck.

Not until Savvy.

"Griffin?" Savvy asks. "Are you okay?"

"He knows the truth," the Butcher says. "This is a farce. He sees it now."

"Griffin?" Savvy asks again.

Griffin envisions several options in this moment. Flipping the table. Asking Savvy if this changes anything for her (she asked him to marry her). Mostly, he tries to get his emotions under control. He doesn't lose that, ever.

Savvy slides a hand over his and it's steadying. "You must have felt like the wedding was your pièce de résistance," she says to Circe. "We'd finally know the truth."

"We were disappointed with how it turned out." Circe smirks.

"That we came out of it alive, you mean?" Griffin asks.

"Of course."

Savvy shifts beside him. He can feel the heat radiating off her. She's as angry as he is. "Why? Why did you need them dead? Why us?"

"All those years ago—we were aging, both of us, and the battles would have taken their toll. So we made a compact in which we shared power," Circe says. "The ritual is specific— two lives taken, two longer lives granted. The power of blood is strong. We kept witches and hunters largely separate and out of the world's eyes for our own safety. Couldn't risk you getting too cozy. The efforts of the coven all those years kept me stable, and the hunters, the Butcher. But then . . ."

"Nothing lasts forever," the Butcher says. "We needed to do it again."

Savvy is shaking her head.

Griffin's emotions are a hurricane. All the good their organizations have ever done—it was in spite of these two "leaders." Not because of them. Never because of them.

"How are you doing, young man?" Circe asks. "I imagine it's quite the shock. Men like to believe themselves incapable of being manipulated. I assure you, it's perfectly normal."

The Butcher chuckles.

The. Bastard. Chuckles.

Sure, finding out that they'd been set up to meet threw him for a loop, but it's not that big a deal. They fell in love, because it's the only thing they could have done.

Griffin shakes off his excess feelings and grins. He catches Savvy's eye and sees relief in hers. "But you didn't."

"Excuse me?" Circe asks.

The Butcher is still grinning, a death's-head.

Savvy has her hands flat on the table and he knows that means she's ready.

"Your plan utterly failed. Sure, there was a blip at the wedding, but it didn't work." Griffin smiles at them. He looks over at Savvy with open affection. "We fell in love. Despite everything you tried. We would die for each other, but we won't die for you. Your way is over."

They sit in stillness for a long moment.

"No, it is not," Circe says, channeling a serious schoolmarm energy.

Savvy drums her fingers on the table, as if she's bored now.

"Yes, it is. I have the quill." She produces it from a pocket in a gesture as much magician as witch, and twirls it in her fingers. "Griffin has your victim Diana's journal."

He produces it from inside his vest, then stows it again.

"We'll destroy it—" the Butcher starts.

"Not without destroying yourselves. No, here's what will happen," Savvy says. "Because we're more fair than you."

This—this they'd agreed on. Griffin jumps in. "You will disappear together. You will leave your positions, and age and die of natural causes. We will have surveillance. There will be no more sacrifices, no more anything. If there are . . . well . . ."

Savvy stows the quill. "If there are, we'll be coming for you and fully justified to do so." Mother Circe's mouth opens and Savvy continues, "And we'll also release the full information about what you two did and have been doing to . . . everyone. Given how much weaker you already are, without the sacrifice you need, I don't think your odds are great if open season gets declared on you."

"Unlike us," Griffin says. "You should've cultivated better friends."

Echoing thunder sounds outside. Lightning illuminates the sky. Circe is gaping toward the window and so they turn, Griffin stashing the book.

The sky outside is filled with witches. But not only witches. The hunters have joined them, their brooms turned sideways to show them aiming Big Rob's weapons into the hut.

Brie, of course, flies closest. "Ready to go?" she asks.

Paris sits in front of her on her broom in small cat form.

He couldn't have timed this more perfectly. Paris must have wanted to make a show of support.

"We are," Savvy calls. Then she hesitates.

"You two will leave in a car," Savvy says to Circe.

"This is my house!" Circe protests.

"It's a familiar and it deserves a choice. You can take Craven with you, should you like."

The Butcher stands and—moving faster than Griffin would've thought he could—removes a hunter's knife from his belt.

Mother Circe gestures at the table and it slides away.

Savvy pulls her wand and holds Circe at bay.

"Bring it, you old bastard," Griffin says, and waves for the Butcher to take his shot.

He hears their friends calling encouragement, but they don't even need the backup. They'll finish this here.

The Butcher lunges at Griffin, who grabs his arm and holds him steady. The knife drops into Griffin's other hand and he slides it between the Butcher's ribs and twists.

The man blinks at him. "You . . ."

"Gave you a better death than you deserved," Griffin says.

A thin line of blood trickles from the Butcher's mouth, and then his skin desiccates as they watch. He's nothing more than dust in seconds. His legend is over.

"You leaving or staying?" Savvy asks Circe, nodding at the floor. "Up to you."

Apparently even Circe knows when she's beat—she doesn't even stop to mourn her partner-in-centuries-of-crime. "Fine. You better hope your allies are as solid as you think."

"We're not-shaking in our not-boots," Savvy says. She looks at Griffin. He reaches his hand out to her.

She puts hers in his. "Should we get her out of here?" she asks.

Griffin keeps her hand in his as he goes over to the window. "Diego?"

Diego is on Brie's broom. How hadn't he noticed that?

They fly closer. "Would you like to escort this woman out?"

But before they can, the house sinks closer to the ground, the chicken legs bending to get them there.

Savvy pulls out her small broom and grows it. "This part I like."

Griffin watches as she goes behind Circe and literally begins shooing her out with her broom, smiling all the while.

Savvy and Griffin stand in the window of the house, watching Circe awkwardly climb down one bent leg to the ground. Savvy pats the sill. "Good house, good chicken," she says.

Griffin puts his arm around her, tucks her into his side. "I love you."

Melissa flies her broom over and semi-crashes into the house. "Why didn't you use me to drain the remainder of her powers?"

"That's what you meant?" Savvy asks.

"Yes, she's still connected to the coven, officially." Melissa grins. "And I am too. You could've tugged on me."

"Feel free," Savvy says. "We don't want her anymore."

"On it." Melissa grins, her head snakes dancing wildly. "Oh, and congratulations!"

"Yeah," Brie shouts, "when's the wedding?"

Griffin gazes at Savvy and his love for her is reflected back at him. "Tomorrow," he says. And then, "Too soon?"

"Tomorrow is perfect."

Their friends send up a cheer and there's only one thing to do. Griffin kisses the soon-to-be bride.

Two Days Ago

34

✦✦✦

The Goddess and the Professor

Savvy shuts the door to their room and plops an overnight bag on the bed beside kitty Paris. "I can't believe we're finally alone."

"They mean well," Griffin says in laughing agreement. His family just left.

A knock sounds. "Don't get comfy," Brie calls. "We're waiting!"

Elle can be heard snorting. "Sorry to say, she's right—no staying with the groom the night before the wedding! You'll see each other tomorrow, at my perfectly planned ceremony!"

The two of them lock eyes and shake their heads. Griffin takes a few steps closer to Savvy, until he can lock his arms in a circle behind her neck. Her hands go to the small of his back. "They wouldn't actually open the door, would they?" he asks.

"Elle . . . no. Brie, yes."

Griffin sighs and sets his forehead against hers. "What if we're quick?"

"Don't even think about it," Brie calls out.

Savvy sighs too. "On the bright side, after tomorrow, we have the rest of our lives for them not to bother us."

"That side is extremely bright," Griffin says. "But they forgot one thing."

"Oh?" Savvy asks, raising her eyebrows.

"The bedroom door locks."

Griffin releases her, and goes over and turns it.

"No fair!" Brie calls.

"Wait in the living room—I'll be out in a few!" Savvy says. "We have to be quick."

"Please, this is the last time I make love as a single man, don't rush me." Griffin grins and reaches out to her.

"Tomorrow *is* going to be perfect, professor? Right?" Savvy asks, sounding almost . . . nervous.

"It's you and me, goddess, of course it is."

Now

35

+ + +

Griffin and Savvy

Savvy is ready to get this party started, but Brie isn't having it.

"You can't wear jeans to your wedding," she says.

"I can and I am," Savvy counters. "This is O'Hooligan's."

Which they're standing outside of. Griffin and his family and friends are already inside, along with Melissa and her mother and the small coterie of witchkin invited. The bridal party has shrunk to just her, Brie, and Elle.

"I don't see why we had to go full O'Hooligan's," Elle says. "I could have found someplace nicer."

"In a day?" Savvy counters.

Elle scowls in admission that Savvy is correct. The Farmhouse still needs cleanup and the full saging treatment, and the barn felt too much like rehashing recent wounds. The brilliant thing about choosing this dive is that they knew it would be available—and they were correct. They're not even being charged extra.

"Besides," Savvy says, "this is where we decided to move in together."

"Okay," Elle says. "I suppose. . . ."

Speaking of recent wounds, Claudia pokes her head out the door and then comes out onto the sidewalk. "Can we talk?" she asks.

"You're not going to try to talk me out of this?" Savvy asks.

"I promise," she says.

Brie and Elle exchange glances and then Elle tows Brie up the sidewalk to give the two of them some space.

Savvy was torn on whether to have Claudia here at all. But she understands her mother.

"I know you know why I'm like this," Claudia says. "I still blame myself. But I'm sorry."

Before, Savvy probably would have just gone with it, grateful for the words. "For?"

Her mother wrings her hands. "For putting my guilt and baggage on you. I shouldn't have done that. I will make it up to you."

"By being the best mother-in-law ever?"

"Yes. And the best mother? To you? I really am sorry, sweetie."

"Good," Savvy says. "I love you, Mom. You can get started by calling all the C.R.O.N.E. chapters and explaining the transition. And why Circe is persona non grata."

"But—" Claudia swallows. Those calls are going to either be okay or create a lot of protest. Probably both. Her mother having to explain that Circe wasn't what anyone believed . . . seems like a good penance. "I'd be happy to."

"But after you walk me down the aisle?"

Claudia's eyes fill with unshed tears. "I'd love to."

Savvy calls over to where Brie and Elle are cooling their heels. "Come on. I have a man to marry."

The two hurry back. Elle squints at her. "Brie is right. Let me just . . ."

She looks around them, confirming that they are alone on the street, and then points at Savvy. The new dress she conjures is identical to the one currently in shreds at Brie's place—well, identical to what it looked like pre-shreds.

Brie squints at her, then points too. Savvy feels the flower crown settle onto her hair.

The door to the bar opens and this time Diego pokes his head out. "You're late."

"We know," Brie says. "Go away."

He makes a face at her and goes back inside.

"You two are getting awfully friendly," Savvy observes.

"Just because we're best friends does not mean I wouldn't murder you," Brie says sweetly.

Savvy bites back a grin.

Inside, the strains of the wedding march start. Brie and Elle rush to get inside before her, but when they open the door a small black cat darts out to Savvy's side.

"You walking me down the aisle, too, Paris?" Her throat burns a little.

Claudia smiles at her and Paris. That missing-something feeling Savvy used to get? She knows, in her bones, that she'll never feel it again.

She and Griffin are going to have a great life, full of love and work. Together.

Griffin's jaw drops when he sees Savvy enter the dive bar, looking like a goddess from an ethereal realm dropped into the grubby mortal plane. Paris prances alongside her. And Savvy's mother has her arm hooked through her daughter's.

He can tell by the smile on Savvy's face that this is a good thing. He's happy about it if she is—Claudia even told him she was sorry earlier.

Auntie Simone is officiating again, and when Savvy reaches the front of the makeshift aisle they've made, she peers at Claudia. "Who gives away this woman?"

"She has more than earned the right to make all her own decisions," Claudia says, and releases Savvy's arm to take a seat at a nearby table.

Paris, seizing her moment, preens and stands on her back feet, growing to leopard size and lifting one paw.

"Clearly Paris approves," Auntie Simone says, and those in attendance sniffle or chuckle depending on how sappy they are.

Griffin thinks it's a good thing he paid the staff extra to take a smoke break out back during the actual wedding. As if Peggy the frog sitting on a table nearby isn't weird enough. But then, Decatur bartenders have probably seen a lot of things.

"You may be seated," Auntie Simone says.

Paris pads over and sits by Jackie, who reaches down and strokes her head.

The ceremony itself is a blur. Griffin's heart is full and he manages to say yes at all the proper moments. They agreed to skip the vows, and make an announcement afterward instead. But the one thing they absolutely are *not* skipping is the kiss.

"You may kiss each other," Auntie Simone says. "Keeping in mind this is a family establishment."

"It is not!" Diego says, scandalized.

Griffin looks at Savvy, his beautiful bride, the love of his life. She looks back at him. "What a remarkable life we're going to have," she says. "Seal it with a kiss."

Their lips meet and there's a fire between them. Griffin licks into her mouth and she meets his tongue with hers, family establishment or not (maybe a mafia family, anyway—this *is* O'Hooligan's). No more secrets between them, no more lies. They're who they are, together.

They pull reluctantly apart. "You want to tell them or should I?" Savvy asks.

"You."

Savvy turns to their assembled people. "The old days of C.R.O.N.E. and H.U.N.T.E.R. are behind us. My mother has agreed to take point on notifying C.R.O.N.E. covens about the truth, and Griffin's brothers are taking care of H.U.N.T.E.R.'s side. That will happen tonight. But Griffin and I want to work together, with whoever will join us. We want witches and hunters to work together."

"But the old names just don't quite work—I want to leave the fact we ever hunted witches in the past," Griffin says.

Savvy beams at him.

"What are we going to be called, then? It has to be a cool name," Diego says, as if that's the make-or-break.

"We're going to be wardens," Griffin says.

He and Savvy were quite pleased when they came up with that, in bed together last night. After celebrating their victory.

"What does it stand for?" Brie asks.

"It's not an acronym," Savvy says. "We'll be Witches and Wardens."

"W&W for short," Griffin says.

"Oh," Elle says.

"I like it," Brie says.

Elle is nodding. As is the rest of the room.

Melissa the Gorgon stands up. "I'm in."

Everyone assembled echoes her.

Just like that, the future stretches out, new and exciting, between Griffin and Savvy. Seems like another prime opportunity to kiss the bride.

Acknowledgments

The first thanks goes to you for reading, as always. You readers inspire me, and I hope I return it back to you. I'd also like to thank my rad in-person writing group, The Moonscribers, the entire community at the Lexington Writer's Room (but especially Lisa and the rest of the board, and all of you who supported us during the aftermath of the fire), and fly-or-dies Kami Garcia and Sam Humphries (I had to make it witchy). My yoga group, which sometimes is the only thing helping me keep it together. And to Creatures of Whim, the local witch shop that has helped with inspiration and gift baskets.

This book wouldn't exist without my extraordinary editors who worked on it, Tiffany Shelton and Jennie Conway, and it would never have gotten to your hands without my fabulous agent, Kate McKean, and the entire team who worked on it at St. Martin's (Mary Moates, Erica Martirano, Oliver Wehner, Ginny Perrin, Susan Walsh, Terry McGarry, Melanie Sanders, and Janna Dokos). Also many thanks to Kerri Resnick for art direction and Natalia Agatte for the beautiful cover illustration.

And, last but not least, to my own herd of familiars and to Christopher Rowe, my in-house Superman fan, who helps keep our circus intact during deadline.

About the Author

GWENDA BOND is the *New York Times* bestselling author of many novels. The Match Made in Hell series, which includes *Not Your Average Hot Guy* and *The Date from Hell*, were her first romantic comedies. She co-founded the charitable efforts Creators 4 Comics and the Lexington Writer's Room and lives in a hundred-year-old house in Lexington, Kentucky, with her husband, author Christopher Rowe, and a veritable zoo of familiars made up of adorable doggos and queenly cats. Visit her online at www.gwendabond.com or @gwenda on Twitter.